AVAILABLE TIME

ALSO BY J. C. DE LADURANTEY

FICTION
Cowards, Crooks, and Warriors
Twenty-Three Minutes

NON FICTION
Making Your Memories with Rock & Roll and Doo-Wop;
The Music and Artists of the 1950s and early 60s

Creating Public Value Through Collaborative Networks

Criminal Investigation Standards (with Daniel Sullivan)

AVAILABLE TIME

A HOWARD HAMILTON RIDE-ALONG

J. C. DE LADURANTEY

AVAILABLE TIME
A HOWARD HAMILTON RIDE-ALONG

iUniverse books may be ordered through booksellers or by contacting:

iUniverse
1663 Liberty Drive
Bloomington, IN 47403
www.iuniverse.com
844-349-9409

Because of the dynamic nature of the Internet, any web addresses or links contained in this book may have changed since publication and may no longer be valid. The views expressed in this work are solely those of the author and do not necessarily reflect the views of the publisher, and the publisher hereby disclaims any responsibility for them.

Any people depicted in stock imagery provided by Getty Images are models, and such images are being used for illustrative purposes only. Certain stock imagery © Getty Images.

ISBN: 978-1-6632-3615-9 (sc)
ISBN: 978-1-6632-3616-6 (e)

Library of Congress Control Number: 2022903392

Print information available on the last page.

iUniverse rev. date: 03/16/2022

AUTHOR'S NOTE

Every person I know who enters the criminal justice profession joins for at least two reasons. To contribute to their communities and obtain employment that provides daily excitement that no other career can provide.

Recruiting from the human race has its pitfalls. They come into the profession wide-eyed from the unemployment lines, college, the military, nursing, aerospace, teaching, the business and entertainment world, and yes, even the seminary.

Seeing man's inhumanity to man in a large city accelerates the experiential base of jadedness. For those mid-sized communities, it may take longer, but it still happens. The carnage of man's inhumanity to man, seen daily, would jade even the most pious. Daily, weekly, or monthly carnage can take its toll on even the strongest. If you ask those who wear the blue, brown, tan, or green uniform, they will voluntarily tell you stories of their adventures on the street. But will you believe them?

Law enforcement is not about race, ethnicity, color, economics, or language barrier. Communities hire their officers to uphold law and order. Many hire from within their communities while others do a nationwide search. Law enforcement is very well trained, and most are very well equipped to accomplish a very complex responsibility. Training takes many forms. The classroom, books, testing, and performance simulations are emphasized along with cognitive skills. Efforts are also made to identify critical thinking skills, communication ability, and a confrontation and restraint perspective.

The search continues for those who can provide an ethical orientation and understand human stress. Only one or two out of one hundred passes the qualifications to police the streets, maintain peace, and control those who violate their laws. It is about policing behavior, observing, and evaluating the response, and reacting to the aberrant behavior in a manner that recognizes decision-making and a positive outcome.

We would all like to have more willing compliance from the public we serve. Policing would be so much easier. We live or work in cities that experience drugs, violence, rage, a loss of community standards and values, or social cohesion, commonly called social anomie. The inhumanity can only be explained by experiencing it.

Not all law enforcement is glamorous. Like a sausage factory, many do not, need not, know how it is conducted. It is not all by the book and sometimes ugly or appears to be taken out of its totality.

In every community, there exists the potential to commit a crime. Some choose to take advantage of that opportunity. Some choose to obey the law, and others choose not to. It is a study of human behavior well outside of the purview of this book.

The underbelly of every community is not known, seen, or experienced by the average person. Nor should it be. Public safety occurs daily without regard to its exposure to the outside world. Only a select few can see and experience what goes on in the streets and alleys at 3 am or behind closed doors on a Saturday night. Law enforcement is one of those.

We judge people by the actions we see them take. Yet, we wish to be judged, not so much by our actions but by our intentions. There is also evil and people who will commit evil acts. We are fortunate to have people who move towards harmful behavior to save us all from it and not turn their backs.

JCD

ABOUT AVAILABLE TIME

Howard Hamilton is a police officer in Orchard Hill. His parents raised him with family values from the 1960s, nicknaming him in honor of a Los Angeles disc jockey from the 1950s and early 60s, H.H., or Hunter Hancock. He was raised in suburban South Bay, went to local schools. He never desired to work in the Los Angeles Police Department, the Los Angeles Sheriff's Department, or any three-letter state or federal agencies.

The music of the 1950s and early 60s didn't interest him like it did his parents. However, the music of the late 60s and all the 70s did. He enjoyed the Eagles' messages, Electric Light Orchestra, the Mama's and Papa's, Spanky and our Gang. He was not sure why but the former opera singer, Meat Loaf, also became a favorite.

For almost ten years now, Officer Hamilton has worked a patrol car on the night or PM shift. He started out working an eight-hour shift with forty-five minutes of code seven or lunch break time. In 2012, the OHPD, after considerable negotiations by the O.H. Police Officers Association (OHPOA) the city established several shifts to accommodate various needs.

Patrol went to two shifts, a ten-hour tour during the week (Monday through Thursday) and a twelve-hour shift for weekend duty (Friday, Saturday, and Sunday).

Before computers, officers were required to determine how much was assigned time. This included briefing, time spent on service calls, code seven, and other assignments given by a supervisor. Observations such as writing traffic tickets, stopping a suspicious person, or anything where the Officer directly initiated the action without being assigned by a dispatcher or supervisor, would become available time. The remaining time would be calculated to determine what was assigned versus how much time the Officer was available for other duties.

Let's do the math. In an eight-hour shift with a total of 480 minutes, code seven would be an unassigned time of 45 minutes with briefing/roll call assigned at 45 minutes. A shift would then consist of 525 minutes. If an officer spent an average of 30 minutes each on seven calls throughout the shift, the allotted time would be 210 minutes. Add the 45 minutes for briefing, he/she would have 255 minutes of assigned time and 270 minutes of available time.

Within this timeframe of 270 minutes of available time, citations could have been issued, observation arrests made, or citizen calls handled. Regardless, the assigned time and the available time would add up to 525 minutes. The same formula can be applied to the ten-hour or twelve-hour shift.

When we examine our work environment, there are times when we are doing what we have been directed to do and times when we have the option of doing what we decide. Many do not have to account for their time in their work environment. Still, others must account for every minute.

What is your "assigned time," and what is your "available time?"

CHAPTER 1

Saturday nights in the Belmont Shore district of the city of Long Beach are not just for the beautiful people. For those who are too young for the bars and nightclubs, there needs to be another outlet.

For Tina, Humberto, and Rodney, nothing could satisfy their need for speed. It was not the drug but the fast-paced roar of an engine and the burning rubber calling Humberto and his friends. It was a high of its own.

Humberto didn't have the only souped-up red Honda Civic, but it was one of the best on the street. Supercharged blowers, nitrous oxide systems, and other high-performance equipment were easily attainable. He could not do much more to the engine, but he could trick it out with undercarriage LED lights. He added flames stenciled on the sides and twice pipes that could emulate a rocket ship when he pushed a button.

Humberto and his friends had raced each other last week, and of course, he walked away with the victory flag. No doubt, they would be looking for revenge tonight.

As dusk descended on this traditional beach community, he was eastbound on Second Street, approaching PCH, and saw his challenger in the rearview mirror, stalking him from behind. It was the unmistakable black Honda Civic with the cat-eye headlights that he ass-kicked last week, looking for revenge. They had no radios to communicate with but didn't need them. Humberto knew all he had to do was accelerate through the intersection, regardless of the color of the light, and the race would be on. The need to keep his victory

1

flag pushed his foot deeper into the gas pedal. Everyone else should and better stay out of the way.

It was already close to dark this winter night, and there was a slight chill in the air. Humberto had his heater on with the windows rolled down. The radio was screaming a forgettable, nonsensical selection of noise that could not even be hummed.

Sitting in the passenger or shotgun seat, Tina had her bare feet resting comfortably on the dashboard, with the heater running full blast, ensuring her comfort regardless of the cold outside.

"Here that motherfucker comes! Here he comes!" Humberto announced to the world, including Rodney in the back seat and Tina now sitting up looking around.

"Where?" Rodney and Tina said, almost in unison.

"Back there, idiots. Behind us." All three looked through the rear window to see the cat-eye headlights of the enemy.

The enemy was coming up fast in the empty parking lane to their right. Humberto accelerated rapidly, announcing that the race was on. The mufflers cracked like a shotgun blast, one after the other. With screaming vocal cords, screeching tires, and the unmistakable smell of burning rubber, they cleared the intersection only by the last second of the yellow phase of a long-ago green light.

His Honda made it to the other side of the intersection before the cross traffic had started up. He hit sixty within forty feet of clearing PCH. Humberto would wait for Enemy to catch him. He knew it would only be a matter of time before they would be side by side with nothing in front of them but dark roads, green lights, and a mythical checkered flag victory once again.

Enemy saw the red Honda Civic he had barely lost to last week and took the parking lane to work his way next to him. He was not going to lose tonight. No, he had thought about this moment since last week.

He saw his chance as Honda red crossed the intersection at high speed with no let up on the gas pedal. The race was on. And it was his turn to win.

Enemy didn't see the traffic light phase—only the red Honda's taillights enticing him on the other side of PCH. The Honda was a magnet that polarized his thinking and his driving. He accelerated along the empty curb lane and concentrated on his prey. It would later be estimated he entered the intersection in full acceleration at over fifty miles per hour into the traffic signal's red phase.

For Humberto and Enemy, it was a means to socialize and show off their hot rod and driving ability. It was their Viagra, the stimulus that propelled them to dare, to take a chance and risk it all for that one sense of a thrill beyond compare.

The Explorer was first in line in the northbound lane of PCH and moved forward, well within the green light phase for that direction of travel.

CHAPTER 2

Clare had just left an exhilarating but exhaustive teacher-training program for yogis. With Howard away for a well-deserved weekend religious experience, she planned to take Geoff and Marcia to a late dinner immediately after class, let them frolic with their friends, and curl up with a recommendation by her book club—*The Dining Car* by a promising new author, Eric Peterson. After seven hours of meditation and holding of yoga poses, that would all happen after a well-deserved hot bath and glass of wine.

Clare never saw the black Honda come up from the curb lane on Second Street. Nor did she see him run the red light or T-bone her car on the driver's side. It all happened before she knew it. Thank God for small favors.

For Clare, it was just her time.

She had thrown her bag containing a mat, yogi socks, a well-worn twelve-foot-long pink belt, a set of blocks, and a change of clothes in the back seat of her Explorer. She then took a long drink of room temperature water from her bottle and put her seat belt on. At 1830 hours in police talk and 6:30 p.m. civilian time, Clare left the yoga studio's parking lot directly adjacent to the Cal State University at Long Beach campus, heading south to Pacific Coast Highway.

She had planned to take PCH through the trendy Belmont Shore this Saturday night, just to see what the beautiful people were doing. It was a twilight night with the sun on its way down, a chill in the air, and streetlights telling everyone that nighttime was soon on its way.

Before starting the car, she had opened her phone to Geoff's number. She intended to let him know she was en route home.

She never made it. Her dream of substituting for Maru on occasion, supplementing the family income, her little escape to a world outside of the family, and her drive to possess a skill few people could master were now on hold. Forever.

Her death would not be an imperfect statistic on Orchard Hill's traffic picture. That would default to the city of Long Beach. For them, it would be an unfortunate by-product of too much traffic and not enough enforcement—at least at PCH and Second Street.

She wasn't texting, doing Facetime, or trying to dial a number. She had just hit *favorites*.

"Hi, Geoff. It's Mom. Just want you to know that—"

CHAPTER 3

It was a late Saturday afternoon, and Howard Hamilton was on his second day of training to be a eucharistic minister for St. Elizabeth's Catholic Church in Orchard Hill. In the early part of January, he blocked off the three-day weekend between the playoffs and the Super Bowl, where there were no games of any consequence to miss. Rex set him up with Monsignor Steve Ryder, coordinator for the Eucharistic minister program at the archdiocese.

The *edu-train-ment* or education, training, and entertainment session, had been skillfully planned by the Manresa Retreat House's staff around the professional football schedule from a Friday afternoon until Sunday, somewhere in the San Gabriel Mountains. Interestingly, Rex would also be a part of the entertainment.

Does the guy ever work? Hamilton mused. Rex Holcomb had retired from the LAPD and been hired back as an expert consultant in satanic cults. He was also a deacon at St. Elizabeth's and doing what he wanted, when he wanted, on his schedule. *Wow, someday,* Howard reflected. *Someday.*

He studied the retreat house grounds and marveled at the immaculate way nature could be shaped. Surrounded by a series of rose gardens with every species imaginable, there were tall, elongated cypress trees that never saw a spider. The forever meandering of boxwoods created one stone walking path after another, leading to a secluded prayer retreat grotto for reflection. It set the tone.

Rex held everyone's attention as he taught the proper method of holding a host, how to stand, and the distance between you and the host recipient.

He was using a video demonstrating how to place the host on the tongue or in hand. The film showed actors dropping the host on the ground, unconsecrated, standing too close and violating the recipient's space, and moving into the person. One clip showed the minister jamming a fist into the mouth of the unfortunate communicant—entertaining and funny for a very sacred procedure: sacred indeed.

Holcomb felt his phone vibrate with a sense of urgency in his right front pocket.

CHAPTER 4

Motor Officer Sergeant Daryl Ussury, supervisor of LBPD's motorcycle unit for the p.m. shift, was the first responder to the scene. He didn't need the EMT to tell him he had a fatality on his hands. He knew it right away. But he could barely tell if the victim was male or female. *Do guys wear yoga pants? Just the mayor of LA,* he thought inside his sense of morbid humor.

He thought not. While the airbag did activate, Ussury saw that the speed of impact took its toll on the driver.

The veteran motor supervisor knew it would be over two hours for the accident investigators from his PD to get to the point of considering the identity of their fatality. He called the on-duty traffic investigator to the scene to start the preliminary investigation. Ussury blocked off the two intersections with flares and cones and ordered a patrol unit to redirect traffic into one lane in each of the four travel directions.

The acrid smell of phosphate from road flares that would light the path of destruction overcame the scene. No one in Long Beach would get to their destination on time this Saturday night.

The EMTs pronounced her dead at the scene. The driver of the black Honda Civic was taken to a community hospital in critical condition. Ussury would ensure he would eventually be absentee booked for felony vehicular manslaughter if he survived. With neither car applying brakes, each felt the impact of speed, crunching metal, and airbags that only helped Party #1, the driver at fault.

Clare would be Party #2 on the report. Not at fault but still deceased. With the witnesses and physical evidence at the scene, there was no doubt about who that was. The souped-up red Honda, Humberto, Tina, and Rodney were long gone, not realizing that they too were a party to a tragedy of the night.

She didn't stand a chance, Ussury thought, hoping the traffic unit assigned to the call would hurry up and get there. With the flare pattern established, he finally found a patrol unit to direct traffic. But this case, with a fatality, needed expert attention by the traffic investigators. It would be much later before the accident's cause and Clare's death would be classified as illegal street racing. Witnesses needed to be talked to, physical evidence examined, and the coefficient of friction forensics applied to determine the speed of vehicles involved.

Early in the investigation, Ussury issued a Sig-Alert to the media announcing the intersection of PCH and Second Street would be cut down to one lane in each direction for at least two hours.

The scene looked like a light plane had crashed in the middle of the intersection. Debris spread from one curb to the other. Most of the jagged metal was in such small pieces as to not be recognized. One could not tell which car was which with the mangled pieces. There were no skid marks because no one other than those who witnessed the tragedy had put on their brakes.

CHAPTER 5

After the traffic investigation team arrived, notified the medical examiner, and took photos, Ussury knew the next steps. It was time to assist with the removal of the body. A blue tarp covered her, so the lookie-loos only had a view of the mangled metal black car against the other black car. Where one car started and the other began was difficult to determine.

The coroner removed Clare from the front seat and put her onto the stretcher. Her purse and cell phone fell to the ground. "I'll take that," the medical examiner said to Ussury. "Her personal property will be our responsibility."

"Can we at least have you consider looking into her wallet for some ID?" Ussury queried. "We can handle notifications if she's local. Save you a lot of time. The car's registered in Orchard Hill, just outside our city."

The ME held on to the purse and placed the phone inside. He then moved the gurney to the rear of his van, activated the handle that let him lift the body into the rear cargo area, and pushed it in as far as it would go. He had done this before, many times. The sound of the door closing was final, very final. He went through the purse and found her wallet and identification.

"Here's her license. You might want to look at this too." Ussury examined the driver's photo and saw that she was more than pretty; she was gorgeous. *DMV did her justice when it came to her photo.*

Clare Hamilton lived in Orchard Hill, about twenty minutes north of Long Beach. After running her license plate, the registration on the car and her driver's license all matched. Of course they did. He almost thought her name was familiar but couldn't place it.

"We can handle the notification if you don't mind."

"No, not a bit," the ME said. "Did you see this?" He handed Ussury an embossed business card. *Orchard Hill Police Department, Officer Howard Hamilton* was the printing with station phone numbers, a badge, an official email address, and a cell phone. "Could be his cell unless the department gives them that too."

There was no telltale writing on the back of the card, asking for courtesy should the need arise.

"Well, he's one of yours, so no problem letting you take care of it, Sarge." He handed his preliminary report to Ussury with the essential information.

"Give it to them," Ussury said, pointing to the accident investigators. "No, I changed my mind. I'll take it." There was no doubt that this ME wanted to leave and get back to the office with his cargo. Or maybe just to his next call and next body. There was room in the coroner's wagon for one more.

"I could no more handle your job than the man on the moon, my friend." Ussury was paying him a compliment that was so often returned with a "Well, I couldn't do yours either."

"Yours either, Sarge," he said, pointing to the piece of paper in Ussury's hand. "Good luck talking to her husband."

Ussury stared at the business card. "This poor guy's life will change forever. Where do I start?" He thought of his daughter, who was still a teenager. So far, he had been lucky, but she was still learning to drive. If she was killed similarly, who would he prefer to tell him? Another ME or a fellow officer?

He contacted his on-duty watch commander and decided on a plan of action after much discussion regarding the situation. The watch commander, Lieutenant Shirley Connor, agreed to contact the Orchard Hill watch commander and be guided by their desires.

CHAPTER 6

Lt. Connor got back to Ussury within twenty minutes with the not-so-good news. Initial efforts to locate Officer Hamilton were not productive. He was not at work; nor was anyone else at home.

Ten minutes later, Ussury received another call from Connor.

"I just got off the phone with Hamilton's Chief. He'll make some calls and get back with me."

Ussury was impressed. "You went right to the top on that one, Lieutenant." There was a short silence on the phone. "Well, Daryl, I can't think of a more important circumstance, absent the death of one of his officers, that a Chief would not want to be notified directly." Everyone was taking a deep breath.

Ussury returned to the cleanup and investigation. He found out from one of the accident investigators that a DUI had crashed through the flare pattern and into a power pole just south of the intersection. They had to call another unit to book the guy and get his vehicle towed away. It was going to be one of those nights. *Sig-Alerts don't matter to drunks.*

Until Lt. Conner could find Officer Hamilton, he needed to wipe away what he had just experienced. Thinking again of his daughter and trying not to put her in Clare's place was tough. He needed to pass the time with something productive or at least distracting. He grabbed a long-handled push broom from a tow truck and started sweeping the glass and mangled metal debris from the streets. He knew that the tow driver had the responsibility of doing that, but he felt it necessary to do something other than think. Or maybe he was delaying the chore ahead of him.

An agonizing twenty minutes later, he was rewarded with some positive news from Connor. "The Chief from Orchard Hill found Hamilton at a religious retreat up in the San Gabriel Mountains. What do you want to do now, Daryl?"

Ussury thought for a moment. "Have you told the Chief that his wife is … she passed away?"

Connor responded quickly, "The Chief knows, but the officer doesn't. Just knows she was involved in an accident."

Another moment passed as Ussury gathered his thoughts. "How about this, Lieutenant. Have the Chief tell the officer, Hamilton—I think his name is Howard Hamilton." Ussury stumbled for the right words. "Have him tell him to meet me at our station. Not the morgue or the hospital but at our place, in the traffic office. How's that?"

Connor responded, "Sounds good, Daryl. How much time shall I give him?" Ussury didn't hesitate.

"I'm going there now, so if he's coming from the San Gabriel Mountains somewhere, it'll be at least an hour on a Saturday night. I'll be fine."

CHAPTER 7

The Chief and his wife had been out to a well-deserved dinner in downtown Los Angeles when he received the call no one ever wants to get. "Chief, this is Lieutenant Shirley Connor of Long Beach PD. I'm the watch commander here tonight, sir, and we've had an unfortunate incident in our city that involves one of your, well, one of your officer's family members."

She explained as much as she knew about the traffic accident and the inability to locate Hamilton to make the notification. She then asked if he could assist in locating Officer Hamilton.

"Let me get back to you, Lieutenant."

They agreed to stay in touch regarding each other's efforts. The Chief contacted Lt. LaBonge at OHPD and brought him up to date.

"Chief, we've door-knocked his house and his neighbor's and tried his cell many times. No luck. Is Clare hurt bad?" The silence at the other end of the phone said it all. "We'll keep trying, sir."

"Dear, remember meeting Officer Howard Hamilton on that case you worked in Rampart?" The Chief referred to a case his wife, a Los Angeles police detective assigned to Homicide had investigated a few months back.

"Oh, I do. He seemed like a nice guy, just a little unsure of himself." His wife now became more curious.

"Well, Long Beach just told me his wife, Clare, was killed in a traffic accident in their city, and they can't locate him. He's not at home. His wife was very active with the other wives, did baking projects for the station and was always available to help in any way." He paused to gather his thoughts. "Wait. I have an idea."

The Chief called LAPD's Detective Headquarters and spoke to one of his old partners. "Hey, Sam, it's Saturday night, and I don't have my handy black book with me. Can you get me Rex Holcomb's number? I need to get in touch with him, and it's kind of an emergency."

He put his hand over the mouthpiece and said to his wife, "You know, taking advantage of relationships is as natural as calling a family friend. There is nothing to going back and rekindling friendships and telling a few tall tales. It's all a part of the folklore. You leave but never say goodbye."

He made small talk with Sam and got the information he so desperately needed.

"Chief, to what do I owe this pleasure?" Rex asked.

"Well, Rex, this one's not pleasure." The Chief explained he was looking for Howard Hamilton and thought maybe Holcomb knew where he might be. Hamilton had confided that he had become friends with one of the Chief's old LAPD cohorts over the past year. The Chief knew that Holcomb was a eucharistic minister and thought perhaps there was a special connection between the two due to going to the same church. "His wife has been in a serious accident, Rex, and we can't locate him to make the notification."

"I know exactly where he is, sir."

"You do?"

"Yes, he's here with me at a training program to become a eucharistic minister at St. Elizabeth's. We're up here at a retreat house in the San Gabriel Mountains. Do you want me to get a hold of him?"

"That would be great, Rex. Give him my cell number and have him call me."

"Will do, sir, and it's good to hear from you. How's the new job?"

"Well, Rex, some days are good, and some are not. This one is not going to be a good day."

Tapping his *recents* icon, he called Long Beach PD back. "Lieutenant Connor, may I help you?"

After talking with the Chief, they agreed that Hamilton would be asked to go to the Long Beach Police Department, Traffic Division. "Sgt. Ussury will meet him, Chief, and take care of business."

"I think I would like to be there as well, Lieutenant. If you don't mind."

"Sir, you're the Chief, and you can pretty much call your own shots."

"I'll see you both in about twenty minutes." He looked at his wife as he disconnected from his call.

"Some days, this job sucks."

CHAPTER 8

Hamilton was having a late dinner in the dining room of the one-hundred-fifty-year-old stone and rock retreat house. Founded by the Jesuits, the Manresa Retreat House was established to honor the Jesuit order's patron saint, St. Ignatius of Loyola. Nestled in the San Gabriel Valley's foothills and overseen by Loyola/Marymount College, the statuesque and beautiful retreat house was open to several archdioceses in Southern California to train new eucharistic ministers. The ministers were desperately needed in a time of reduced vocations for the priesthood.

Howard was finishing his dinner, sitting alone in the corner of the dining area, when he saw Holcomb approach. He had just finished a quick two-mile run in the mountains before sitting down for dinner.

"Rex, thought you were through with us for a while."

"I was, HH, but I need to talk with you for a moment." Holcomb took a deep breath. "May I sit down? Not sure how to say this, but Clare has been in an accident. I don't know the extent of her injuries. Long Beach PD requested you go to their station. That's about all I know."

Probably to give her a ride home.

"Wow, Rex. She's a very cautious driver, so I don't know how such a thing could happen. Give me a moment to process this. My head is here at the retreat. Now I don't know what to think. Should I call her?"

"Howard, she may not be able to get to her phone if she's hurt. Otherwise, she would have called you. I think you should go to Long Beach and meet there."

He stared at his almost finished dinner, trying to think of his next move.

Hamilton advised the training director that he would return after taking care of some personal business with family. He didn't elaborate.

The drive from the San Gabriel Mountains to Long Beach was a straight shot south on the 605 Freeway. Los Angeles freeways were always crowded, but he moved with the traffic flow this Saturday night. Random reflections of what they were going to do with just one car and two teenagers captured his thoughts. Maybe, just maybe, if she was not too banged up, she would eventually be able to get back to her beloved yoga teacher's class.

He walked casually into Long Beach PD's front lobby after parking in the visitor's stall across the street from the police station. He had come in a back way or the way police cars entered with prisoners. He had booked a person into the LBPD jail and only knew the back entrance, the unofficial entrance. Entering from the front door was new to him.

The lobby was foreboding and dark for a Saturday night, as if the police department was closed. But who closes a police lobby? His thoughts were scattered.

In the lobby, he was met by a uniformed motor sergeant who introduced himself as Daryl Ussury. They exchanged an accommodating, professional greeting that only those who bleed blue can do. Ussury had taken his helmet off, but the telltale signs of his motor boots, the sergeant stripes, and symbolic gold wheel with an arrow on his sleeve left no doubt as to his assignment.

"Do you need to see my ID, Sarge?"

"I don't think so." Ussury motioned for him to follow into the Traffic Division office.

"Come on in here, Officer Hamilton."

Hamilton put his badge and ID holder back in his pocket. He was escorted into a comfortable reception area generally reserved for victims and witnesses. The lighting told him the offices were closed.

"Why bring me in here?" he muttered. "Where's Clare?" He was a bit perplexed and unsure why he was where he was.

"That's what we need to talk about." Ussury remained businesslike but decided to take off his cop persona for this one.

CHAPTER 9

Ussury paused, struggling to get the right words out. He was at least fifteen years older than Hamilton and outweighed him by fifty pounds, but it felt like a father-son talk, not officer-to-officer. He had not faced this much personal anguish in his memory. He took his hands off his hips and went right for eye contact. He needed to look Howard directly in the face to take the next step.

He thought back to how he saw her, her head and what was left of her face against the steering wheel and airbag. Unfortunately, only her husband knew her as the striking, petite, and nurturing wife, mother, and lover.

Their eyes met, both holding still for that indescribable moment. "Clare's not here, Officer Hamilton."

"Why are you calling me that? My name is Howard, and I'm not on duty."

"I know. Just out of respect, I guess."

"Respect? Why? Where's Clare? Is she in the hospital? Or is she …"

The words just hung there. Lifeless in their way. Right away, he knew the answer to his futile but necessary question. He had tried to answer that question before as well. Where was Geoff? Marcia? Oh, God, no! Not his Clare!

Silence engulfed the room that was getting smaller with each breath. Almost instantaneously, the oxygen was sucked out of the room. Neither one could breathe. Ussury knew this would not be easy, but he did not anticipate the next question so fast. And it was not a question but a statement, a command, a persistent demand. He told himself to keep eye contact.

Should I touch him? Hug him?

Ussury reached out and held him by his shoulders, with a gentle firmness that only said, "I'm sorry."

But Howard didn't want to breathe. He wanted just to be suspended in that rarified air that says, *Let's keep things as they were, not as they are or how they are going to be.*

CHAPTER 10

"I want to see her, Sgt. Ussury, sir. I want to see her. Please. I have to see her."

It had not registered completely. *Where are Marcia and Geoff? They should be here. Where is my mother? Her parents? They should be here. Why do I have to carry this load?*

The Sergeant did not respond.

"I want to see her," he said in a much quieter tone.

"No. No, you do not," was finally the reply.

But it was not just a reply. It was more like a command.

"I do." Silence.

"Howard—may I call you Howard?"

Hamilton nodded.

"When did you last see Clare?"

"Why does that matter?"

He repeated the question.

"Friday afternoon, before I left for … for my religious instruction at the retreat house. So what?"

"Do you remember what she was wearing? How she looked? How she smelled? How she smiled?"

"Yes, of course. Why does that matter? I don't get it."

Ussury was now staring directly into Hamilton's eyes with a powerful but foreboding look of comfort. "So, you remember what she looked like on Friday night? That's good because that's exactly how I want you to picture her."

Ussury was continuing to hold Hamilton's shoulders with a caring but firm grip. Neither had moved even one inch.

"Not the way she is now. I want your picture of her to be the beautiful, caring wife and mother she was. Not the way she looks now." Ussury was picking and choosing each syllable, each word. He knew each phrase, each choice of words would be a timebomb set to go off if not selected carefully.

"Why? Why can't I see her?"

"Trust me on this, Howard. You do not want the last picture you have of her to be the condition she is in now." Ussury took his first complete breath in the last ten minutes.

"She is dead? Isn't she, Sarge? She is."

It was finally getting to the first level of reality he possessed at that moment. This door, this chasm he had walked into, alone, was beginning to take shape. She was gone, not to the store, not to church, not to yoga. She was gone. Gone.

—————— CHAPTER 11 ——————

Howard needed to release some tension. He opened and closed his eyes and paged through his and Clare's lives—the ups, the downs. His mental trip to their past was all a positive experience that only he could see, yet others were surrounding him all the way. He was in another zone, unaware of where he was, what he was doing, or what was to come next. He was not in the traffic office of the Long Beach PD headquarters. No, he was somewhere else.

His eyes closed, and his mind and heart were a million miles away. He was sitting comfortably in a soft, overstuffed sofa that had seen better days, looking straight ahead but seeing nothing, firmly placing his hands on his thighs, with his fingers wrapped tightly, like a vice grip.

Ussury left the room quietly. He could see he had at least done no harm. Leaving the room was the next essential step in his delivery of grief.

He did not know how much time had passed. Minutes, hours, or days? He heard voices. Someone was talking to him. Who was it? "Howard? Howard? Are you OK?" Who was that? He didn't know and didn't care.

It was Father Art, Rex Holcomb, and the Chief, his Chief. Where was he? Why were they there? He looked up to see no one. Their mouths were moving but said nothing.

Then he heard it. "Daddy, Daddy." Marcia rushed to him, threw her arms around his neck, and shouted in his ear, "Daddy,

Daddy." That was all. Geoff just stood there, saying nothing, as if the numbness of it all had yet to sink in.

The group hug lasted forever. Rex and the Chief backed out of the room and motioned for Father Art to stay. The reality for the Hamilton family, or what was left of it, was starting to settle in.

Father Art broke the silent grieving with "Let's pray, shall we?" Everyone reached for everyone. They found their hands touching someone else. They did not know whose hands they were holding, but it didn't matter as long as they were holding someone's. And that was where the comfort would begin.

The depth of Howard's sorrow, of their collective sorrow, was very personal. He never thought that this tragedy, this ungodly event, would happen in the Hamilton family. He could withstand losing a grandparent or even a parent. But not the love of his life, not like this. The series of events and their inevitable transitions occurred in distinct but subtle ways. By definition, death was beyond his control. And, of course, he thought he could control everything. He was invincible and thought his family was too. But not this time.

The event, or whatever one would call it, was quick—too quick. Clare's death, as sudden as it was, required control—of emotions, feelings, frustrations, and the desire to change, change just one thing, the outcome.

Futility set in. Managing life was not possible. Howard Hamilton had no idea of the psychological transition process he was going through; nor did he know what was ahead for him. He kept looking around. Howard knew he was in a police station, but this was not his station. Where was he?

He could not think this one through to where he would be next week, next month, next year—hell, tomorrow. Father Art had told him that at some point, he would have to let the sorrow go. Let the hurt just hurt. Let the end be the end.

"The first step is to see the future," Father Art told him. "Your old reality of Clare is just … just gone." Father Art was efficient as he placed his hands on the tops of the Hamilton family's hands, clutching one another.

"You need to get to a neutral zone, where you are not in your new world yet but no-man's land. It's a place where God just lets you be. To be with yourself. It is a place where you recognize that the old must give way to something, something else. But we don't know what that new is going to be."

Howard knew that Father Art had his best interest and that of his family in mind. But he also knew that it would be up to him, the single parent, to lead his family into an unknown future that had yet to be written.

"Don't rush. Stay in your neutral zone. Go back to the sorrow, but then return to the neutral. If you become confused, that's OK. It doesn't mean that there is something wrong with you. God has a plan for you and your family, but don't rush to it. You'll only jeopardize your future."

What did Father Art mean by that?

Howard would contemplate that statement several times. Was it to do nothing? To vegetate, just exist, or wallow in his sorrow? Or was it meant to do anything he wanted, if it was legal, moral, and not dangerous? He had no idea and was not going to ask for clarification. He was lost in his world of confusion.

There would not be a new beginning for him, Marcia, or Geoff. There could be no new beginning because he would never end his sorrow, his grief, and later, much later, his anger.

The three of them lived. Clare did not. They were together as a family, minus one. No. More than one, even if the number four was all they had been. One plus one, plus one, plus one was not just four. It was so much more. Three was three, but four was exponentially more, regardless of the math.

They all denied their new reality. There would be no future as a family of three. Anxiety was the only constant. The shock was always going to be there. They would see her in all they did. If they stayed in her house, she would be in every room. They would walk into the kitchen, knowing she was no longer there but fearful that she may be there. It was all just a dream.

Perhaps the emotion that would never leave Howard, Marcia, particularly, and Geoff, to some extent, was the frustrations that would follow. Who would buy the food, do the laundry, vacuum, pay the bills, or wash the dishes?

The confusion that was to follow would go on and on for months, maybe longer. The challenges that would face them each day as they went forward would add stress of immeasurable intensity. There was nothing left. The arguments would turn to sorrow, grief, anxiety, and shock, all over again. It was a cycle that would continue in what was left of the Hamilton family, minus one.

CHAPTER 12

Howard's hands were still gripping his thighs. Tightly. He was not in the conference room of the Long Beach Police Department. Where was he? He looked around. People everywhere. The fragrance of flowers everywhere. No one was talking. Soft guitar music was playing in the background. He was dressed in a shirt and tie, a suit—a black suit. The numbness came to him quickly.

He stared straight ahead. There was a presence he could sense. He glanced up and strained to see Jesus on the cross. He turned to his left. Marcia. He removed his hand from his thigh and patted her on the knee. To his right must be Geoff, he thought. It was. He was in church; he had to be in church.

The medication he took at the direction of Dr. Sullivan was doing the trick. All he had to do was go through the motions, look straight ahead, attempt a feeble smile, and move on after today. Clare's day. Her day was to be celebrated and recognized as the architect of his life. His kids' lives. Where was the emptiness he was supposed to feel? It wasn't there. He could only think, turn around, and recognize his familiar surroundings. He was at St. Elizabeth's. His church; their church. The Hamilton family church.

St. Elizabeth's was not an old, majestic basilica or mission. It was one of the new Catholic churches constructed in the latter part of the twentieth century. Some would call it modern or at least transitional, but it was more than just cement, wood, and glass. There was a powerful reverence when one walked in. It felt like a church should feel. God was present. Perhaps it was the size of the crucifix that hung behind the altar. It was bigger than life and very imposing. One could not look at it without feeling the pain and suffering it portrayed. And when the whole choir sang, it radiated positive energy that ensured a religious experience. It was where angels sang.

But not today. Today there were just the three in the front row. Clare was lying in repose in front of them. Just below the altar. From his seat, he could see her profile and her hair. Her hands were resting on her upper stomach, holding her mother's rosary. She was wearing her Nordstrom best. No black. A muted floral pattern had been purchased for the holidays. The holidays that were not to come. *We must remember to take the rosary from her to pass along to Marcia.* From where did that thought come?

Bentley, the family golden retriever, was lying in front of the casket, guarding her. He did not need a leash because his master was right next to him.

Father Art and Deacon Rex started the high mass, and someone he could not remember was supposed to do the first reading. He had no idea who it would be.

Then John Walker walked to the pulpit and spoke about the twenty-third psalm, but Hamilton only saw his lips move. His brother did the second reading, but he heard nothing. He had been to Catholic funeral services, Protestant ones, a few Jewish and nondenominational services. They seemed to be all the same.

He had written his comments, knowing he would have to read them. He was not going to tear up or lose his place as he had seen others do. That's why he had written it days before, set it aside, and then went back to the meds. That was the only way he could function. Perhaps those tears would come later. Not now.

He talked about her childhood without him in it. He talked about her schooling, hobbies, and contributions to the community. He talked about how hard it was to get that first date. Three contacts just to get her number, leaving messages that were never returned and getting frustrated but never quitting. He talked about where they went on the first date. Her girlfriend Lynn had insisted he keep calling her. He talked about their perfect home, their perfect yard, their perfect life, built by Clare; he and the kids were just grateful recipients.

As he stared into the haze of his meds, the audience appeared as cardboard figures. Just photos of people on a stick like he saw when he worked the Oscars one year. They would stick a photo of someone on the seat to make sure the room looked full, even if it was not.

CHAPTER 13

She was cute and fun, the family metronome. She kept the heartbeat of the house moving. After family, her next love was yoga. He talked about her goal of being an instructor and working with Maru. He glanced at the third row and saw Maru crying on her husband's shoulder. Howard paused.

"It's OK, Maru. She's with God now and still doing the downward dog." For many years, Maru was Clare's yoga instructor and mentor. She sat up straight as he called her name.

Howard felt like he had to explain. "Clare saw no conflict in the enjoyment of yoga and her Catholic upbringing. She was pursuing what everyone pursues, serenity and calm, peaceful meditation. It was prayerlike." He left it there and continued.

"Her meals were legendary in the family, on the block, and at the Department. She was an incredible cook who knew just the right balance of carbs, protein, and fats to make the perfect meal even better. I've already lost five pounds, and she's only been gone for less than a week."

He stopped, stepped back from the podium, and broke down just enough to lose his place. And his mind. The best part was that he was among friends. That was the worst part as well.

The silence was a tribute to his sorrow. He apologized to Clare, not the audience. He knew she would be upset, so he took several deep breaths, smiled at Geoff and Marcia, and continued.

He continued apologizing, this time for his shift work, not being home at night, and not being there on holidays.

"She had to pick up the newspapers from the driveway in the morning, keep the kids quiet as they got off to school, and put up with my stories. And of course, not being home on time. She did, however, love the OT—I mean the overtime, for you civilians." That brought a few smiles from the audience, who understood.

"She was the family doctor, and we were her patients. She was always a healthy one. Never sick, she ate right, read health magazines, and would know more about medicine than any doctor. And, and …"

He stumbled over his words, trying to get back on track.

"The four of us were a perfect match. Clare had a love of life and patience when we were idiots. She was just fun to be around. That's why I always wanted to be home. And now she's gone. My work was just that. I always wanted to be home."

He paused again to catch a breath.

"I viewed our family relationship as a mix of *Camelot* and *Mother Knows Best*. Wait, wasn't that *Father Knows Best*? Not in our house." He pointed in the direction of where the Chief and his wife, the LAPD detective, were sitting. "I would get better career counseling than any Chief could give me—sorry, Chief—and she would help with many of my on-the-job decisions, better than any supervisor."

He knew he had gone on too long, so he tried to find a way to close.

"She was healthy, vibrant, an outstanding yogi, mother, and wife. I never realized or thought that life as we knew it would end so quickly and soon be just a memory."

He waved his arms to the stilled audience that was hanging on his every word.

"All of you, many of you, had the opportunity to know her. We've all heard about filling the dash. Well, Clare was filling it with a love of life, her family, God, and ..."

He had to stop again.

"It seemed like we just got started ... and before you know I ... the times we had together as a family ... are gone. I want to close with a quote from Dr. Seuss, who said, 'Don't cry because it's over; smile because it happened.' Clare happened." He turned, gesturing with his outstretched hand to the casket with her body lying in repose.

"Death is always so sad because of our love and affection for that one particular person. To take the sadness and tragedy out of death, this one, you would have to take the love out of life. One never knows how long we have. We never saw this one coming. Never."

He slowly walked from the podium to the sound of a silent audience, an audience that could now take a breath and continue their sorrow as well.

CHAPTER 14

There was no mention of how or why Clare was gone. Lieutenant Rikelman's words echoed in Howard's mind as he readied to process out of the church.

Rikelman had reflected on the loss of so many OHPD members in the last year by several means. Clare's loss was not from a gunshot, cancer, or a heart condition. It was a tragedy of the street.

It doesn't matter how they die, Howard. They're gone, no matter the cause.

His trancelike state would wear off in a few hours, but for now, leaving the church to the waiting hearse was like something he had already rehearsed in his mind.

Howard was listening to the singer strumming his guitar. He slowly moved from his comfortable seat in the front row and stood facing the casket with Geoff and Marcia. He knew the song but didn't know who was singing it. It was from the 1970s by an Irishman named Gilbert O'Sullivan. *Clare, the moment I met you ...*

Just get this part over with, he thought, *and do not look up.* He nodded to those who reached out for him, seeing John Walker, maybe Lt. Rikelman, and who was with Rikelman? Vivian Hayes, the widow of Charles "Gabby" Hayes? The same Vivian who lost her husband to a heart attack in court? No, it couldn't be. It had to be the drugs.

He saw himself holding Marcia's and Geoff's hands, or were they holding his? He saw people with faces but was unsure if they were real.

Two ladies approached him with outstretched hands as they placed the coffin, no Clare, into the hearse to ride to the burial site. Did he know them? They called to him.

"HH. HH, we know, we know." Who were they? He vaguely recalled their faces, but they were just people who would eventually go to the cemetery. All he cared about was having this day over and being alone with his kids.

It would be days before others would tell him there were over one thousand attendees at the church. He was confident he had been in St. Elizabeth's, but he could not describe anything. Friends, family, uniforms from agencies other than Orchard Hill, those he worked with, churchgoers, yogis, and strangers to him but not to Clare.

On the way to the cemetery, it started to rain. How prophetic. Rain. Clare's ideal weather. *Let it rain. Let it fuckin' rain.* It was her way of telling the world and him that she had arrived at her final resting spot. She was happy. Not to be away from family but to be in that next station some have a belief in, others are not quite sure about, and still others deny.

Hamilton smiled at the rain, knowing she had sent the message.

He reflected on a discussion he and Clare had the last time it rained. "Howard, how can someone be an atheist? I mean, I guess I understand that some people grow into moving away from God. But why go through life denying his existence to yourself and others, as well as the hereafter? I would think that if there was a God, and he was forgiving, and there was heaven, you would want to hedge your bet and believe in him. The alternative is a disaster."

Once again, Clare had the last word. The rain was her way of saying, "See? I told you so."

The three of them hunkered down in the back seat of the stretch limo along with his mother and Clare's parents. The eye contact among the six of them told it all—nothing to be said. Everyone let a small glimpse of a smile walk gently across their faces as they looked to the rain for solace.

The drive was effortless. The procession moved slowly and methodically, with the only sound being windshield wipers. Motorcycle escorts leapfrogged to block traffic and allowed all who followed to break traffic laws in her honor.

If only they had been there that fateful Saturday night. To stop traffic, to pause while she effortlessly drove through the green light. The irony did not escape Howard, but his silence assured that everyone in the limo knew it was for Clare.

CHAPTER 15

The limo and procession of cars crawled through the gates of Queen of Angels Cemetery. They passed other grieving families burying their loved ones. A distant volley of gunfire and the sighting of military uniforms announced to everyone the message of another veteran who had gone to eternal rest. Both Marcia and Geoff flinched at the gunshots—gunshots that Howard would turn into a salute to his Clare.

That eternal rest Clare talked about happened only to other people. Not to the Hamilton family. Yet it had happened to his aging father just a few years ago. But not to youthful exuberance. Not to her …

The invisible umbrella holder walked them to the gravesite. Geoff walked Bentley by his side. Father Art and Deacon Rex said what they had to say, placed a crucifix on the casket, and stepped aside.

The Chief walked up to the Hamilton family and gave his condolences. Howard was surprised at the next event.

As the Chief bent down to talk so only the immediate family could hear, Donny Simpkins—yes, the Donny Simpkins, Howard's best friend on the job—slowly walked over to the Chief. Was he dressed in full uniform and—what? He was wearing his hat. His police hat. The one he said he would never wear. He approached the Chief, handed him a box, saluted in that slow, methodical manner, and made an about-face, leaving the Chief back on his knees in front of the Hamilton family.

"Howard? May I call you Howard?" he asked. The nod was sufficient.

"This is the flag that was flying at the station, our station, on the day of ..." He stumbled for just the right words. "On the day of the accident. We, the Department, wanted you to have it."

Marcia, Geoff, and Howard placed their hands on top of the flag together. And then there was the collective flood of tears.

But it wasn't over.

The Chief stood, tall in uniform, and faced the family and the flag with that same, slow, and painfully symbolic salute. The three of them just looked down at what was lying on Howard's lap and were interrupted in their solitude by the clearing of someone's throat.

It was Sergeant Ussury, the motor sergeant from Long Beach PD, the one who found Clare as no one else would ever see her.

It was Sergeant Ussury's words he would and could not ever forget. *You must remember her the way you saw her that morning. Not how she is now.*

He, too, had a strangely shaped box. "Your Chief and I had the same idea. This flag is from the Long Beach Police Department. It was flying at our station that evening. We wanted you to have it as a token of our sorrow for your loss."

The bond was there, never to be broken. There is no brotherhood or sisterhood like that of law enforcement. Howard knew it, but here it was, on full display, for his family, friends, and, yes, even strangers to see.

The haze was wearing off. Did he want his senses to return? He wasn't so sure. Not yet, not right now.

The line formed with condolences that were like a broken record. But they were still necessary, even essential. He wanted to hear them all from fellow officers, family, neighbors, fellow worshippers, and strangers. The two women appeared again, right behind Lieutenant Rikelman and Vivian.

He now put two and two together. It was Amanda Johnson and Yvonne Woodrow. The two other widows from Orchard Hill PD. Amanda's husband, AJ, had been shot and killed by a robbery suspect. Yvonne's husband, Clyde "the Glide," had been accidentally shot during a hunting accident in Catalina by Donny. What they said now made sense. "We know. We know."

Yes, they do, he thought. *Yes, they do.*

CHAPTER 16

The next thirty days following the memorial service were a blur for the Hamilton family. The emptiness at home was readily apparent to all who entered. There was no new routine, at least not yet. Mom had always done this or that. The family dog, Bentley, was also in mourning. He went from room to room, searching for someone who would never return.

As a family, they were still figuring out who would do the laundry, start the dishwasher, vacuum, and change the sheets. No one knew or, for that matter, cared—at least not yet.

Multiples of the death certificate would be issued. Insurance companies were to be notified, and accounts were changed, updated, or canceled.

The family would continue going through the motions for almost a year. That was the process of mourning. School days gave way to holidays and a summer trip that never happened. Work was work.

Leave me alone, let me drive aimlessly around the city of Orchard Hill, and give me time.

That was all Howard Hamilton, widower, could ask. And space. More space and distance, more distance, arm's length relationships—it was all anyone of them could handle for now.

Periodically he would flashback to the services and listen to the song "Clare" by Gilbert O'Sullivan. It was soothing in its way. He eventually bought an album with the artist's collection of hits, to find the song had been written to honor O'Sullivan's niece, a young girl. But for the most part, the lyrics still fit. The more telling song on the album was "Alone Again, (Naturally)." Much later, he would find that *Clare* was spelled the Irish way, *Clair*.

There would be no arrests of any magnitude for almost a year for Officer Howard Hamilton. He had nothing but assigned time to answer the radio, do what it told him, and get through the day. He knew it, his supervisors knew it, and of course, the Chief knew it. Leave well enough alone, and the Hamilton family would come out of it. Life, as they knew it, would go on.

They had reached the acceptance stage with both impatience and skepticism. What was the future to hold as a family, as a husband, daughter, or son? There was no hope for the future. At least not yet. There was no natural energy, no ups, no downs, just day-to-day existence. Would there ever be energy like they had? Would they ever be a creative family that was filled with enthusiasm? Only tomorrow could tell but not today.

Howard spent time at the station working out in the very spacious weight room, equipped with everything needed to buff up and stay in shape. He cleaned his locker for the umpteenth time. He had become the talk of the Department. His patrol bag became a department store of items: Purell sanitizer in a spray bottle, latex gloves, N 95 surgical masks, and his best binoculars to spy on the bad guys someday. His use of baby wipes became legendary as he cleaned the steering wheel and microphone before going into service each day. He was seen walking around the offices, wiping telephone receivers throughout the station.

His Vertex bag was top of the line. It became known as the "Gucci bag" because of its quality and craftsmanship. He even bought himself an expensive toy to put in the secret pocket—a night vision monocular because he knew he would eventually get back to his beloved night watch.

His motions were becoming more purposeful. He developed the best reference guide for every possible social service in the county. He had an answer for every conceivable question a homeless person could ask—or anyone else in distress, for that matter. He photocopied protocols from OHPD General Orders for procedures to utilize in officer-involved shootings, SWAT activations, and natural disasters. They were all laminated, with a checklist to follow should things get heated.

He had a personal CPR mask, EpiPens for opiate overdoses, and a box of Tylenol, not for a citizen but him. The headaches were continuing. It had been over a year. He was allergic to aspirin and ibuprofen, so only Tylenol. After the zombie pills given to him by Dr. Sullivan immediately following Clare's death, the most powerful thing he wanted was Tylenol. And Wild Turkey, 110 proof, on the rocks. And perhaps a touch of red wine.

Of course, he added extra AA, AAA, and nine-volt batteries, four boxes of ammo, and a buffing brush to keep his boots clean and remove an occasion crumb from the uniform. He had zip ties, a hundred-foot skein of 550 paracords, and enough yellow "Police Line—Do Not Cross" tape to conceivably handle the most significant crime scene. His coup de grâce was a package of dog treats for all angry or unhappy dogs.

If necessity were the mother of invention, then preparation for any eventuality was the father of readiness.

CHAPTER 17

His attention to detail made him a combination of a role model, laughingstock, and perfectionist, all rolled into one. It was just his way of channeling action to things that he viewed as housekeeping, order, and clarity. Clare would be proud.

That, unfortunately, was last year. This year would challenge even the sanest of beings, let alone the Hamilton family. Marcia had withdrawn from a world where mom ruled and took each day as dread and doom. On the other hand, Geoff took off on his own to explore sports, running track at school in the spring, and thinking about football in the fall.

Howard was all over the map. He had lost his compass, his mapmaker, soul mate, and his significant other. Without Clare, HH shot gunned planning, created chaos for the family, and became unpredictable. The kids found they could not count on him to keep them on course because he had no course. Bentley was his only constant. He was always there to hang out. That was what goldens did. There was what lay ahead today and maybe just a little bit of tomorrow. His workouts were his respite.

January crawled into February, and work was, well, work. They wanted him in detectives, narcotics, and even in the strategic planning unit responsible for writing policies and planning for the Department's future. Hell, how could he plan for the Department's future if he could not plan for his own?

The only constant in his life was work, getting the kids off to school, and Peet's for that caffeine fix. Probably in that order.

For now. He was back on the night shift, so he could get the kids jump-started in the mornings. Off by at least three in the morning, he could get some sleep for a few hours, make a decent breakfast, and catch a few more winks after they left. Working a four-ten shift meant he could have up to three or four days off in a row and act somewhat like a normal dad—whatever normal was.

The problem with days off was too much available time to think. Any plan was not worth thinking about. Should he get a new mattress? Clare was always there every night. No matter how many times he washed the sheets and pillowcases, her smell on the pillows, the concave impression on her side of the mattress—they were still there. She was still there.

CHAPTER 18

It was his first day back to work after a few days off. He went to the briefing, sat in the back with the other veterans, got his equipment in order, and checked out his favorite black-and-white Dodge Charger. He became more comfortable with the latest piece of mandatory equipment, the body-worn camera, or BWC. A stationary camera was in his black-and-white, and the BWC became just a part of the uniform. He just had to remind himself to turn it on at the appropriate time.

Roll call had advised the watch of a few burglary suspects and an auto theft ring from Chicago collecting vehicles off the street like hotcakes. *Must have a place to get rid of them,* he thought. Maybe on his next shift, he would come in early and talk to the auto table to see what they had regarding types of cars, locations taken, and other MO information—something to prompt his interest anyway.

He pulled into Peet's for his five o'clock fix. He put his earpiece in, so he could hear the police radio, preferring to go inside instead of the drive-through. He scanned the entryway, just as a matter of routine, and saw many usual customers. No one piqued his interest— that is, until he saw … way back, toward the rear of the reception area where one would order, something that caught his eye. A male in a T-shirt and Levi's was walking to the employee's entrance back office. It looked like the guy was trying to either reach in over the Dutch door or grab something with his back turned.

He decided to walk casually in the direction of the employee entrance and make his presence known. Good thing that he did because the male turned to face him in a rather "you caught me" manner. Hamilton knew him right away. "Michael? What the …" Then he saw Sophia on the other side of the door.

It was Alcazar, his first trainee who had just gotten off probation and was obviously off duty. Then he figured it out. He was grab-assing with Sophia and probably kissing or whatever they could do in the secluded nook.

"Hey, Mike, put your pecker back in your pants, bud." Howard looked around to make sure no one else heard him.

"Oh, sorry, sir, I mean HH." No doubt, Alcazar was embarrassed and looking for a way out. Howard was blocking his way. The uniform was working its magic.

"So," Howard said with a slight grin, "this thing getting serious? Or are you just messing around?"

"I don't know, sir. Jeez, am I in trouble?" Michael backed away and fell over a tall waste can that was ready to go to the dumpster.

"That's a good question, Officer Hamilton," Sophia said, looking sternly at a humiliated and mortified Alcazar. "What do you have to say to the nice Officer … Mic? Huh?"

She was trying to suppress a laugh and search for some assurance regarding their relationship at the same time.

Sophia and Michael had met months ago when HH and Alcazar were first teamed up. As his field training officer, or FTO, Hamilton worked with Alcazar after graduating from the academy and felt like he had mentored him into becoming an exceptional officer. At least until now.

Michael recovered, wiped himself off, and tried to regain his composure.

Sophia glanced at Alcazar. "I have to get to work, you two. Mic, we'll continue this conversation when I get off work. Officer Hamilton, your usual? I'll get it."

Sophia put her apron on with her name embroidered on the front and went to her barista duties.

"Care to sit and have a cup, *Mic*?" He started to laugh again. "Or maybe some hot milk?" He laughed again at the inference of immaturity he was trying to make.

Hamilton pointed to an open booth.

"Sorry, Howard. Just, she gets the best of me, and it comes out that way. I like her, but ..." With his head down in an apologetic manner, Michael shuffled in his seat, trying to calm down. It was the most sincere he had seen Michael.

"But what? There shouldn't be a but. She either is the one for right now or not." Howard worked to maintain the upper hand.

"She is," he said, clasping his hands and continuing to avoid eye contact.

"I know. I can see that. Can't you?" Howard realized it was time to let up.

"Can we change the subject, HH?"

"Sure."

They both walked to an empty table while Sophia prepared their coffee order.

"I haven't seen much of you after we went our separate ways with me going to other training officers. You were the best, HH, and I'm not blowin' smoke. I learned more from you." He trailed off. "What I want to ask is, is ... how are you doin,' you know, with Clare ... not around anymore? Jeez, I don't know how to say it or ask it." He ran both hands through his hair as if to sweep cobwebs from his brain.

"We're OK. Thanks for asking."

"Anything I can do to help?" he offered, fully thinking he knew the answer.

"Yes, there is, Mic or Michael. Whatever your name is. Now that I'm single, you better scoop Sophia up, or *I'm* comin' after her."

"Oh, no, you don't, sir."

"Just kidding, Michael, and quit calling me sir. But it is time to make some decisions. By the way, how's your mom? Still sleeping in her bathtub?"

Michael and his mother, Lillie, lived in a gang-infested neighborhood in Wilmington. Due to the drive-by shootings, she had taken up sleeping in her cast-iron tub with a mattress that created comfortable protection.

"I think I have her convinced to sell. It hasn't been easy, but with the job," he said, referring to his newly spawned career, "she realizes I won't be home like I was." He was now much more comfortable and made eye contact with HH.

"Understandable," was Hamilton's typical one-word response as he nodded agreement.

"Just wanted to get off probation, make sure I had a real job, and then work on her to move."

"Good. I like that type of thinking." The mutual smiles rekindled the bonding lost for a moment.

They worked on the bottom half of their coffee, and Hamilton made a motion to leave.

"Just a word to the wise, Michael," he said, holding his hands in the air as if to stop Michael from getting up. "Don't do too much grab-ass off duty. I would bet some people here know who you are or think they do. Save it for the privacy of your own home, or car, or whatever. People are weird. You know?"

"Yeah, I got it. I should have known better." Michael reverted to his sheepish look.

HH saw his submission and tried to salvage the conversation. "Hey, just remember, a hard pecker does not have a brain."

"Roger that," Michael said, laughing but still a bit ill at ease.

CHAPTER 19

They parted ways, with Michael and Howard both saying their goodbyes to Sophia. Michael gave Howard one of those looks, *Not sure if you meant anything by that remark about Sophia.*

He was walking rapidly back to his black-and-white when a voice called to him. "Officer Hamilton? Is that you?" He pulled out the earpiece to his radio.

He turned around and was surprised at who had beckoned.

She was dressed in casual workout elegance. She wasn't smiling. For almost two years, Amanda Johnson had nothing to smile about. Her husband, Officer Andrew Johnson, or known in the OHPD family as AJ Foyt, had been killed by a robbery suspect. Hamilton had been there immediately after the shooting and could do nothing to save him. One round in the ten-ring. He was dead upon impact. His bulletproof vest was hanging over the passenger seat. After a rigorous workout in preparation for a tryout at the local NFL Combine, he had taken it off.

He recalled seeing her at AJ's funeral, but it was somewhat hazy as to whether he saw her at the service for Clare. Perhaps. She had seen him as she entered the coffee shop, recognized him immediately, and followed him out.

She extended her hand. "Amanda Johnson, AJ's … wife." The hesitation was almost natural, as she had not referred to her husband by his OHPD nickname to anyone.

"Amanda! Of course. How are you doing?"

Howard was a bit taken aback by the greeting but scolded himself for dropping his guard. He should have been much more aware of his surroundings. Standing next to his patrol car, HH reached in to see if his MDT had given him a call. He turned up the radio slightly, set his coffee cup on the hood of the trunk, and for whatever reason he did not know, reached out to give Amanda a brief hug.

"Thank you," she said somewhat shyly. "It's been a while. I don't know if you remember, but I attended Clare's service about a year ago. How are *you* doing?"

"I'm ... I'm OK. Still adjusting. But you. You look great. Glad to see you taking good care of yourself."

The clothes were trendy but fashionable. Her hair was in a bun. She sported running shoes with shorts down to the top of her knees and an Under Armour, almost T-shirt that barely covered her breasts but not much else. A bead of sweat rolled slowly down the side of her cheek.

"Just came from the gym." She wiped the droplet with a finger. "How are your kids?"

He had heard the question more times than he could count. He replied with his standard line, "Geoff is doing great, and Marcia is still a work in progress."

"AJ, Andrew, always spoke highly of you, Officer Hamilton. He said he wished he could have had you as a training officer."

"It's Howard or HH, Amanda. Come on!"

"Hard to do that. AJ wasn't even off probation yet, so everybody was sir this or sir that."

"I know. It's our culture, but he was looked up to also. Sharp guy, looked good in a uniform, kept in shape, and did what he was told. My kind of boot." They both laughed.

"Well," he said, looking around the parking lot. "Can't be seen talking too long to a pretty girl. Might get in trouble at the shop."

They laughed again. "Good to see you, Amanda. Really good to see you. And thanks for coming to Clare's service. It meant a lot."

"I think, well, we have a bond now, from the Department, I mean." She said it perhaps without thinking, but he got the message.

"We do, Amanda. Thanks for saying that. Even though Clare wasn't a member of the dDepartment, she was one of us. Part of the OHPD family."

"Always will be."

She made a move to leave, and they both stumbled over "Great to see you." One hug as friends was all either could take.

Time to go to work, he thought. *Time to go to work.*

CHAPTER 20

Weeks passed. Time moved like the wind. There was no way to control it and yet no way to follow it, see it, or slow it down. He knew she was gone. He reminded himself more than once the emptiness was her absence, but it was also her presence. He still walked into rooms expecting to see her, smell her, and feel her there. Days had turned into months, and months had transitioned to the first anniversary.

It seemed that people gave him way too much space: his family, the kids, fellow officers, supervisors, and even the Chief. No one was asking how he or the kids were doing anymore. It was now just a bad memory, a memory that he would live with forever, but they, whoever they were, would get to go on with their lives.

The people he wrote tickets to, gave directions to, or problem solved for, at least temporarily, cut him no slack. They wanted immediacy. "Fix it now. Could you not do that to me? You can't do that, or I won't do it again, sir."

They couldn't have cared less about his situation. Even if he were to tell them, and he never would, it was his problem, not theirs. He, Geoff, and Marcia had overcome their series of conflicts and waves of anger. Now he was a single parent, a widower keeping things together, maybe not with Gorilla Glue but at least with Silly String.

Not giving a shit about others was the hallmark of today's society, so he might as well fall in line. He didn't want to be in charge of anybody's life, let alone his own. *I didn't choose this life. It was chosen for me.*

The phone calls kept coming. Donny was almost a daily chat. Nothing sappy, just checking in. He even got a periodic call from Donny's girlfriend, Officer Pat "the Wolf" Wolford. The three of them held the secret of HH catching the Wolf giving Donny a blow job in the workout room at the station in the middle of the night. That bond would never go away.

Red Walker stuck Post-it Notes on his locker with brief updates on the detective spots opening up. Howard wasn't sure he was ready just yet.

It was hard to practice officer safety. He was in a modified zone that permitted him to function but not always think ahead or be aware of his surroundings. He would find himself gazing at a tree when he should have been looking at the road. He would sense he may have run a light or not stopped at a stop sign. His autopilot was on most of the time. Maybe it would get him through this.

When he interacted with the public, it was like going through the motions. Robotic. Mechanical. *Yes, sir, no, ma'am. Yes, as a matter of fact, I do have my camera on.* He knew he was vulnerable, but there was not much he could do about it. *Just stay safe*, he told himself, *and don't do anything stupid.*

The casseroles stopped coming from neighbors after a few months, but his mother still brought fresh-baked chocolate chip–oatmeal cookies every few weeks or when the supply ran low. The kids' friends took turns picking them up for school and made sure they did not wake him in the hustle-bustle of the morning rush.

He knew it was time to get back to what mattered. And what mattered was work and family, maybe in that order or maybe not.

CHAPTER 21

She had more energy than someone on speed, meth, or any uppers. That was because she loved her job. Mary Ann Kowalski ("Don't call me Marianne. It's Mary space Ann") felt she had reached the highest level on Maslow's hierarchy of needs, self-actualization.

Unlike many of her classmates from high school, she went right to college on a softball scholarship. Excelling at first base since Little League made her a sought-after athlete. She was and always had been big-boned or hefty. Not an hourglass shape by any means, but what she did not have in looks, she made up with in personality.

She didn't date much—well, if the truth be known, not at all. She heard the whispers of "Is she gay too? Everyone else on the team is." God, no. Just not interested right now. A negative experience when she was thirteen delayed any interest in boys or men.

It had taken her a long time. A bachelor's in biology, rejected from all nursing schools, opting to petition, and be placed on a waitlist if someone dropped out. They did. She got in, excelled in the classroom and residency, and the rest, as they say, is history.

She spent three wonderful years in the emergency room on the night shift in a hospital just adjacent to the ghetto. Gunshot wounds, stabbings, traffic accidents, overdoses all came in droves—every night. The shifts went as fast as Olympic sprinter Asan Bolt did the hundred meters. Every night was a repeat performance. The experience level piled on, with the three years being like nine in any other hospital.

She finally looked for an area of specialization. Selecting pediatrics, she landed a job close to home at a local children's hospital and adjusted to young people's life-and-death trauma.

Mary Ann had read somewhere that putting off a family and relationships until one was professionally settled meant that her original calling was not family but a substantial career. It was based upon the theory of the *Phantom of the Opera*. As she had read, Christine's calling was singing. She had to choose between Raoul and the phantom. The phantom was not a person portrayed in the stage and movie versions but a calling to commit to one's craft. In the case of Christine, it was her singing.

The phantom just symbolized the highest level of commitment to one's chosen profession. Some answered the call, sacrificed other priorities, and heeded the call. Others did not take the route demanded by the phantom and never challenged themselves to go to that next higher level.

Five years and many memories later, she briefly entertained pursuing a physician's assistant or PA education. But she loved being with and caring for her patients. Nurses were in charge of doctors, while PAs worked for the doctors. She opted for administrative credentials and made sure she excelled in the pursuit of even more education. But a few things were missing— namely, a child of her own and a man in her life. And, just maybe, in that order.

Her inner strength came from two strong-willed parents who could not survive each other's drive. They had taught her that she could do it all. Have a baby and then look for Mr. Right. Her medical contacts made it easy. In vitro fertilization, or IVF, was natural. So was the sperm bank. Let them know what sex—and bingo. Nine months later, much to the chagrin of her family, Ann Marie was born. She was healthy, feisty, and full of energy. Just what the doctor or nurse had ordered.

CHAPTER 22

She took time off from work and applied for director jobs with a regular day schedule. Her nursing school professor found her the ideal position at Rosecrans Presbyterian Hospital. After a year of playing mom, it was time to get back at it. The family finally fell in love with Ann Marie. Her mother, sisters, and nieces all chipped in to accommodate her new duties. But there was one more thing on her list. She never felt the loneliness of being a single parent. The family had filled every need. But …

And then it happened. Not what was expected but just what she wanted. The hospital had just delivered a new batch of medical residents from the University of Southern California's medical school. As Director of Nursing, she knew her hospital, rightfully positioned in the South Bay and adjacent to the ocean and upscale homes, was a sought-after site for the new crop of medical students.

She knew the drill for them, as she had seen it a dozen times. The key for first-year residents was the diagnosis. Follow a veteran orthopedic surgeon, internist, or gastrointestinal expert around with a clipboard, take copious notes, and hope you were not called upon to offer your opinion. At least not first anyway.

He was about the same height as she was and pleasantly plump but not morbidly obese. She found opportunities to follow his group around at least once a day and made sure she was doing her rounds at the various nursing stations at the same time he was.

No eye contact. He was intently concentrating on the doctor in charge and the various patients. Not by name, just by symptom.

Wavy, jet-black hair, right-handed, glasses but not too thick, a stern look, and no ring on the left hand. He was of a mixed-race, she opined, maybe half-white and half-Asian? Maybe not. But what culture? Chinese, Vietnamese, Korean, or Japanese? Maybe Hawaiian?

For about a month, she stalked the new medical team as they continued their rounds. As an efficient administrator, she obtained his personnel medical file somewhat surreptitiously, just to find out his name and a few other things.

She found out his name was Jung Song, but he went by James Song to Americanize himself. He was not married. She looked at his date of birth and realized he was older than her by a few years. *Hmmm. What was he doing all those years? He does not look that old.*

She still wasn't sure of his origin, so she contacted one of her nurses and tried to bring his name up casually. Shazam! The name was Korean. Now she would brush up on some greetings and phrases just to break the ice.

It went from *ahnyong hasimnikka kim sun sang* or *hello* to *ddo bebkep sumnida and see you again*, to *im nida Mary Ann, I am Mary Ann.* It progressed to *pyol myong I itsumikka, do you have a nickname,* and a response of *James* to *junhwa bognoga mu ut imnika? What is your phone number?*

They would frequently meet for coffee and exchange greetings in his native language but would have more intimate conversations in English. In the next few months, she exhausted her vocabulary with *tang sin un cho hun sa ram imnida, you are a good man,* to phrases she would have to look up in her Korean pocket dictionary. She researched the Korean culture to find that family and honor were the most treasured traits. Not surprising.

What did *tang sin un dae dan hi a rum dap sumnida* mean? She found out to her embarrassment that it translated to *you are very beautiful.*

It was sometime early in the relationship that she decided to start working out. She wanted to be desired, and being healthy was the first step. Walking at lunch, going to a gym on days off, and eating more healthy became her mantra. It worked.

In six months, the relationship had blossomed. James had only a few months left in his residency. One day, he used a phrase that she did not have to look up: *na rul sa rang hamnida* or *do you love me?* Mary Ann was ready with a response that shocked her consciousness as well as James. "Mul ron sa rang hamnida," or *of course, I love you!* James responded with *chong mal*, "Really?" They both responded with *a I ko ma war a ch amjul gop da.* "Thank God. How pleased I am!"

They laughed at each other's attempts not to speak English. Each of them had delayed any feelings until their respective careers were well in place. It was time to take it all to the next level.

CHAPTER 23

Hamilton knew he was in a funk. And he wanted out of it. Work had not been satisfying lately. Geoff and Marcia had settled into a rhythm and seemed to be adjusting well. Marcia was still the silent one, and those waters, he knew, ran deep. He thought of inviting her on one of the four-mile runs he mapped out for himself at the beach.

After almost a year and a half, it was time for them to release those pent-up emotions. But, and it was a big *but*, the Christmas holidays were here—all of a sudden.

The Hamilton family would work to get through the first of many Christmas holidays without Clare. But not well. Crying and laughing were the center point of any discussion. Family photos were placed strategically throughout the house, in their car, even taking center stage before their driver's license.

Geoff had decided to enroll in a basketball camp, and Marcia was going to a cheerleading camp. It would be almost a week by himself. And he could not stand it. Where could he go? And what could he do with them gone? More working out? More Wild Turkey? What happened to just the red wine he and Clare would share way too often?

It was his third day of playing the bachelor role. Cooking for himself, cleaning the house, and doing a bit of yard work. He searched the garage for the Christmas decorations and finally found them neatly stored. Some were in the garage, but even more were in their spare bedroom closet.

He was developing a rhythm of his own when he returned from work. That rhythm did not extend to work, however. It was becoming too mundane. There was absolutely nothing exciting in his life.

He was concerned that he would let his guard down at work when it mattered. The vigilance he once had on the street was just not there. He was grateful that Orchard Hill was the type of community where willing compliance with the law was the rule for most. The best he could do right now was just persuasion, advice, and warnings. He didn't have the fortitude to enforce or arrest, and he knew it. At least not right now. Maybe he should consider an inside job or investigations. Narcotics, Detectives, or even a squint or staff assignment would refresh his energy for police work.

He was cleaning the kitchen for the third time that day when the doorbell rang.

Who could it be? The kids were gone, and bills had been paid. A solicitor? He casually strolled to the door with a dish towel over his shoulder, thinking of how to say no, he did not want to buy anything, without offending.

He was shocked to be met by Amanda Johnson, AJ's widow.

"Amanda! What a surprise seeing you." He stood in the doorway, looking through the screen door, somewhat dumbfounded as he was trying to piece his thoughts together. *Has she been here before to see Clare? Why now and why here?*

"Are you going to invite me in?"

"Of course, come on in. Let me wash my hands. Been gardening and housecleaning."

J. C. De Ladurantey

"You're keeping the house nicely. Oh, my, I see you're decorating for the holidays," she said in a hushed tone, looking around to see a staged home that could be ready to sell. Nothing was out of place.

"We try. I mean Marcia, Geoff, and I. I just realized it was Christmas, so ..." The thoughts and words drifted away.

There was no handshake, hug, or anything suggesting a friendship. Both felt very awkward.

Howard directed Amanda to the living room couch. He walked quickly to the kitchen to scrub his hands and get rid of the dishtowel. Bentley moved from his normal resting position in the kitchen and walked back with Howard to the living room. He sniffed at Amanda's feet, then casually lay down on her right side, across from Howard.

He sat in the chair adjacent to the sofa directly across from her. Then, somewhat as an afterthought, he immediately stood up again. "Well, I see you made a new friend. I'm sorry. Can I get you anything to drink? Water, a Coke, wine, or beer?"

"Water would be good." She smiled and looked around, gazing at the paintings, furnishings, and tchotchke decorations. She reached down to pet Bentley, who reciprocated by licking her hand. She focused on the pictures of Clare but did not comment.

He returned from the kitchen and handed her a small, chilled bottle of water.

"So, what brings you to ..." He stumbled, trying not to place her on the defensive. "How did you find me ... ah ... us?"

"I hope you don't mind," she said rather shyly, "but I asked Janet, the Chief's secretary. She and I have become friends over the ... incident with AJ, and I asked her for your phone number and address." She took a long drink of water and asked for more.

Howard returned from the kitchen and reflected on AJ and what he remembered about him and Amanda. He also still had embedded in his mind the picture of AJ's bulletproof vest draped over his passenger seat.

AJ was the son of a black mother and a white father. He had joked that Amanda was the other way. Her father was black, and her mother white. It made for a blended family of a unique nature, and they both wondered what their kids would turn out to be and what box they would mark regarding ethnicity on the next census.

Amanda was striking. She had the Halle Berry or Mariah Carey look—fair skin, Caucasian features, but the copper tone that said something else was there.

"I hope you don't mind." Again, concern marked her face.

Howard could tell she needed some assurance. Access to the home information of police officers was very protected. Janet knew that, and so did Amanda.

Howard decided to change the subject. "Want to see the house?" he offered as he swept his arms around to give her a sense of comfort.

"Sure," she said with relief.

The tour didn't last long. He showed her the kids' rooms, family room den, even the garage, and his pride and joy, the English garden backyard he had just started. The short hallways and close quarters made moving through the home difficult without bumping into each other on occasion. Clare's photos were everywhere. Somewhat awkwardly, he walked by the master bedroom, not even commenting on it.

They returned to the living room and took their respective places. Amanda's next question shocked him.

"How are you doing, Howard? I mean, it's been almost a year and more since …" She let that sentence trail away. "It's been over two years for AJ and me …"

He decided to interrupt. "I know, Amanda. I know." They both stared off into a space that each knew was for comfort. They had been there before.

"I know it's hard, really hard, but nothing is going to change what is, and that is they are both … no longer with us." The silence was deafening.

They both started to talk. Trying to change the subject, he said, "Looks like you're still working out. You look great. I'm running and lifting but have not gone back to yoga." More silence.

"Have you gone to counseling?" Amanda asked.

"Just once, to get cleared to go back to work. The Chief asked if I would do it. So I did."

"The Department has been so good to my parents, AJ's, and me. Janet and the Chief check in with me at least once a month, and …" She drifted again.

Howard held up his hands but remained seated. "Hold it, Amanda. Why are you here? I mean, why look me up, get my home address, and knock on my door, and now you're sitting in my living room?"

It came out so much harsher than he intended.

"I better go," she said. But she didn't move. Gazing down at the floor, she was trying to collect her thoughts. They both sat in silence.

"I'm sorry, Amanda. I guess I don't understand."

She looked over to him, sitting with frustration and confusion written all over his face. There were tears in her eyes. "I thought, I thought we had a connection. Something to share. To just be, you know, friends."

"We do, we are, but …"

"OK, let's start over. Can we?" Was he trying to salvage something here?

She stood to go, this time grabbing her purse.

"You and I have had the worst day of our lives. Separately. Losing someone is not easy. I just thought …" She trailed off again, wishing she could finish what she had so clumsily started.

CHAPTER 24

Howard realized what was between them. "I do feel a bond with you, Amanda. We've both lost our first love under violent circumstances. Just being in each other's presence, we both seem to have a rush of guilt, shame, and at the same time maybe a level of abandonment." He could not look at her now.

"Hey, I have all of that and more. I'm scared, frustrated, and confused. Maybe that's why I came here." Amanda turned away to make sure no eye contact was possible.

This is Clare's house. He wanted to say it but held that thought back. *It is her domain. She is here, or at least her spirit is.* And Bentley is or was her dog. There was too much anxiety in the room.

Two minutes of silence in a room filled with only two people is not possible. The one minute plus allowed both Howard and Amanda to regroup just a little.

"How about another water? The bottles are small." He finally broke the silent bond that had formed due to the intimate but somehow trusting silence.

"Do you have a bottle to go?" She smiled in her eager but shy way, sending the message it was time to leave.

Howard slowly walked to the kitchen, opened the refrigerator door, and stared for just a moment too long. "Something wrong in there?" Amanda called.

"No, not at all."

He walked her to the door and reached out to gently touch her elbow as she reached for her car keys.

"Hey …" He placed his arms around her shoulders. She wasn't very tall, so his arms enveloped her in what they both needed most. She hugged, and he hugged—comfort from someone who knew.

The embrace was one of friendship, close friendship. Howard and Bentley walked her to the car, past the boxwood bushes that outlined the walkway—the boxwoods that he and Clare had planted together. They had grown and were now touching to form a perfect hedge and pathway.

He opened the driver's side door, and she sat down. Neither wanted to speak. Howard finally broke the quiet with just two words. "Thank you."

She smiled, started the car, placed it in reverse, and backed out of his driveway. Howard and Bentley followed the taillights until her car turned the corner and was out of sight.

CHAPTER 25

Mary Ann and James's dates were short but sweet. Hospital schedules did not always conform to each other. She purchased a condominium a few minutes from the hospital, close to her sisters and mother. James took to Ann Marie. He was a natural.

But who was Jung Song? She was to learn he was a very complicated and diligent person. On one of their frequent dinner engagements, he shared his early experiences.

"I was raised in the United States as a first-generation American. My parents immigrated to the States after the Korean War. Dad was in the South Korean Army and rose to the rank of *Sojang* or Brigadier General."

"A General? Wow, very impressive, James."

"It gets better. He left the military, attended law school, became an immigration specialist, and was appointed to the Los Angeles County Superior Court in downtown Los Angeles. My mother chose to stay at home and raise three kids. After we all graduated from high school, she taught in the Koreatown area of downtown LA. Stayed in what is now known as Koreatown."

"Koreatown? I didn't know there was such an area. Where is it?" Mary Ann was going to dig into his background as gently as she could.

"At the time, it was a relatively small area. You know where the Wilshire district is in LA?"

"I think so. I may have been there for a job interview once."

"Well, it's in the area around Union, 3rd Street, and Pico."

She still wasn't sure where it was but encouraged him to continue.

"Well, I decided to be an Anteater."

"What did you say?" She laughed. "I'm sorry. You were an Anteater?"

"Yes, UC Irvine," he said, referring to the school's mascot. They laughed together. "I did my premed there. But I wasn't happy. I was restless and wanted to visit my home country. I enlisted in the Korean Army as a young Sowi or Junior Lieutenant with my father's connections. With my premed background, I rose to *Sangwi* or Senior Lieutenant and then to *Taewi* or Captain. Just one year later, at the age of twenty-six, I became a *Teajwa* or Senior Colonel."

Trying to coax him to continue, Mary Ann showered him with praise. "James, that is very impressive. You amaze me."

"I studied the relationship between South and North Korea extensively and was assigned to Paju, also known as Panmunjom, a border village north of Seoul open to tourists and just across the border from North Korean artillery sites. While their cultures may be similar, their politics definitely were not."

She brought out the best in him as he continued to respond to her encouragement.

"Between you and me, I longed for escalation and conflict between the two countries but chose to keep those thoughts and desires silent. I'm not a fan of the North Korean government and its assassins, so I needed to keep quiet and decide my next steps."

"What did you do? I hope you weren't too vocal about it."

He shook his head to make his point. "No, because of my relationship with the United States Army's various members, I became interested in returning to the US to finish my medical education. Working through my Dad, I applied and was accepted

71

at the University of Southern California Medical School. I'm sure you know, but the Trojan alumni organizations are very influential. I had all the qualifications to get in. First, my alumni father, second, my military record, and lastly, my academic record in premed." He emphasized the three by holding up a finger for each to count his blessings.

She just stared at him with pride, beaming at his accomplishments.

"At twenty-nine, I ultimately came back to the US, completed medical school, and was considering an area of specialization when I got assigned to Rosecrans Presbyterian Hospital for residency. Then I met you. End of story."

"Not the end, James, not by a long shot."

CHAPTER 26

The kids came home within an hour of each other, and all was right with the world—at least the world at home. Everyone caught up on each of their camp adventures. Geoff touted the hazing he was put through at basketball camp and how it would never hit the papers or TV, but he passed with flying colors.

Marcia opened up. "Dad, you've started decorating for the holidays. I was thinking of doing that when I got home. Can I help?"

"Maybe we can do it together."

Work was another matter. He tried to get back the enjoyment of the uniform, the "unknown trouble" calls and dealing with the occasional domestic violence case, traffic, tourists, and PD drama, but it still felt a bit hollow.

The dolphins were talking about a lot of movement of people in the department. Transfers, promotions, and retirements seemed to be constant. The dolphins became the term of endearment for the OHPD grapevine. Someone visited Sea World to find out that dolphins gossip in their language. It became the mantra for the Department that information, regardless of truth or fiction, was the dolphins talking.

At least in the Department, Donny, his best friend, had taken a job as a detective trainee on the auto theft table. His acumen for sniffing out stolen cars was legendary, so it was a natural fit. John "Red" Walker was still working homicide, and perhaps it was time for him to make a move. But where?

He couldn't or wouldn't work Narcotics due to their crazy schedule and the kids needing him wherever they were in this world. After ten years in Patrol, all he had to do was ask, or at least put his name on a waitlist, and he would get selected for some specialized assignment.

⸻ ◆ ⸻

It was just another shift on Patrol, and he was getting ready for briefing. The internal intercom announced, "Officer Hamilton, can you call Janet in the Chief's office?" The oohs and ahs from the locker room were relentless. "Fuck you," he mouthed but did not speak to anyone watching. Of course, he would never use such language anywhere but there. He might use it to get compliance on the street or banter with his buddies, but it would never be brought home. Never.

He decided to walk up the flight of stairs after briefing to see what she wanted. The elevator was for the public.

"Officer Hamilton," she said, bright-eyed and cheery, "how are you and the family doing?" Janet was one of the most straightforward people he had ever known. She said what needed to be said, very matter-of-factly and never with remorse.

"The Chief's not here right now. Can I talk to you in his office?" She didn't wait for his approval but walked into the office and expected him to follow. Once he did, she closed the door.

"Listen, Howard, I did something that's been bothering me, and I need to let you know. You know Amanda Johnson, AJ's wife?"

He knew where this was going but decided to play coy.

Janet let her glasses dangle from their jeweled clasp around her neck. "Well, she came up here last week and was talking to the Chief about something and, in front of the Chief, asked me if she could have your address and phone number. I felt like he would approve, so I just gave it to her. I hope that's all right."

She was almost violating his personal space as she leaned into him to get his approval. It was more of a statement than a request.

"Did she say why she wanted it?"

"I thought it was because of something that she had talked to him about. That's why he didn't say anything. I'm sorry if I did something wrong." Howard was going to leave it as it was, with Janet not knowing Amanda had already taken advantage of the information.

"It probably has something to do with … you know, what happened," Howard said to ease her concern.

"Well, that's what I thought too," she said in relief.

"Well, if it's OK with you, can you give me her contact info? It's only fair."

He returned to the streets with a whirlwind of thoughts.

CHAPTER 27

James Song opted to take an internist position with another doctor after he completed his residency at Rosecrans. The private practice was located on the east side of Los Angeles in a community dominated by Asian cultures, predominately Chinese and Korean. Monterey Park was not far from downtown LA, distance-wise, but traffic-wise it was ugly. He was still renting an apartment in El Segundo and would make the drive to his new office on freeways that never quit, day, night, during the week or weekends. He was considering moving closer to his work.

Things were going very well for him. He saw his parents and brothers frequently. They enjoyed Mary Ann and Ann Marie, and he was adjusting to the chaos of her extended family. There was no discussion of moving in with her or marriage. He assumed that would happen eventually.

Mary Ann decided to broach a very sensitive subject on one of their many dinner dates and stayovers. They had just finished dinner at one of their favorite sidewalk hangouts for sushi, having devoured kimbap, gimbap, and norimaki.

It was an early winter evening. Many of them were like summer nights in Southern California, even if the rain was on its way later in the week. They always got the table at the end of the row for privacy.

She called him Jung when they were alone together but referred to him as James when they were in public.

"Jung, we've talked a lot about your past, with school and your involvement with the Korean Army. And I see why you never became serious with anyone before us."

"Yes, well, it just never would work out. I dated in high school and college but just for fun."

"I know and see that. I just wanted to talk a bit about me for a minute, OK?"

James looked directly at her. "Go on."

Mary Ann took a deep breath. She searched around the sidewalk café to make sure there was no one eavesdropping. "Here goes. I was thirteen at the time. My folks were together then, and we always had these family gatherings on the weekends, primarily Sundays, because of everybody's schedules. My mom's sister ..." She paused to collect her thoughts and take a breath. "My mom's sister had a longtime boyfriend. He was about twenty-seven or twenty-eight at the time. Everybody liked him, but I thought he was creepy." She was looking him straight in the eye, trying not to blink.

"Well, at first, it started with him touching me on my arms, hugging me for just a little bit too long. I think you know where I'm going with this."

"Go ahead, Mary Ann. It's OK." He was in counseling mode now. He stared at her to intensify his listening, reaching out to hold a hand.

"He would find a way for us to be in a room together with no one else around and try to touch me, you know, in my private parts."

"Did you let him?"

"Well, not exactly. I was so embarrassed that I did nothing. Nothing ..."

There was an emphasis on most of the last word, but then it drifted away, trying to make the thought go away with it.

"Anyway, over some time, it kept getting more frequent. It was like every Sunday; he would see me and find a way to get us alone. It was a big house, and there were many rooms."

James decided that the best thing to do now was to remain silent and let her talk. He looked around the restaurant to make sure no one was listening. "This all went on for over a year. That person would reach under my panties and …" He could see she was fraught with emotion in just telling the story—more than likely for the very first time.

Her story was repelling James. He was trying not to be revolted or nauseated—not at her but the circumstances. He had never encountered anything like what he heard in his own culture. *Perhaps it happens, but maybe it's just not discussed.*

"Can I ask some questions yet?"

"Please do. I've never told anyone about this. Not my dad, a priest, or even a girlfriend."

He was thinking about what she told him and realized he wasn't listening to her anymore. He didn't have to. He squeezed her hands tightly in his. The closest table was now empty, so he felt more comfortable consoling her.

"Everybody looked up to him in the family. He never married her, but I don't know why. I haven't seen him in over a decade, but … but …"

He raised his hand in a manner that signaled he had heard enough. "Who is this guy?"

She hesitated. "Names aren't necessary, Jung. Please, I just needed to tell you how sensitive I am about intimacy. That guy is a nothing, a total nothing."

"OK, I got that, Mary Ann, but you don't know who else he … he …" Jung was fumbling around for just the right and sensitive phrase. "You don't know if he ever touched anyone else, do you?"

"I don't know and don't care. I know I wasn't strong enough to do anything about it or tell anyone until now. Please, don't think bad of me, please."

"For goodness sakes, none of this was your fault. Don't you see that? You were thirteen, young, and had no idea. He had no honor, no respect for you. This guy, this predator, was an adult. A responsible adult. He did know better." His empathy was turning into a wave of seething anger.

He sat up straight and let her hands go. It was then he contemplated his next move, but he wasn't going to let her know. "You're right. I don't want to know who he was or is."

Both let the quiet of the moment envelop them with the exterior sounds of the street, patrons moving chairs, and waiters hustling to serve others.

He decided only to go a little further. "Have you ever gone to counseling?" He was trying to continue his eye contact and not expose his internal rage.

"No, not yet, but I think I see a need if we're going to go further with this relationship." She sat there with her hands in her lap, looking at him with pleadings dripping from her eyes. "What do you think?"

Jung nodded his head. "I think ..." He paused for a long moment that let her know something else was coming. "I think it would be good. But somebody neither of us knows. Can you do that?"

"Of course. Of course." He tried not to appear patronizing.

"Good. Don't tell me about it. That will be between you two, all right?"

"I understand. Can we let this matter go? For now?"

He would not let it go, but there was no need to tell her.

CHAPTER 28

It was Sunday, so that meant a Kowalski family gathering. There was no mandatory appearance required. Just if available, food would be on the table at six for whomever. James loved the tradition and always looked forward to Mary Ann's family gatherings. His own family was much more traditional—invitation only, with the dress attire specified. None of that for the Kowalski's.

Mary Ann called to say she would be late and to go ahead without her, and she would eat later. "Drive carefully. I think it might rain," he cautioned.

He showed up a little early and helped her mother set the table. He had been accepted into the family as an individual and not just as her boyfriend.

"How many tonight, Mom?" He had gotten used to calling her that after he stumbled around with Mrs. Kowalski, Helen, and then, well, Mom.

"Six or eight, not sure, but there'll be enough. Do you like lasagna?"

"I do. It's a part of our heritage, you know." They laughed.

"I'm afraid to fix anything … anything Asian for you. Not sure I could meet the standards that your family sets."

"Oh, I'm sure you would, Mrs. Kowalski—I mean Mom. I'm sure you can whip up just about anything."

"You're kind, James, too kind."

"Are your sister and her husband coming?"

"Oh, yes, they're here a lot. I don't think Ron and Kate are doing well financially, you know. So, any big meal helps."

"Oh? What does he do?"

"He sells cabinetry to the construction industry, but I'm not sure how good a salesman he is."

"They've been married for a while, haven't they?" He knew where he was going with this line of questioning, but she didn't. He selected the dishes to be used for the Italian-style meal that had been planned.

"Almost nine years. We all thought my sister would marry her other boyfriend; we all liked Paul even better than Ron."

"Why was that?"

He was going to keep the questions open-ended for now. He put the water glasses on the right side and at the top of the plate and the knives and forks in their respective Emily Post positions. Forks on the left on top of the napkin and the knife on the right. The cutting edge of the knife was facing the plate.

"They just seemed to get along so well. Paul had a great job, was making good money, and then … then they just drifted apart. Don't know why." It wasn't a question—more of a statement.

"Oh, yes, Mary Ann mentioned him," he lied. "Paul, Paul …" He stumbled like he knew the name.

"Paul Svenson. He was Dutch or Swedish or something like that, I think."

"Oh, that was it, Svenson!" he exclaimed as if it had just come to him as well. "What did he do that made him such a hotshot?"

She looked out the long driveway with headlights bouncing like a pong game and announced, "Oh, it looks like they're here. Thanks for the help, James."

Paul Svenson. Maybe that's all I need to get started here.

Online would tell the tale. But Jung Song wasn't done with this, not by a long shot.

CHAPTER 29

Howard decided it was time for a family meeting. It was one of many things that had been allowed to slide since Clare's passing. They always had them, and then they didn't.

During the fall, Friday nights didn't work because of school football games. OHHS made it to the CIF playoffs, so each week was filled with championship possibilities until they lost, which they finally did, in the quarter finals. Geoff had opted not to play with pads on and chose basketball instead. Saturday mornings wouldn't work for Marcia, but Howard didn't know why.

Saturday-night Mass at St. Elizabeth's was very routinized, but just for three now. They decided on Sunday brunch at the Cheesecake Factory. They could talk through their omelets, eggs Benedict, or just some great French toast.

They had gotten through Christmas with fewer tears than last year, and New Year's Eve would probably be just as sad, Howard knew.

It was the same booth they always got when they went out as a family. Saturday-night Mass at St. Elizabeth's and Sunday brunch, either at home or the Factory, had been a staple part of the Hamilton party of four for over ten years. For the very first time, it would now be Hamilton's party of three.

The hostess and waitresses were always the same for the Sunday schedule. And they all knew about Clare. There was no "Where's the wife?" or "Just three today?" They all gave a smile of pity. It was the silence about her that still permeated outside the home activities, even after eighteen months and especially during the holidays.

"What's up, Dad?" Marcia was the first to break the quiet as they scooted into the large half-circle booth that could probably seat six or eight.

"Oh, nothing special. We just hadn't had a family meeting in, like, forever."

"How are you doin', Dad?" she asked.

"I'm doing OK, Marcia. But just OK. And you guys?" He swept his hand around the table to signal some level of inclusiveness.

Geoff chimed in. "Mom trained us well, Dad. I mean, I miss her and all, but I'm getting by. Almost two years now. Geez."

"I know," Howard mulled as they looked at the extensive menu the size of a novel.

They ordered their usual, and all three went for the coffee like it was their addiction. It was. Caffeine had become the family vice. *If you must have one, make it coffee* was their mantra.

They talked about their week and what was ahead for each of them for next week and New Year's Eve. They all agreed to stay home and watch the ball drop New York time and style.

"There's something that we have to discuss though."

Howard said it like he had developed an agenda for a staff meeting.

Marcia and Geoff looked at each other with an "I told you so" gaze.

"OK, I'm thinking about applying for a different job in the PD. I've been in Patrol for almost ten years. Somebody laughingly said that it wasn't ten years, but one year ten times. I guess I got good at it, but maybe it's time to think about other things." Their food came, and everyone grabbed for the ketchup at the same time.

It was Guy Coyle who told him about the "one year ten times" thing. He had not told the kids about his new friend from LAPD. He had told Clare, but maybe someday he would explain the Guy Coyle relationship. Not yet.

"Well, at least we agree on one thing," Howard said as they laughed and opted to let the lady of the house take the first squirt.

"So, Dad, going to be a big-city detective?" Marcia asked.

"I don't know. I've thought about putting in for that, for the Narcotics/Vice Unit, or even a regular staff job writing and developing policies. I also thought about just staying in Patrol and taking the next Sergeant's exam."

He paused to take a breath and a bite of omelet.

"So, what do you guys think?"

"Wow, Dad. Detective work sounds cool." Geoff reached for the jelly.

"Here's my problem. I'm not sure what jobs are open, but I can put my name on a waiting list when a position comes up. The problem is I don't want to apply for everything. Just one of them. Geez, I could even consider riding a bike—I mean a motorcycle."

"Jeez, Dad. Sounds too dangerous for us," Marcia said very seriously.

"And I'm not too crazy about just writing tickets and investigating traffic accidents."

Geoff and Marcia looked at each other and shook their heads. Howard missed the obvious sentiment they had about traffic accidents.

"What kind of hours are the other jobs, Dad?" Geoff was quickly going to move on for all of them.

The waitress asked if they needed anything else. "Coffee," they said in unison.

"Well, the Narcotics job is tough. You go to work and never know what time you go home. If the case requires surveillance, it could take you away for ten or twenty hours or more. Hard to say. Could work holidays, miss games, but make a lot of money in overtime."

"How about the staff job?" Geoff kept prodding.

"Day watch, Monday through Thursday or Tuesday through Friday. Four ten-hour days. Weekends off. Holidays off unless I want to work some overtime in patrol."

"That sounds good to us, Dad," Marcia said.

"Yeah, but it's boring. And it's not the street. It's not police work. At least not yet. Not sure I'm ready for a pocket protector–type job."

"So, what's left?" Geoff asked as the plates were being cleared.

Howard summed up the discussion and settled another question at the same time. "After all of that discussion, it comes down to stay in the uniform or take a serious look at detectives."

They looked at one another in agreement as the waitress asked, "Any dessert? Cheesecake to go?"

"If you have a pumpkin cheesecake with a graham cracker crust, we'll take one to go! Case closed. Huh, kids?"

CHAPTER 30

For the last few months, Lieutenant Ib Rikelman had been recruiting Hamilton to apply for a Narcotics/Vice Unit position.

Rikelman was a workaholic. HH knew that. But he was also persuasive in just about everything he did and everything he wanted. Rikelman wanted HH in his unit and was going to do whatever it took. The bulldog, in his tenacity, was not to be challenged, even by the Chief of Police. Howard had seen it firsthand many times. Ib Rikelman wasn't just feared. He was also dreaded.

Most people at OHPD would rather go head-to-head against a terrorist or a barricaded suspect than tangle with him. He was going to get his way, no matter what. Fortunately for the department, he could convince anyone of anything, given the time and energy. There was never a doubt as to his loyalties. It wasn't ego, power, or even influence. He would just wear you down until you succumbed.

Rikelman had a plan for Hamilton, and HH just had to go along to get along.

It was a change of shift as he prepared for his umpteenth night in uniform. Rikelman caught him in the locker room. He looked around to make sure there was no one within listening distance. He did not want an overhear for what he was going to say.

"I want you in the unit, HH. I know you can't handle the long hours of working dope, but maybe you can learn the ropes differently. The Chief and I have talked, and your ten years on the street, coupled with your strong integrity that we've seen time and again, puts you in a unique position."

Hamilton knew better than to interrupt Rikelman when he was on a roll.

"You're a leader in your quiet way, but you still have a lot to learn. I want to give you that chance. Are you with me?" Rikelman could stare through anyone like a rottweiler ready to devour raw meat.

He nodded.

"The Chief and I have come up with a position in my unit that is perfect for you."

"What is it?"

Rikelman looked around to make sure there was no one within hearing distance. "First, let me tell you what it entails." He was not going to put everything on the table just yet—but enough to entice HH.

"You get to name your hours—any ten you want on a four-day schedule. Come and go when you want but put in the time. We know you and your work ethic, so that's not going to be a problem." Rikelman paused to see if he had the fish nibbling on the bait. He did.

"Second, if you don't grow your hair long like the rest of my degenerates, you can work OT in Patrol when you need it." Another pause to let that sink in.

"Third, no suit like the detectives, but dress business casual. You may or may not do some undercover. It depends."

"You still haven't told me what I would be doing, Lieutenant."

"I'll get to that, damn it, HH. I'll get to that."

There was going to be some silence now on both sides. They stared into each other's eyes, neither wanting to back down from their positions of strength.

"You're a member of the Peace Officers Association. The damn POA. But you're not one of the rabble-rousers they have."

"OK."

"Let's go to my office." Rikelman was looking around like there were spies everywhere.

Rikelman left first. Howard acted like he was putting something back in his locker and took the shortest route to his office. The Lieutenant closed his door and went directly to his chair, sitting back with his hands in a steeple position.

"The department is becoming, how can I say it, divided, HH. Have you noticed?"

"Well, no, but I've been a bit distracted from all the garbage around here."

"We know."

Hamilton could see that Rikelman was going somewhere but was still uncertain where this was taking him. "Who is *we?*"

"The Chief and me. He's a good Chief. Don't get me wrong. He's the best thing that's happened to this department in a long time. But some people want him out of here."

"Why?"

"Why? Because they want to get rid of him. They want him gone. Certain people don't like the fact he came from LAPD and their ways, and they don't like some of the new things he's doing to get close to the community."

"Wait a minute, Lieutenant." HH held up one hand to build some distance from where the conversation appeared to be headed. "Who is this *we* you refer to, and who is the *they*, if you don't mind me asking again?"

"I know you've been dealing with your problems, or I'm sorry, your issues at home and that … HH, but let me bring you up to date about what's going on here."

He had been talking to Rikelman for almost an hour. HH was still not sure what the hell was going on.

CHAPTER 31

"The Chief has been here now over three years. They think that's enough."

"Excuse my French, Lieutenant, but again, who the fuck is *they*?"

Rikelman leaned forward to keep his voice down and still get his point across. "The POA, your POA, and two city council*men*." Rikelman put just enough inflection on the *men* in councilmen for HH to get it.

"You don't have to tell me. I know."

"They," Rikelman said, putting his fingers in the shape of a quote, "don't like the changes in the disciplinary system, his closeness to the community, and, most importantly, the fact he's from LAPD. Here to fix us."

"And these two councilmen have *your POA* in their back pocket."

"They contribute to their campaigns every election, go on fishing trips, and are backing one of them for state senator. With your dues money, I might add." More silence as the wheels were now turning in both heads like the windmills in the Palm Springs desert.

HH finally broke the silence. "Is there enough *we* to counter the *theys*?"

"I think so, Howard, but I don't know. They want someone from inside to be selected as Chief, somebody they have influence over, someone they know."

"I see." But did he?

"We got off track here a little bit, Howard. I'm in the process of taking one of my vacant positions, the one that Tremaine filled before he retired. I'm calling it an Intelligence Officer," he said, again using the Texas-style horn symbol for quotes on his words.

"Go on."

"The job will be to float between narcotics and vice, collaborate with the county drug task force and the Sheriff's Department and any other agencies we might joint venture with on investigations. If we had any issues within the department that needed looking into, like internal affairs stuff, you could be used. I'm not going to write that in the job description. It'll be a bit more nebulous than that. You would report to me and only me. I shouldn't say that chain of command wise. Barber will be your supervisor, but you'll get your assignments directly from me."

"Uh huh," was the only reply HH could muster at this point.

"So, think about it, HH. Get back to me ASAP if this is something you want to do. But ..." He looked him directly in the eye as only Norman Bates would. "You need to be here. Understand? And do not—*do not*—tell anyone about this."

"Yes, sir." It was all he could say to someone like Rikelman.

Howard's head was spinning. He never understood politics or police organization theory. He was just a street cop for crying out loud. Time for a visit to his LAPD mentor, Guy Coyle.

Coyle was a retired LAPD lieutenant who had moved into Orchard Hill after a divorce. They had become fast friends, and Coyle always had sage advice.

CHAPTER 32

Jung Song's practice was thriving. In just six months, he was seeing patients almost every hour. New immigrants found their way to the San Gabriel Valley, and he was the only Korean doctor for miles around. They would bring in their first-generation American-born children, even though he was not a pediatrician.

He tried to speak English to them, but he would revert to his home language when all else failed. His immediate success allowed him to pay off his student loans and purchase advanced scientific medical equipment within three years. He was confident that he and Mary Ann would soon be married. While he loved Ann Marie, he wanted his child to add to the family.

The last month had been a whirlwind. Finally, he decided to sell his El Segundo condo. He found the ideal place to live and perhaps entice Mary Ann to move in, even before they were married. It was a glass and steel high-rise complex of four replicas of four buildings, with downtown Los Angeles views. Each building had seven floors with a front lobby. Even the elevators had breathtaking views. He selected the fifth-floor condo with a view from every room, seven minutes from his office.

He was alone at the office on a quiet Saturday morning. Dressed casually, he was catching up on paperwork, dictating reports, and researching children's diseases.

He was deep into the internet on Web MD when he decided to try something. He typed in the name Paul Svenson, thinking he might find something on this egregious animal who had violated her chastity and changed Mary Ann's life forever.

There were three different Paul Svenson's in the Southern California area. How could that be? Was the name so familiar, like Smith or Jones, Wang or Kim, in the Netherlands? He looked for more details. How about someone around Orchard Hill or at least the South Bay?

Something caught his eye. It was a press release dated over two years ago. It related to a mudslide that closed principal streets in Sparrow Hill, directly adjacent to Orchard Hill but much more affluent. The homes were multimillions instead of the one to two million in the rest of the South Bay. All because they were in the hills. Just about everyone had an ocean view with large lots.

Sparrow Hill was one of those communities about which everyone said, "Someday I'll live there." He grinned at the notion that many people lived on "Someday I'll" but rarely got to live the dream. But he and Mary Ann would. He had plans, but first he had to take care of some personal business.

The press release was not as impressive as the person who had signed it and was shown being interviewed by the media. Mudslides of any nature caused havoc in many communities, but only a few areas could bring traffic to a halt in the South Bay, and Sparrow Hill Road was one of those. People used it to get from one end of the region to another, particularly during rush hour traffic. The press release and interview were conducted by none other than "Paul Svenson, press information officer for the Sparrow Hill PD." Could it be him? Was he that lucky so quickly?

There was a video attached to the information. James clicked to see what the guy looked like. His excitement turned into a tense study of the video and the on-screen speaker. His age seemed about right. From the vague description given by Mary Ann, this could be him. He smiled at the screen as he took down information that was scrolling on the screen. It was him. He knew it. A cell phone screenshot immortalized his photo for the next step in his plan.

CHAPTER 33

Guy Coyle's home was the epitome of the Craftsman-style bungalow that flooded the real estate market after the turn of the twentieth century. But he had taken it to a new level. What else was a retired lieutenant to do but putter in the garden, paint and repaint the exterior, and furnish the interior to his liking?

Hamilton made the phone call that got time with Coyle. But he couldn't resist a smile as he pulled to the curb to see, just a few houses from Coyle's house, the neighbor's trash cans still out. Guy told him he had conjugal visits with the widow who lived there, but only when the trash cans were left out. It was Coyle's job to take them to her backyard and enter for a visit.

His footsteps took him up the irregularly shaped pavers that made a winding path to the front door. The enameled white paint smell was in the air. It had been done for probably the second time on the trim facia boards, window frames, and front door.

This home could be in a magazine.

He knocked three times on the exterior screen door and announced, "City police!"

"Got a warrant?" was the reply. Howard stepped in to give a manly hug to his best friend of the moment. "Howard, how the hell are you, bud?"

They had met several times after Clare had passed, but there was still that bond about being alone without companionship. Coyle had been divorced for almost seven years, but Hamilton viewed divorce somewhat like the death of a spouse, except that in divorce, the other person was still alive. Both hurt but in different ways.

"What's on your alleged mind, Howard? Want some coffee or water?"

"Water will do."

They walked to the kitchen. Howard got his ice water from the refrigerator dispenser of a new Sub-Zero, and Guy made a quick Keurig coffee.

Coyle was rapid-fire talking. "You look great, HH. Have you been working out? You're a bit more buffed than the last time I saw you."

"Yes, sir, I have. Running and lifting some weights again."

"Keep it up, bud!"

Hamilton got right to the point and talked about his meeting with Rikelman and the Narcotics/Vice Unit's job offer. Coyle let him talk uninterrupted.

"Is that the job I should take or maybe an inside staff/squint job? Or maybe motors? Or just stay in patrol?"

"Only you can answer that, Howard, but let's see what we have here." They walked to the living room, which was only a few feet away in this two-thousand square foot bungalow. Howard still marveled at the remodel and the furnishings. Right out of a *Restoration Hardware* catalog. It looked like he had added a room or had gotten one of the bigger homes on the block. But the masculinity of strong farmhouse wood furnishings spoke volumes.

Coyle thought for a long moment before he began his counseling session.

"First, let me paint this picture for you. Perhaps it'll help you decide. You know I spent over thirty years in LAPD. As they like to be referred to, the City of Angels is also the city of devils. We house some of the most vicious, unforgiving, and loathsome, evil people to walk the earth. And in large numbers."

Hamilton sat back for what he knew would be a lecture with no notes from someone who knew.

"We have serial killers, people who mutilate, shoot, molest, and rape in numbers unimaginable. Most of the time, we contain them within the city limits, but sometimes, like the Nightstalker, they transition outside our borders to the county or other communities. Or even Orchard Hill." He stood up to get another cup of coffee from the kitchen but continued.

"I moved here because of your City's reputation for being a safe community, after I read your Chief's interview when he first got here."

"Oh, I know where you're going on this one, Guy. Of course, you're talking about the pie crust, aren't you?"

"Yup. He said something like, and I will try to quote, 'Orchard Hill is like a pie, and we are in the center of that pie. So, we patrol the crust to ensure we protect the interior, which is our city, from the communities that surround us."

"Yeah," Howard responded, "and he got in a lot of trouble for saying that!"

"The media will always try to twist words into what they want it to mean, rather than the intent. Of course, you know that by now."

Howard nodded.

CHAPTER 34

HH put aside the ice water. It was time for a second cup of coffee for the day.

"That's what made me look at your city for retirement. I looked at your stats and felt like LA didn't bleed over into your city, even though you border them on almost two sides. You do patrol the crust, and I liked that."

"So, where is this going, sir?"

"No sir, Howard. I told you, Guy." Another nod.

He had been scolded, just as he had done with Alcazar, his first trainee. But in any paramilitary organization, everybody above you was always a sir.

"Let me get to a point here. You have almost ten years in a beautiful city working patrol. Your city has had a few blemishes but nothing like what I experienced. You made your choice to work here, and I respect that. It's a different kind of police work. Well, that ten years has now come around to bite you in the ass. Ask yourself, was it ten years or one year ten times?"

"You've said that before, and it does stay in my head when I think about it."

"Again, only you can answer that. Patrol serves an instrumental purpose in our line of work. It lets you see the streets, curb to curb and sometimes inside those homes and businesses that try to hide their failings. That's what gives you experience. And now, if you took that job, you get to see the underbelly. What else is hiding in there."

"What do you mean, hiding?"

"You've done mostly preliminary investigations—the tip of the iceberg. You were the crime fighter, the warrior, the frontline soldier that protected the streets because the streets were yours, not the criminal element. You can't eliminate crime, but you can control it. You can prevent it sometimes, or you can predict it. In your city, in patrol, it was your presence, just your uniformed presence, that deterred much of the crime. Here, you can provide services and enforce the law. They go hand in hand." Guy was trying to get off his soapbox but had just one more message for Hamilton.

"You told me about your satanic cult killing and the big drug deal you worked. For OHPD, those only come around once every five years or so. You got lucky to be involved with both of those things. Great experience."

"I know."

"In LA, those things happen almost daily. They might sneak over to cities like Orchard Hill occasionally, but we dealt with that shit day in and day out. And they still do."

"Talking like a college professor now, Guy. Quite a lot of insights here."

"Don't let me lose my train of thought here, Howard. You've hit me where I'm most vulnerable, talking about our work. There's a lot of support to let that blue suit out there be the front line, that thin blue line. Here you can be a guardian, if you will, and sometimes also be a warrior but not every day."

"I get how that makes sense."

"Well, here is where it gets interesting." Coyle went for the third cup of java. "I don't see you as a dope cop. Somehow that doesn't fit my image of you. Whatever job you take next, you may not ever make an arrest again. Not directly anyway. A staff job would ensure that, unless you were off duty and had to take action."

He returned from the kitchen. "But in detectives or intelligence, you have to build a case from almost the ground floor." He looked directly into Howard's eyes to see if what he was saying was sinking in. "Let's take that intelligence job that your Lieutenant offered. Not every department thinks that progressively. That's smart for an agency your size."

"But we're not the CIA or FBI here, are we?" Howard was about to take a bite of the golden apple.

"Yes and no," Coyle responded.

"Let me paint this picture. And I apologize for the length of this discussion, but ..." He paused to tuck in his T-shirt after getting up and down too many times.

"Intelligence in police work is nothing more than gathering information. LAPD's gang unit, the CRASH teams, were designed as street intelligence units to identify all the gangbangers, not just make arrests. When the shit hit the fan, they knew who was who in the zoo. That's what intelligence or information is. It's knowledge of the past and present, analyzing the potential problems and handling that information to a conclusion—or just maybe putting it in a someday file for the future."

There was to be no more coffee.

"I think I know what your Chief and Lieutenant have in mind for you. Listen to them, not me. Look for something you can get your teeth into, something that will consume you a bit. You need that now. Take care of your kids, have some great memories of Clare, and get ready for a new adventure. Oh, and have a great new year."

Coyle put a soft arm on HH's shoulder as they walked to the front door.

Howard then realized it was New Year's Eve, eve, the day before, the day before. He had a lot to think about. But maybe not that much.

CHAPTER 35

Song was not angry. He was not emotional. What Mary Ann told him, in excruciating detail, was just wrong, so wrong. There was a line that human beings should not cross, and this was one of them. How could he violate an innocent young girl? Svenson had no honor or respect for women, and he would ensure a price would be paid. Just as in his military and medical training, he would be methodical in his plans—nothing in haste.

His work at the hospital had been all-consuming. In private practice, he oversaw his clock. Yet he loved every minute of being the medical resource for people in need. He could answer even the most complicated questions, make the correct diagnosis, and put his patients at ease, just as he did with Mary Ann.

Sparrow Hill. What was that city all about? His research found it was one of the most iconic locations in the world, hidden along the coastline of California but possessing wealth and acclaim reserved for only the most prestigious communities. It was a Mediterranean revival-style city, tiny but mighty and influential.

A peninsula like no other, the community had rolling hills, ocean views from every corner, and a school district rated as one of the highest. SAT scores were off the charts. A prestigious college and three high schools produced some of the world's most outstanding achievers, thinkers, and doers.

Since the 1920s, Sparrow Hill, named after its most famed estuary, had been a landfill. The property languished until developers saw the potential for a Marineland of the Pacific. The wealthy and famous gravitated to its cliffs, expansive land, astounding coastline views, and perhaps even a few mysteries hidden in secret beaches.

James would use the skills he inherited from both his parents and his training— imperturbability, listening skills, and perhaps a little investigative work to find out more about Sparrow Hill and, yes, its police department.

It didn't take long.

⸻⸻◦⸻⸻

He stopped by a local hospital for a meeting with a few colleagues. They researched new medications for attention deficit disorder and other youth-related maladies that he had expressed interest in. Finally, he was seated in the cafeteria with several pediatric specialists who were discussing their weekend.

"Oh, you should see the whales we saw from our front window this weekend. They were spawning and jumping, and it was nature at its best," exclaimed Dr. Ben Samuels to anyone at the table listening.

"Where was that?" someone asked.

"From my place in Sparrow Hill," Samuels offered.

"You live in Sparrow Hill?" another asked.

Samuels went on to admit he did. "I guess I'm part of the lucky sperm club. My dad left us the family home after his passing. Anyway, the whales were active this weekend. That's why they used to have an aquarium down the hill called Marineland."

"Tell us about the Hill," James probed. He figured it was a simple question but one he was more than just a little bit interested in.

Samuels went on about the community and how the biggest problem was traffic. "Getting off the Hill is a pain in the ass," he joked. "Forty minutes to get here, and most of it was stop and go on the city streets. Once I hit the freeway, I'm OK, but boy, stop signs, soccer moms, and police radar keep you moving, but too damn slow for my Porsche."

James decided to take that opening for another open-ended question. "Do Sheriffs or private security patrol them, or do you have your own police department?"

Samuels had the floor now, and he was not going to relinquish it.

"Well, we have our private security, but we also have our PD. But they're just about like private security. I doubt whether they make many arrests. I mean, look who lives there. Not many criminals in those homes." The laughter encouraged Samuels to continue. "There's always been a big discussion about just giving up the PD and going with the Sheriffs. We don't need it, but you know what? They're ours, and most of my neighbors enjoy the quick response when we need something. You know, checking out a suspicious person or controlling our neighbor's kids speeding on the streets."

James could not resist one more question. The information he needed was coming quickly anyway. "What do they do all day?"

"Well, when we go on vacation or leave town for a long weekend, they do vacation checks, take in our newspapers from the driveway, and check the house. Outside of that, I don't know."

It was time to get back to work. But James got the information he needed. And he knew what the PD did, or at least he knew what one of them used to do.

It doesn't sound like Svenson is a real policeman anyway, he reflected.

CHAPTER 36

What was not to like about what Rikelman had proposed? That was the question Howard asked himself. He desperately needed a more substantial distraction than what Patrol was providing. He had made up his mind, but he still had a family to consider.

He tried to keep a schedule with the kids. If he was going to be home by six, so would they; otherwise, they were on their own. The key was constant communication, by email, text, or actually talking. What a novel idea.

Tonight was dinner at home with a combination of takeout, homemade salad, and the cheesecake left from Sunday. Some traditions needed to be kept.

He explained the job in ways they were going to understand hopefully but kept it open-ended. He was not going to decide without their input.

"But, Dad, will you still get to wear a uniform?" Marcia knew how much he loved the streets. "Eeeew! Does that mean you have to wear a suit and tie? With a gun on your belt and handcuffs? Will you come home like that every day?"

"They said if they need me, I can get some patrol OT, but a lot will depend on what I have going. No suit and tie most of the time. Just business casual."

"Will you be undercover?" Geoff asked.

"Maybe. I just don't know that much about it right now. But I'm assigned to the Narcotics/Vice Unit, so I assume so."

He caught Marcia looking away, her expression serious. Did she think about the time he found her in a marijuana den at her friend's house? Or was it when she turned in the guy who brought the weed? Did she remember that it was Lieutenant Hospian's stepson? He did remember she blamed him for getting the guy bounced out of school. All of that seemed like so long ago.

The kids looked at each other and laughed.

"What's so funny?"

Marcia could not resist. "Dad, you've always looked like a cop. How can you go undercover?"

"I don't know all of that yet. I must go to some training and just get my feet wet. Listen, I'm leaning to take it, but I wanted to hear from you. It has to be a family decision."

"Dad," Geoff said, "it's your decision. Not ours. But we'd support you in whatever you wanted. I think Mom would agree with that. Or would have …" That pause lingered a bit too long.

Marcia jumped in to break the unease. "Can't wait to hear some different kinds of stories. Maybe being a detective is just what you were destined to do."

They were maturing right in front of him. He knew it would be only a matter of time before they were out of the house and living their own lives without him.

CHAPTER 37

Over the years, the Hamilton family welcomed Australia, London, New Orleans, and New York celebrations in the new year. But not LA's. Hugs and plans gave way to bed and quiet time. This year, Howard was to work on New Year's Day but not the eve.

On Monday, he would start the new job and hang up the uniform, at least for a while.

He decided to make two phone calls, first to his mom. His mom had also gone through a lot. Losing his dad and then Clare was not easy for someone with a heart condition. He never wanted to let too many days pass without reaching out.

The second call was more of a hesitation. It was ten thirty, and who knew where Amanda Johnson would be? He turned the volume down on the television and punched in the number Janet had given him, unsure if it was a landline or cell. It went to voice mail.

Probably right, he thought.

His text haptic chimed.

"Howard, was that you?"

He texted, "Yes."

The phone rang.

"I didn't want to answer because it said, 'Unknown caller.' Sorry."

"Just wanted to call to wish you a happy, well … a good New Year."

She laughed. "You can't say happy New Year? You can be happy, can't you, Howard? I know I can."

"Well, I guess it's better than Thanksgiving. Of course, I don't or didn't have much to be thankful for then."

"Yes, you *do*. You can be thankful. You can be happy. Your children are beautiful people, and your family is still a family. Where's Bentley?"

"He's right beside me and heard your voice. You guys must have bonded. Boy, didn't want to make this a downer call. But sorry. We keep getting off on the wrong foot."

"Well, let's get on the right foot." It almost sounded like an order. There was a short pause, telling Howard something was going on, but he was not sure what.

"Here is what you do. Get a glass of wine. Then after you finish that, pour yourself another one. It should be midnight by then. Call me back, and we'll celebrate the new year on Facetime." She hung up.

CHAPTER 38

They were only three-ounce pours. Hamilton was not that much of a red wine drinker, so he decided to take it slow. At 11:59, he hit *recents* on his cell and turned down the television again. He wanted to see the partying going on but not take part in it. It didn't matter the channel. They were all showing the Big Apple countdown and then switching to local events.

"Wasn't so sure I'd get a call back."

"Why not?"

"Did you have the wine?" She wasn't going to answer his query.

"Yes but small pours."

"What channel do you have on?"

"Doesn't matter. They're all covering it."

"Let's just watch the ball drop together." She wanted to take back the "together," but it was too late.

Each was in their respective thought track. As the countdown continued, their mental pathways took different directions. When the New York crowd hit ten and started the countdown, they could hear each other breathing lightly. The slight slurp of their drinks wasn't bad manners, just perhaps an unspoken message that relaxed the other.

The ball dropped on Times Square, and, as usual, the celebration began.

"Happy New Year, Howard."

"Happy New Year, Amanda."

They glanced at each other on their phones and could hear they were watching the same channel. The silence was deafening. It screamed at each of them in a cacophony of sounds. They heard it in their heads and in their minds, but not for others to hear.

For each of them, it was pain, anguish, and a release.

Was it one minute? Two or five? Neither knew.

He broke the stillness that was covering the wireless connection. "Thanks, Amanda. Thanks."

He was sure she knew what the thanks were for, but it was only his speculation.

The festivities continued on the screen, but there was a different mood in their respective settings.

"What's on tap for New Year's Day for you and the kids?" He could see she was all smiles when she mentioned the kids.

"Well," he said, sitting up from what had become a slouch on the couch as he muted the volume, "I'm going to be working my last day of Patrol on New Year's Day because on Monday I start a new job."

He saw her face get serious again. "You're not leaving the department, are you?" He could see and hear she was a bit startled.

"Oh no, nothing like that. I'm just going to an investigative assignment at OHPD. I would never leave the job. Never." Howard waved his arms across the screen to make the point. He wasn't sure he meant it as it came out, because he didn't want her to think about other ways to leave. He hoped she did not pick up on the misstep.

She relaxed again. "Sounds exciting. Do I get an update on it once you get settled in?"

"Oh, I don't know about that," he said, feigning a bit of a stern attitude. "It's very top secret." Then he smiled into the phone to let her know he was joking.

"What could be so secret in OHPD, Howard?"

CHAPTER 39

He thought about the conversation with Amanda more than he wanted to.

It had been one of his first New Year's Eves not working. Seniority had its benefits but getting New Year's Eve off was a privilege for very few in his line of work. New Year's Day was a different matter. It was going to be his last tour of duty in uniform for a while. He would start the new adventure on Monday. Today would be it for Lincoln 75.

But the day was proving uneventful. It was Orchard Hill and not LA, so what should he expect? Two traffic stops to give both drivers a warning, only because he hated writing tickets. Citations just pissed the citizen off and only made the sergeant feel like he was doing something. At least now, the Chief had changed the policy so that even a warning would count as an observation activity he could count against his available time. He had to show some activity.

Two domestic violence calls, a lost child that, thank God, was found before he got there, and a stop for a Peet's coffee marked the early part of his day. There were the usual waves and "thanks for your service" comments. He hated the phrase. It always sounded a bit too condescending. He developed a response that always brought a smile. "You're worth it." At least they were waving with all five fingers.

He drove in the neighborhood near his own home and spotted a car double-parked on the street, with the driver's door open. He put his bar lights and flashers on, parking offset but directly behind it to ward off any other oncoming traffic.

He got out of his car to check it out. There was no one in the car. Instead, the engine was running with the keys still in it. Then he heard a loud cheer and handclapping from a group in the house adjacent to both cars.

He activated his body camera and walked down the concrete side yard toward the backyard. Loud voices and unintelligible noises were coming from the rear yard. He gently placed his hand on the butt of his gun. It was just a habit.

He turned the corner just as the group cheered again. It then got tranquil as someone spotted him and yelled, "Officer, can I help you?"

It was an outdoor backyard party with a big-screen television, food on every table, and beer poured from a keg. A family gathering to watch the Rose Bowl game! After all, it was New Year's Day.

He announced that someone left their car in the middle of the street, double-parked with the door open.

He didn't know the family or anyone else at the party, so he added in a more official voice, "This is the best ticket I've written all day." Everyone turned to look at the obvious one at fault. There were couples and kids, but no one looked familiar. Finally, a young Asian man stepped out of the crowd.

"Officer, I am so sorry. Let me move the car. I was just unloading when USC scored, and I ran back here to see what was going on."

The only noise was coming from the TV and kids who didn't grasp what was going on.

Hamilton took the lead and walked back to the street with him.

"My name is James, James Song. It's my car, and, well, you heard my lame excuse. I'm here at my almost fiancée's relatives' house and just got carried away."

They talked for a few minutes as Song continued to apologize. Then he moved the car and went back to where Hamilton was standing. Howard reached in his car to grab his ticket book.

"You know, James. Today could be your lucky day." He held the ticket book in front of Song's face.

"I've been on the streets for almost ten years. I hate writing tickets. It's the worst part of a great job. Monday morning, I start a new gig in detectives. I don't want to end my shift on the wrong note. So, have a great day."

CHAPTER 40

The first Monday in January coincided with the new OHPD schedule. Hamilton was going to get in early, but first he had some big decisions to make. For the last ten years, he had gone to work in a T-shirt and Levi's, then got to the locker room and put on the uniform, dressing in a suit only for court.

Sometimes the big decisions were hard. He stared intently at his closet.

Today, HH had to decide whether to wear his Costco Grizzly Mountain woven short-sleeve shirt or his new Untuckedit shirt given to him by the kids for Christmas. He went with the Untuckedit. While it was a bit tighter around the waist, the style still hid his gun and ammo pouch. It was still weird.

He walked in the back door of the station before the shift change. There were a lot of new faces on the day shift. Newbies were still on probation, some just getting off their training cycle and being thrown out there as a one-officer unit for the very first time. He looped his identification card around his neck, just so those strange faces would know who he was.

Day watch had what had affectionally been called the maggots. The slugs with seniority, pretty boys and girls, those wanting to mingle with the detectives, and the new kids getting their feet wet for the first time with the sun up. He did the casual greetings to more strangers than friends and worked his way to the Narcotic/ Vice office. More than likely, he would be the first one in. It was only seven o'clock in the morning.

But there were Barber and Rikelman. It looked like they had never left.

"Hey."

Barber looked up. "Welcome aboard, Howard." Rikelman never looked up. "Let me give you the cook's tour here."

Barber and Howard had worked together in Patrol and on a big narcotics case that led to John Bresani's death and a ton of dope seizure.

Barber dropped his pen on the desk to send the message that he was paying attention to Howard. "Here's your little corner of the world." Barber waved his hand at a small desk in a corner with bookshelves above it. "No windows but plenty of reading material. Your files are in the desk drawers. I'll spend some time with you this week, but I want you to get settled in. Here's your computer."

He pointed to a Microsoft Surface. "You can use it as a desktop or take it with you. I'll give you the passwords and sites you need to know. You're slated for intel school in a few weeks, so don't get too comfortable."

Rikelman stepped away from his work, taking the cue that it was his turn to engage. "Coffee's over here, gun locker here, and your wall locker is over there. A combination is on the inside of the desk drawer. If you bring your lunch, we have a small fridge but keep it clean. We always have water." He pointed to a wall at the entrance of the office. "Sign in and out board is right there on the wall, and Joanie will get you all the keys you'll need."

Hamilton and Rikelman went back a few years. There was much mutual respect from their past experiences, but his nickname, Norman, came from troops of long ago, who dubbed him with the moniker based on the character in the old Alfred Hitchcock movie *Psycho*. Norman Bates was the split personality that was stern but gentle, and when you least expected it, he went batshit crazy. Howard and everyone else at OHPD knew never to call him that. He may have known about the nickname but rue the day anyone would call him Norman to his face.

And you did not want to be around Norman. But Rikelman—and do not ever call him by his first name, Ib—was a predictable manager who loved controlling and pushing the envelope simultaneously. That's what made him easy to work for, most of the time. But when he was Norman …

CHAPTER 41

The first week flew by. HH was into all the reading material, manuals, and websites. It was as if he was back in school. It was almost as much academic work as his bachelor's degree. But that was not his most significant adjustment.

After this week, he was going to attend an intelligence school at the LA Sheriff's Academy. The STAR Center, as it was called, was in Whittier. The sheriff took over a high school campus that had lost student enrollment and was shut down by the school district. They converted it to their version of a police academy with in-service classes like Intelligence, Vice, and Narcotics.

He remembered he worked with a female detective, Bonnie Carvin, from Whittier PD on the Bresani capper. She had been assigned to the LA DUECE multijurisdictional narcotics task force that worked out of Star Center and was as sharp as they came. Impressive knowledge and an excellent resource for him perhaps. *Sometime soon, I'll have to look up what DUECE means,* Howard reminded himself. *Damn acronyms anyway. We're crazy for them.*

About eleven thirty on the first day, he asked his first stupid question.

"What time is Code 7?"

The office was half-full of some of the narcs working, while the other half took the first week of the year off. Generally, there was too much overtime and no money at the end of the year. Time off was the only way to level the playing field. Orchard Hill's dope dealers would have free reign.

"What did you say, Hamilton?" The "Everlys," Don and Phil, posed the question together, just like the real-life duet they were.

"Code 7?"

"You eat when you want to. This isn't Patrol where you have to ask. Just eat. Did you brown bag?" Don was relentless in his sarcasm.

"Just askin', dickhead," was Howard's response. "And no, I didn't, but I'll bring one tomorrow, fill it with dog shit, and light it on fire on top of your desk."

The room roared with laughter. Finally, someone from the corner retorted, "You'll fit right in, Hamilton."

"Knock it off, you guys," Rikelman yelled from his office.

So, this is how it's going to be, Howard thought. *Just have to man up.*

CHAPTER 42

The four days of driving to STAR Center from the South Bay was miserable. He was not used to the bumper-to-bumper traffic. Moreover, he was late for the first day of class, so he had to leave home earlier in the following days to get there on time. Working in the city he lived in was a big perk, he realized. So how was he going to fit in a workout? *How do people do this shit?*

The school was worth it. Howard packed two three-inch binders with handouts, new manuals from the Feds, and a ton of websites, links, and confidential information only known to the intel community. While unsure what he would do with it all, he gladly left on the fourth and final day with a new round of energy for the job.

He stopped by his new digs to drop off his books and take stock of his new assignment.

"Got an assignment for you, HH," Sam Barber said in a very bland manner.

"Let's do it," he responded. There was no "How did the school go, Howard?"

Barber closed his door. "I know you know this, but I gotta say it. You were chosen for this new spot for several reasons."

Hamilton nodded but was just going to let him talk.

"You've shown your integrity, know how to take risks but be prudent about it, and, most of all, you're a self-starter. You can't just wait until we give you something. We want you to look at things on your own. That's what this position is all about. Snoop and poop.

Most important, though, keep the Lieutenant or me apprised of what you are doing. We may point you in one direction, then the other. Understand?"

"OK."

"Take some notes, Howard. I want to get you moving in the right direction. I need you to keep in mind that anything we give you stays with you. No sharing of info with Simpkins, Walker, or even Bennett, or any of your other friends in the department. Got it?" Barber made sure they locked eyes with the unwritten contract.

"Of course, sir."

"I'm going to give you some necessary information to work with, and while this isn't a test, I do want you to keep either the Lieutenant or me apprised of your progress."

"Got it."

Barber placed a manila folder in front of him with only a few pieces of paper inside. "The place is an outdoor swap meet–type operation. It's tricky, HH. The entrance to this business is in Orchard Hill, but the parking lot where the activity occurs is in the county. Don't ask me how that happened. I don't have a clue. Just worked out that way."

He went to a map behind his desk and pointed to the approximate location.

"We think the place is being used to launder counterfeit jeans, CDs and pirated movies, among other things. That's the info we have. I need you to do a workup on the ownership, corporation, or whatever the business is and perhaps pay a few visits to get the lay of the land. No enforcement, no arrests, or seizures, but find out who all the players are. Look for deliveries, movement of merchandise, and anything else you think is appropriate. But keep the Lieutenant and me informed. Any questions?"

"Not yet."

"See you on Monday, bright and early."

Test number one, he assumed.

CHAPTER 43

He was still going through withdrawals. He was a night shift warrior, not a day watch maggot. He would have to adjust, so this weekend was to be decompression time. Maybe the kids would help prepare him because he just did not think he was cut out for this.

Barber had given him reading material that he could review at home, so no need to sit in the office when he could be home.

Marcia and Geoff were maturing right before his eyes. While he had been playing cops and robbers at night, Clare raised them both to be responsible people. He saw that now.

He did not have that much impact on them, but maybe his career choice put them in a situation where they did not want to dishonor the family name. It was like the selection of his profession had helped to rear them. Was it possible? Regardless, he knew it was not his day-to-day parenting skills that had made the difference. Now, it had to be. There was no one else to blame.

Reflection was just looking for happy memories. Howard had plenty of memories with Clare over the years. When he received that call from the Los Angeles County District Attorney's office that the suspect charged with her death would be sentenced, it didn't matter. He wouldn't even tell the kids. The matter was over.

CHAPTER 44

Monday, Monday. Can't trust that day. The Mamas and the Papas made the song famous, but the words meant a lot more today. Barber's conversations had been somewhat troublesome. *You can't trust anybody—can't share your investigations or even stories about them.*

What will we talk about at Home Plate? Having beers with the guys was not going to be as much fun. This shit he was getting into sounded way too cloak and dagger, so sharing his work would be out of the question. And he didn't even know anything about what he was going to be doing.

With his first investigation about to get underway, he needed to get organized. He remembered some of the critical information in the intel class that started with "write everything down"—and early in an investigation, because you don't know where it will take you.

He gathered his raw information from Barber and set up a *chrono,* or chronological log for his first case. He developed a numbering system, discussed it with Barber, and showed him, step by step, the logistics of his efforts. He created an online log for each day and each activity associated with each investigation and refreshed it periodically throughout the day. He was anal like that, so it did come somewhat naturally.

He earmarked a list of sources of information. Forwardedge and Google Earth were his first stops. He downloaded aerial photos of the address from Earth and researched who owned the property through tax records. Two corporations held ownership as an LLC partnership. No names. He had to go deeper.

Maybe I'll just go out there and take a look.

"Hey, Sarge, do we use our own vehicle, or do we have any plain cars? How about a camera? Video recording devices?" He already had a set of binoculars and a monocular in his ditty bag.

Barber threw him a set of keys. "It's Shop 828. Parked on the side, away from public view. It still looks like a UC 'cause it's a Charger. Just not black and white. Sign out for it and check the gas and mileage."

It was a two-door, but other than that, it was almost as sharp as his Shop 885 black-and-white. It did not look like the car had been driven much. It was a few years old, but the speedometer only read twelve thousand miles. There was no junk in the rear seat, but it sure needed a wash and detail. Just like in Patrol, he checked the trunk and found an old briefcase with a name on it he knew had retired last year. He would give it to Barber when he got back. He lifted the back seat. *No contraband, thank goodness.*

The location in question was a fifteen-minute drive from the station. It bordered LA County and Orchard Hill with some of the strangest gerrymandering lines he had seen. He pulled into the driveway of the address and saw that it was a converted drive-in theater. There was nothing more than a large parking lot with a few small buildings on each side that probably were the ticket booths and snack bars.

An old sign was leaning on the retaining wall that surrounded the asphalt Sundown Drive-in. It brought back memories of his parents bringing him there when he was maybe eleven or twelve.

He would fall asleep in the back seat while they enjoyed a movie and popcorn.

It was a Monday, and most of the activity took place on the weekends, he assumed. He walked the property. It was weird that one part of the lot was in the city, and the other went to no-man's land in the county. He searched for the property lines and found them. There were little green metal bolts plugged into the concrete that only engineers and architects knew.

He looked around and saw no one. So, playing a game in his mind, he hopped on one foot in Orchard Hill and then the other in the county. Orchard Hill, county, Orchard Hill, county. Like a hopscotch player.

He would have to be here when the operation was in full swing. It did not look like the old snack bar or entry booths were used for anything. Some of the humps or berms of asphalt used to park at an elevated position for viewers to see the screen were still there, but the speaker posts were long gone, as was the giant screen. It was still a scene from the past.

What does this place look like on the weekends? What does the future hold for this piece of turf?

CHAPTER 45

Hamilton returned to the station to continue his investigation of the Sundown property. He could sense the electricity in the air as he walked into the rear detective squad room.

"HH, did you hear?" Red Walker had seen him come in the side door.

"What?"

"You better sit down. Harvey Stevens is dead," Red said in a monotone fashion, like he was delivering a death notification to a deceased family member.

"Sergeant Stevens?" Howard looked him directly in the eye with not a question but a statement. "Fuck. He just retired. He was getting a divorce from Val. What the?" They looked at each other for answers, knowing that neither had any.

Walker kept talking, even though Howard did not ask any questions. "He electrocuted himself in his garage while he was packing his shit to move out. The floor was wet; he was barefoot and must have had a frayed chord nearby." Walker said it with just a touch of southern twang to bring happiness to the situation.

Stevens was one of the most revered field supervisors OHPD had. He had been a field training officer years ago and was caught dating his trainee, Valerie. They married. He was ultimately promoted to sergeant, and they lived happily ever after. Stevens announced his retirement, and everybody was looking to attend a great retirement party. Then Val, who became a great detective, announced she was leaving. Word got out they were getting a divorce, so the retirement party was canceled.

Walker went back to his more somber tone. "Hermosa PD is handling it because they lived there. But it looks like an industrial-type accident."

"Does the shit ever stop here?" Howard said to no one in particular. "Let me know if you hear anything about a service, Red. I got work to do."

Walker looked at him quizzically, "What work? Are you in detectives now?"

"Today's my first day, working in Narco/Vice."

"Finally, HH. Glad to hear. You deserve something good happening to you."

Johnny "Red" Walker had been the OHPD gunslinger, who got in more shootings than anyone in the Department's history. Had he been in LAPD, it would not even be on the radar screen, but for OHPD, his actions had been noted by many who had concerns about his so-called death wish. Hopefully, his last shooting had been his final one, because the powers that be had decided to take him out of uniform and hone his skills into a homicide detective. And detectives in OHPD had never been in a shooting.

At least not yet.

CHAPTER 46

Hamilton walked to his new office and immediately saw Barber. "I guess you heard, HH?"

"Yeah. Not the way I want to go. But who can pick and choose?" Nothing more was going to be said on the Harvey Stevens matter. Maybe later.

He walked back to his cubby hole and opened his computer.

"I loaded some sources on your system, Howard. Because what you're doing is new, and we have no precedent for what you will be doing, we'll go slow. Start you out with Lexis Nexus, some county databases, and state stuff. We'll get into the Feds later. There are some sites we pay for and others that are free. You don't have to worry about that part." Barber wasn't expecting a response and wasn't disappointed.

HH did a local search for a business license on the address and was surprised there was not one. He called the city clerk's office at the city hall and verified that no one had taken out a license. County records did not show a permit either.

The California Department of Corporations and Secretary of State showed the property owned by Sundown Enterprises and Sunset Enterprises, a joint venture LLC or limited liability corporation. So, what and who were Sundown and Sunset? He downloaded the Secretary of State Statement of Information, but it only listed the person filing the form, Jonathan Pritchett, general counsel. He was listed as the manager with an address in Sparrow Hill, an office suite number A-13. It was dated over five years ago.

But why no business license?

He went into the United States Department of Treasury website and searched for the IRS information, headquartered in Cincinnati, Ohio. Both Sundown and Sunset Enterprises had separate tax identification or EINs, with the Sparrow Hill address listed.

He drilled down inside Forwardedge and found it. There were more LLCs with the exact attorney's name and the names of other corporations. There were three listed for each enterprise. He jotted down the names, checked the state records to make sure somebody was paying sales tax, and moved on. He would put together his version of a Murder Book, but it would not have all the blood and guts or intrigue of a homicide. At least not yet.

Lieutenant Rikelman tapped him on the shoulder. "Hamilton. Chief says the City Manager would like to talk to you. Can you break away?"

"Sure. Should I call him?"

"He wants to see you in his office."

"What about?"

"How the fuck should I know, HH? I'm just the messenger boy here."

"OK, sir. Just thought I would ask." He did not want to poke the Norman Bates bear.

So, what could the City Manager want with him?

CHAPTER 47

Hamilton put a sport coat over his shirt to better hide his weapon. It would be just a short walk to the city hall, and he tried to recall the City Manager's name. It was Rollins, Howard remembered. Before Clare's death, they had met when he responded to a call that involved the CM's wife.

He didn't know first names, but he wouldn't use them anyway. Instead, he grabbed his trusty notebook in case he needed to jot some things down.

He decided to take the route to the city hall through the front lobby of the police station. As he walked his way through the well-appointed grounds, he could not help but notice a few things for the very first time. First, there were concrete lighting posts staggered from the entrance to the parking lot in front of the station. The public would not realize it, but those light posts were concrete balusters whose base went at least five feet into the ground. Second, there was no way a terrorist could drive a car bomb to the front door or get anywhere near the facility.

As he continued his walk, he saw the identical balusters throughout the grounds that covered the Civic Center. The public had no idea how well fortified the Civic Center was. Only good planning or terrorist prevention through environmental design could be credited with this effort. Hiding in plain sight on the night shift did not give him this perspective. He was getting a lesson a day on the city government. He already saw things differently in the daylight.

He entered and took the elevator to the second floor after checking the marque for the city manager's office. "LeRoy Rollins" it said in gold letters, with his staff assistant's name just below.

The last time I was in city hall, I was sworn in for the job. He flushed at not knowing much about his city.

As he walked down the hall on the second floor, he saw photos of all department heads, including the Chief. He saw three men in suits and ties, a woman in a business suit, and a classic-looking grandmother, well dressed and trying not to smile. They were listed as the City Council. Names were inscribed in gold leaf.

"Mr. Rollins will see you in a few minutes, Detective." *This receptionist is right out of central casting,* he thought. She knew who he was by the calendar in front of her rather than him identifying himself.

"Officer Hamilton, good to see you." Rollins stepped out of his office and stuck out his hand for the politically correct handshake, firm but not aggressive. He placed his hand on Howard's shoulder and, with the other, closed the door.

He pointed to the visitor's chair and took his place in the more comfortable armchair, setting his notebook down on the small coffee table. "First, let me say how sorry I am about the loss of your wife. It can't be easy, raising two kids without a mother."

That was straightforward, Howard thought. He remembered seeing the City Manager and his wife at the service.

"Thanks for attending her service, sir. It was nice of you, and the flowers you sent were beautiful."

Orchard Hill had sent a standup wreath full of a colorful array, with her name, *Clare Hamilton,* spelled out with tight bud roses. He thought back on that for just a moment.

The momentary silence engulfed the room, and both men honored it.

"Officer Hamilton, I just wanted to personally thank you for what you did for my family and me a year or so back."

Howard recalled getting a radio dispatch to a restaurant where the manager had detained Mrs. Rollins. She patronized Della's Kitchen often and each time walked out without paying. The manager knew who she was and would contact Rollins, and the City Manager would square up with him each time it occurred. Howard recalled the manager telling him that other customers were aware of her actions this last time. He felt it was his responsibility to call the police to resolve the problem. Howard got the call.

"I love my wife and knew she had this … problem. I confided in the Chief after I received the call from Mr. Guerra. We all agreed you could not have handled the situation any better. I thanked you then, and I thank you now."

His phone rang, but he ignored it.

"She's been in therapy for this sickness, and I think we've turned the corner. I guess I enabled her a bit because I just contacted the stores and restaurants she frequented when this first started. I just took care of it. After the fact. Probably not the smartest thing but …" He drifted off, not knowing where to go from there.

"Well …" Hamilton fidgeted in the seat, trying to adjust his holstered gun so it wouldn't catch on the arm of his chair.

"Sir, she was very cooperative, and the manager was very understanding."

"I know and appreciate that, Howard. Can I call you Howard?"

"Yes, sir. You can call me anything but late for dinner." Howard tried to make light of the situation. Both gave appreciative smiles.

"Let me explain something, Howard. Yes, Barbara's fine now, but had it been any other officer or any other restaurant manager, this thing could have been headlines in the *Daily Wind*. Or the *Times*. And I would not be here. You handled this extremely sensitive issue quietly, and I truly do appreciate that it wasn't shared with the world."

"Only Clare, sir. I tell her, ah, told her everything about my shift."

"Well, I thank her too, Howard. That's why when the Chief casually advised me he was creating a new position in the department and putting you there, I could not have been more pleased."

He now saw the issues a bit more clearly. What happened in Orchard Hill stayed in Orchard Hill. If possible.

"Can I share with you one of our culture issues at the PD?"

"I would love to hear it."

"Well, we have a saying that the dolphins are talking."

Rollins frowned but let Hamilton continue.

"One of the guys went to Sea World a few years ago and found out that dolphins talk among themselves and gossip. PDs are notorious for spreading rumors—who is doing what, who is sleeping with who, and you know."

"I do."

"I can assure you, sir, the dolphins never got this. Not even a hint of it. The Chief and I made sure."

The phone rang again.

"Somebody wants me, Officer Hamilton. Thanks for stopping by. And thanks again for everything."

CHAPTER 48

The walk back from city hall was much more comfortable than the one to it. He was starting to see that information about the past, present, and even the proposed was critical. Gathering information that turned into essential intelligence meant evaluating, analyzing, and using the information. He learned it in class, but he was now seeing it in a different light.

If the Chief told Rikelman to let me know the City Manager wanted to see me, how much did Rikelman know? Sergeant McGinty was at the call where Mrs. Rollins was detained, and then Captain Markham called him in to thank him for handling the delicate situation. The critical factor here was, who knew what about Mrs. Rollins's situation?

Could his knowledge of the situation make him vulnerable in the politics of Orchard Hill? What other pieces of information would he be privy to that could be construed as tactical or strategic intelligence? His attendance at the intelligence school had to be balanced with his real world there in the city.

"How was the meeting with the City Manager, Hamilton?" Rikelman asked as he entered the office.

"Good. Nice man."

"Can I ask what it was all about?"

"Geez, Lieutenant, if I tell you, I'd have to kill you. You know how that goes." He laughed at one of the first lines he'd learned in the class.

"Got it." Rikelman smiled the menacing Norman Bates smile.

"No, seriously, sir. He wanted to ask about, about how I was doing, you know."

"Thought so."

"He also knew about this new job here. Interesting, huh?"

"There are no secrets in Orchard Hill, Hamilton."

Wanna bet? he thought. "Guess not," he quipped.

CHAPTER 49

James and Mary Ann were making plans, short-term and long-term. Everyone at the hospital was ecstatic about them. They each had finally found their soul mates, and James was sure to be the next medical superstar. The short-term plan was to live closer to work for both, and the long-term plan was for him to grow his practice, not just in the Korean community.

But there was other work to do as well, at least for James. His off day was Friday. Mary Ann was working but would be home by three in the afternoon. He found PCH and drove north to the outskirts of the South Bay. He used MapQuest to locate Sparrow Hill City Hall and quickly wound his way through the circuitous streets to its hideaway.

The buildings were classic old Spanish architecture, updated for earthquake standards but still looking as if they were from Marbella, Spain. The highest structure was two stories. It was subtle elegance at its best. The pavers that led to the city hall entrance looked and felt like they had been laid hundreds of years ago—worn but solid and unmoving.

He gathered some handouts about the city. Public Works, Planning, Parks, and the PD were within steps of one another. It was typical of city governments today to be on a ten-four plan. According to the notice, the city hall was closed every other Friday. This was one of them.

The public is easy to train.

He was ready to depart, having just enough information to understand this community, when a notice posted on the window got his attention.

On Friday, February 14, city offices
will be closed all day.
City officials will be conducting
a team-building workshop to better serve our community.
The city of Orchard Hill will be providing emergency services.
We apologize for any inconvenience.

There was a number posted, advising who to call in case of an emergency. James wrote it down. The city of Sparrow Hill was very transparent in its operations. And that was just fine with him.

CHAPTER 50

"Lieutenant Hobson in Patrol wanted to see you, Howard," Joanie casually mentioned as he walked back to his office.

"Got it."

He decided to call Hobson on the Watch Commander's internal line.

"Hey, Detective," Hobson jabbed.

"Yes, sir, Lieutenant, sir," he laughed, mocking the reference to detective.

"Need some help. I talked to Rikelman, and he said you might be able to help us once in a while. For some OT. That is if you haven't let your hair grow yet."

"No, sir, I'm good to go. What do you need?"

"Can you work a p.m. night shift on the fourteenth? Got some coverage problems."

"Sign me up, sir. Ka-ching. What day of the week is it?" He looked at his calendar.

"It's a Friday," Hobson responded, just as he confirmed.

"Great. No problem. It's a day off anyway."

"Thanks, HH. Glad to see you haven't forgotten your roots."

"Never, sir. Never."

It had only been a few weeks, and it seemed like forever since he had suited up. *Maybe I need that once in a while. You can't lose the edge.*

CHAPTER 51

Another week flew by. Howard developed the profile on Sundown and Sunset Enterprises. He found the owners through the Department of Corporations and jotted their names in the chrono. The only common name was the attorney.

"Lil from the city manager's office for you, HH," Joanie said on the intercom.

"Detective Hamilton. May I help you?"

"Detective, this is Lil, the city manager's receptionist. You left something in Mr. Rollin's office. Your notebook. Do you want me to bring it over or …"?

Shit! "No, ma'am. I'll come to get it." He hung up quickly, looked around to see if anyone overheard, and ran out the door to the city hall.

He couldn't remember what was in it. *Fuck, fuck, fuck* was his only thought for the moment. He raced past the light pole balusters he had admired on his first trip to city hall this day, not taking notice this time.

He quickened his pace, trying not to look conspicuous. He used the winding stairs that arched up to the second floor, stopped to catch a breath, and smiled at Lil, the receptionist.

She smiled as he reached out to accept the package. His notebook was wrapped in a city envelope, taped, and had his name on it. Lil looked to be about in her midtwenties, probably a recent college graduate learning the ropes of municipal government, or just biding her time until Mr. Right came along.

Howard smiled back, thanked her, and reflected on one of Donny Simpkins's great lines, "She is one potato chip away." Of course, everyone in the know knew what that meant, at least at Home Plate, the OHPD watering hole.

Hamilton decided to calm down a bit and stepped into the hallway before he opened the package. The City Manager had put his business card on top of the notebook with a brief note. *Be careful out there, Howard.*

"Yes, sir," he muttered to no one. "Yes, sir."

He walked past city officials' photos and decided to linger a moment before returning to the office. He probably should get to know who these people were at some point. He didn't vote in elections, trying to stay below the radar screen in this quiet city.

He saw the honorable mayor's photo, Martha Gottlieb. He looked at the other four: Don Diego, Doug Frankel, Ronald Watson, and Lee Straus.

Typical politicians, he thought. *Typical.* He was unsure whether the balusters surrounding the Civic Center were to keep the terrorists away or keep secrets of the city hall inside.

CHAPTER 52

Everybody knew someone in the underground—even Dr. James Song.

Everyone had a past—some darker than others. James needed contacts in the underground Korean community. And he knew who to call. The second-best way to know and understand a culture was to study it. The best way was to be born into it. He had been.

He put out feelers in his community, and it was not long before he found him. Unfortunately, his friend from grammar, middle school, and high school, Daniel Pak, did not make the grade. James remembered him as being against school administrators, authority, and, most notably, his family values, customs, and traditions. The rumors were that Pak had moved into the *am-si-chang* or black market. He knew Koreatown because of his business connections, owning a fancy specialty store in his old neighborhood but choosing to live in Monterey Park.

Pak established himself as a high-end *ya-hooe-bok*, owning a men's dress suit shop, selling to the same community he had shaken down just a decade before turning legitimate. Well, semi legitimate.

They met for cocktails in a quiet nightclub overlooking a golf course in the City of Industry. It was neutral ground for what was to be the topic of conversation.

"Ka-jok-dul-un o-tto simnika?" *How is your family?* After catching up on fifteen years of separation, they watched the golfers tee up. James shared his military experience, and he tried to get Pak to tell him what he only heard in rumors.

Some of their friends were marginally successful in becoming Americanized, others adapted more quickly, and still others never did adjust. His friend Pak was a rebel, against all authority and traditions.

James had grown up in a very young Koreatown, USA. Being steeped in the customs and culture from childhood, his friends were primarily of the same ethnicity. Most acclimated to the middle class very quickly. The eldest in the family always took the lead, whether it was in business or education. For James, it was natural. But unlike his birth country, he would not commit to an arranged marriage.

Pak, James recalled, started a group of his peers into low-level crimes in the neighborhood surrounding 8th Street and Irolo in downtown Los Angeles—the beginning of Koreatown.

After high school, they parted ways, James to college and Pak, well, to the street. It was there that the group he formed was converted into a gang. The Korean Killers, or KK, started with street crimes and grew to more sophisticated shakedowns or Korean businesses' protection. Typical, low-level organized crime. His language of choice was from Seoul, not America.

James got right to the point. "I need someone to work with on a project I have. Do you still have connections?" For the keywords in their conversation, they reverted to the Korean language.

"For what?" Pak asked.

"I need somebody with a *ya-p'o*, or *gun*, and willing to use it."

"How much are you willing to pay?"

"Money is no object, but confidentiality is." James was getting right to his point, and Pak could read through the words not said. James's eyes told him everything.

"I'd do it for you, James. You know that. But I can get you somebody for sure. When do you need this done?"

"Ballentaindei. Valentine's Day, a week from Friday."

"I'll make the call and put you in touch this weekend."

"Tang-sin-un cho-hun sa-ram imnida, Daniel." James smiled. *You are a good man.*

They continued watching the golfers with interest.

"Do you play?" James asked.

"I do," Pak quickly responded. "It is part of my business to stay close to my customers. Fortunately, many of the people we grew up with have the money and the time to do so. And you?"

"Not yet, Daniel, not yet. But soon."

They parted ways with a phrase they had both grown up using, "Si-jak-I cho-u-m yon ban-un song-gong-i-da."

A good beginning is half the battle.

CHAPTER 53

Having a three-day weekend off every week was going to be different. Howard had to plan his days using a more extensive calendar than marking days he worked and his days off. Planning in this job required even more engineering. Workouts were going to be a bit easier to squeeze in. He would like to work Patrol occasionally, not so much for the OT, maybe a little, but more to keep up his street skills. He had a couple of hours of work looking at him but realized he needed to do something.

"Hey, Sarge." He looked at Barber, noting he was the only supervisor in the room. "This assignment on Sundown. Can I get some OT this weekend? Need to see it in action, and, well, they're only open on the weekend."

"No problem, HH, but you can put in for the OT or just adjust and come in later one day. Your call."

"Sounds good. I'll let you know how the weekend goes."

He went back to work on the Sundown project, doing a spreadsheet on Excel to list the names he had recovered from the Department of Corporations. Working in his cubicle offered him the privacy he needed. It also covered his frustration at not being as adept at computers as he would have liked.

Barber bounced back at him. "HH, in that class on intel, did they talk about the LA Clearinghouse?"

"Yeah, I already entered the address in but am still working on getting some names together. Should finish that part today."

"The only reason I mention it is the Clearinghouse keeps track of all investigations going on across jurisdictions. All over Southern California. If there is any agency working on it without our knowledge, we need to know. And they need to know what we're doing. Deconfliction is important. I don't want you running into a DEA or DOJ investigation. Have you heard anything since you entered the info?"

"Nothing yet but can't do much with just an address."

He glanced back at his screen. What was bothering him was the only name he saw thus far was Jonathan Pritchett's, the attorney. The rest were more LLCs. So far, his spreadsheet read:

Company	Names	Incorporation Date
Sundown Enterprises	Jonathan Pritchett	September 2016
Sunset Enterprises	Jonathan Pritchett	September 2016

He laughed to himself as he looked again at his open page. *This is stupid; I don't have anything here.*

He drilled down to the Sundown name. There were three more LLCs: Sunrise, Moonshot, and Moonrise Enterprises. He added them to the spreadsheet. All incorporated in 2016. He then pulled up Sunset. Three more LLCs: Moonstruck, Satellite, and Moonwalk Enterprises.

He added those names to the list. When was he going to see names other than Pritchett? He went back to Lexis Nexus. No luck. He found another database, AutoTrack XP, and hit paydirt.

He printed out the results. Names, business addresses, and tax ID numbers were there. Now he was getting somewhere. Or was he?

CHAPTER 54

He had a list of names that amounted to a football team roster. Who were these people? The names sounded familiar, but he wasn't to the point of identifying them yet. First, he needed to develop his corporate list, then break it down by name.

By EOW, he had at least developed his first matrix. Barber and Rikelman were gone, so he had no one to discuss it with. Instead, he stared at his finished product:

Company	Names	Incorporation Date
Sundown Enterprises, LLC	Jonathan Pritchett	September 2016
	Managing partner: Tobias Spacek	
	Partner: Douglas Frankel	
	Partner: Mark Ryan	
Sunrise Enterprises, LLC	Jonathan Pritchett	September 2016
	Managing partner: William Marcus	
	Partner: Ronald Watson	
	Partner: Tobias Spacek	
Sunset Enterprises	Jonathan Pritchett	September 2016
	Managing partner: Ronald Watson	
	Partner: Beverly Sieman	
	Partner: Mark Ryan	
Moonshot Enterprises	Jonathan Pritchett	September 2016
	Managing partner: Mark Ryan	
	Partner: Douglas Frankel	
	Partner: William Marcus	

Moonrise Enterprises	Jonathan Pritchett	September 2016
	Managing partner: Beverly Sieman	
	Partner: Tobias Spacek	
	Partner: Ronald Watson	
Moonstruck Enterprise	Jonathan Pritchett	September 2016
	Managing partner: Sylvia Crest	
	Partner: Douglas Frankel	
	Partner: Mark Ryan	
Satellite Enterprises	Jonathan Pritchett	September 2016
	Managing partner: Douglas Frankel	
	Partner: William Marcus	
	Partner: Tobias Spacek	
Moonwalk Enterprises	Jonathan Pritchett	September 2016
	Managing partner: Tobias Spacek	
	Partner: Beverly Sieman	
	Partner: Sylvia Crest	

Hamilton would need some help with this, but no one was in the office, so it would have to wait until Monday. *Can't trust that day!* The desk vibrated with his phone, and he saw who was calling.

CHAPTER 55

"Amanda Johnson, how are you?" He smiled into the phone.

"How did you know?"

"Got you on speed dial too."

"I've moved up in your world. Thanks."

Howard was a bit surprised she had followed up after their last conversation on New Year's Eve. "Well, you were always up there, Amanda. To what do I owe this pleasure?"

"Where are you?"

"At work."

"Don't you ever get a day off?" She was probing now.

"I have a new job, and yes, I have the next three off ... wait a minute; I think I still have to work on Sunday, but never mind. What's up?"

He told her a bit about the job but no more than what anyone else knew. Everything was just too new.

"Well, next Friday is the fourteenth. And it's also Valentine's Day. Thought we could have dinner or something just to, you know, not be alone."

He mulled that over for a little too long. "Howard, are you there?"

"I'm here. I just did a little flashback, that's all. Thank goodness it isn't Friday the thirteenth. Right now, I think I would prefer that."

"*Howard*." Amanda dragged out the name as if to scold him.

"I know. Sorry. But, hey, did you know how Friday the thirteenth started?"

"I don't care about the thirteenth. I'm more interested in the fourteenth."

"Well ..." He paused for too long. Amanda was going to fill the void.

"Well what, Howard? Do you have another date that night?"

"I'm working Patrol. We're shorthanded, so I signed up for some OT."

"But you're in detectives now."

"I know, but they need me here." He paused again. "Maybe Saturday."

There was silence. "Are you just making that up to not see me?"

"No, Amanda, of course not. Let's just plan on the fifteenth instead. OK?"

She still felt like she was being put off, and he could tell. She was needy, he thought. A bit too needy. How could he salvage this?

"I promise we'll go to dinner, and I'll tell you how Friday the thirteenth came about and why it's unlucky."

She was withering right before his very ears. He knew she was convinced he was fabricating working Patrol to get out of being with her on Valentine's Day.

He had to end this charade. "Hey, got to go. I'll call you during the week, and we'll do something."

CHAPTER 56

Sunday will never be the same. It was not the Mamas and Papas but a soundalike group, Spanky and Our Gang, that sang another salute to a day of the week. He knew the Bee Gees had "Saturday Night Fever," and ELO had "Tuesday Afternoon," but did anyone write songs about Wednesday or Thursday?

After Saturday-evening Mass at St. Elizabeth's, he sat down to dinner with Geoff and Marcia and let them know he was getting up early on Sunday to "run some errands."

There was no shower. With an old LA Raiders baseball cap, jeans, sunglasses, an oldies rock and roll T-shirt, a Levi jacket, and running shoes, he was ready for his first undercover assignment. His off duty, snub nose Smith & Wesson with a ten-point grip was tucked in his backside, still in its pancake holster.

After Clare's accident, he had replaced her totaled Explorer with a Lexus SUV. He didn't ask if he could borrow the Charger from work, so he decided to use his private vehicle. *No risk*, he thought. *And not going that far.*

It was six thirty in the morning when he pulled into the side street adjacent to the Sundown. He was surprised at what he saw. There must have been over fifty motorhomes, RVs, and pickup trucks already inside the lot. It appeared they were setting up shop, with pop-ups to protect from the sun and beach chairs lined up for the proprietors to sit and watch the shoppers. Others were lined up on the street, waiting to get in.

How had he missed this city within a city all these years?

He took a few photos of the entrance with his phone to document how the place looked when open for business.

He noticed that not much of the activity was visible from the street. So how did people know what was inside? Too many questions.

He looked like a worker. With a one-day stubble on his face, his dress code was just like someone who could help set up and tear down. He strolled through the makeshift aisles that coincided with the lanes where cars would park when it was a real drive-in.

It was an out-of-doors garage sale but with items that appeared to be seconds or unsold merchandise from every outlet imaginable. He saw hanging baskets of flowers, from fuchsia to impatiens. There was fresh fish on ice, vitamins, CDs, DVD movies, and blue jeans.

His mission today was to look, listen, and absorb.

It appeared they were still in the process of setting up. Howard saw the sign that said "Open from 7:30 a.m. to 3:00 p.m." Not seeing any food vendors yet, he had time for a Peet's coffee. He walked back to his car, drove about three blocks, picked up a coffee and almond croissant, came back, and parked in the lot across the street that looked directly into the driveway's ingress and egress.

He decided to walk back in with coffee and croissant in hand. As he entered the gate to get in, another unkempt individual asked for an entry fee this time. Five dollars. His hands were full, so he had to set down his breakfast, dig out his wallet, and pay the entry fee. They stamped his hand. He only had his police wallet with his department identification and badge, so he had to do a sleight of hand to make sure no one saw it. He made note to dig out one of his old wallets for next time.

Who uses wallets anyway?

He felt like everyone was looking at him as if he was in uniform. But, no, he was just paranoid, he thought. He would have to get used to being a Joe citizen if he was going to be successful in this job. He walked the aisles with other patrons, stopping, touching, looking for sizes—just a typical shopper.

The clothing vendors were in two aisles. The CDs and movies were in another aisle, way in the back. He spent time in the two clothing rows, examining jeans in various sizes from various makers. The names appeared to be familiar, but he didn't know one from the other. However, he did recognize some brand names.

He would have to research the various types of jeans manufacturers to get an idea of what he needed. More homework. There were no barcodes, no price tags or anything to tell the potential buyer they would get a bargain.

Every vendor had a small credit card machine, a receipt book, and a small cashbox. For the most part, it looked like an all-cash business. He decided to continue walking around and found an RV that appeared to be the vendors' registration center. A male Hispanic in his fifties was sitting at a table, handing out forms, and his partner, a female in her forties, who looked like a trailer-trash washed-out meth head, was taking the registration money from each vendor who lined up.

Had he arrested any of these people?

Excellent system, he thought. His head was on a swivel, moving from side to side. That was when he spotted him.

CHAPTER 57

The guy was dressed almost like he was. He wore jeans, an untucked T-shirt, sunglasses, a Rams baseball cap, and running shoes. He was casually leaning against the RV like he owned it or was guarding it. His eyes were in constant motion. He was watching the crowd, the cashbox, and searching every face and what each person was carrying. He was security. But he was also Carl, Carl Peters.

Oh, fuck.

He walked away as if called by someone else, making sure Peters didn't see him. *Peters is the fucking OHPD POA vice-president! What is he doing here?* Hamilton answered his own question. *He's a hired gun, providing security for this operation.*

His thoughts were immediate. *Are there other guys from the department here? What the fuck are they doing? Do they have work permits? What if they get in a shooting? Did they see me?*

He decided to go to the back row where the CDs and DVDs were. There were not as many people there, he had noticed. At least not yet. The crowds had not made their way to the rear of the parking lot. He acted like an interested customer, browsing everything from sheet music that had more than likely been photocopied to CDs from the 1970s and color reproductions of the jackets and disks with homemade labels.

Everything here is junk, and people are buying it.

He walked to the two pop-ups that displayed signs announcing DVD movies. He saw the same thing. There were old Steve Martin movies, some soft porn, and westerns. Westerns? Where did they come from? He saw *Star Wars* and other sci-fi labels and even a *French Connection* DVD starring Gene Hackman. One of his favorite oldies. All for five dollars each.

Who buys this shit?

He got down to the end of the last row and saw another familiar face. He was dressed in jeans and a T-shirt, untucked to hide the gun. The requisite sunglasses, King's baseball cap, and running shoes labeled him as a cop—OHPD. It was none other than Alex Aguilar, big-time POA loudmouth.

What the fuck?

Time for him to leave. Hamilton walked the perimeter to look down each aisle as he made his way to the front entrance. He was confident the OHPD guys had not seen him, but he didn't recognize anyone else. *Who else is here?* He did a mental headcount of the number of vendors and made his way to his vehicle, parked across the street.

It might have been three hours of overtime, but it was years in lessons about what was possibly going on in Orchard Hill. *Sundays will never be the same.*

CHAPTER 58

Monday morning could not have come soon enough. He was in by seven and finalized his chrono for the last week. He cleaned up the spreadsheet to make it presentable to Barber and Rikelman. He hesitated to add the POA names but opted to use first name, initials, and last instead.

Right at 7:30 a.m., Barber and Rikelman walked in. Behind them were a few of the other narcs who had been on vacation the previous week.

"Hey, Lieutenant, Sergeant Barber, can we meet?"

"Jesus, Hamilton, let's get settled. Get the second cup of coffee and take a look at the weekend logs. How about eight o'clock?"

He should have known better than to jump on Rikelman like that the minute he walked in. Unfortunately, he had been too hung up on passing his anxiety off to a higher level and failed to test the waters early on a Monday. Instead, he went back to his workstation.

Patrol was always the twenty-four-hour pulse of a PD, and Orchard Hill was no exception. But if you were not in Patrol, working a staff assignment, Detectives, or other specialized units, events occurred while you were off duty that everyone needed to know.

On Mondays, everyone went in to check the twenty-four-hour log. If you had been on a three-day weekend, you would need to check three twenty-four-hour logs. The twenty-four-hour logs were prepared by the watch commanders who worked the weekends, in conjunction with the dispatch center, who entered everything into a formatted email for all to review. It was essentially a giant cut and paste.

One could never miss a beat in OHPD. Everything was documented and reviewed for accuracy. Well, almost everything. Otherwise, the dolphins would eat it up.

"OK, Hamilton, what do we have?" Barber knew that Howard was holding on to something that didn't make the twenty-four-hour log.

Howard started slowly. "Well, Sarge, as I told you, I decided to visit that address in question." He glanced around the room to see if anyone was listening.

"Can we go into your office? Better yet, can I send you a spreadsheet I've worked up, and we can discuss it on *your* computer in your office?"

He jumped back, did a quick email message, and walked into Barber's office after closing the door.

"As I said, I took a few hours yesterday and visited the site in question. Last Thursday, I worked up a spreadsheet with what I found regarding the ownership. I thought it was simple, but it got a little complicated after a while."

Barber just nodded for him to continue. "I just sent you the first go-around on the sheet, and I haven't sent you the chrono yet. I wanted to talk about that."

"OK."

"Bring up the email I just sent you."

Barber clicked on it and reviewed the data. "Hey, that's impressive. You've ..." He paused. He looked closer, taking his time to digest what was on the screen. "You've got two names here that interest me."

"I know," Hamilton replied.

Barber sat back in his chair. "So, tell me about your visit to the site."

Hamilton gave him a summary of his observations. "Then I saw those two."

"Frankel and Watson? There?"

"No, Peters and Aguilar. Who are Frankel and Watson?"

"Doug Frankel and Ron Watson are two of our City Council people. So who were you talking about?"

"Peters and Aguilar. From the POA."

Almost in unison, they said, "Holy shit."

Monday, Monday. Can't trust that day.

CHAPTER 59

For the next hour, Hamilton and Barber reviewed what they had. "You found no business licenses for any of these guys?"

"Not in the city or the county."

"Who're the other players? Pritchett, Spacek, and everybody else?"

"Haven't got that far, Sarge. Still work in progress."

"Well, right now, just keep digging. I'll fill in the Lieutenant. It's all good information, but we need just a little bit more. I'll find out if Peters and Aguilar have off-duty work permits. I can do that easily without stirring anything up. You're pretty sure they were working, huh?"

"No doubt, sir. They didn't have their shopping clothes on, but they did have their backups."

Barber looked at Hamilton almost like he was imitating Norman Bates too. "Hamilton, this is like Vegas. Do you catch my drift?"

"It stays here, sir. Got it." No dolphins were running there.

Hamilton went back to work.

Between AutoTrack XP, Lexis Nexus, and Google, he was able to locate information on everyone. There was not much he couldn't get from those databases with six billion records and twenty-five terabytes of data.

Tobias Spacek was a former Montebello police officer, but he only worked there for seven years. He quit and went to work with William Marcus, the former mayor of Thousand Acres in north county. Marcus had retired from Glendale PD and then got into politics. It looked like he enticed Spacek to leave the cop shop in Montebello early and make his money in a security company they had formed, Specialized Security Industries or SSI.

With Marcus's political contacts, they landed big contracts with PGA West, AIG Concerts, executive protection, the Golden Globes, and the Academy Awards. In addition, their very upfront marketing scheme bragged they employed either retired or off-duty cops. The strategy brought built-in integrity and, of course, concealed weapons.

Was it possible Beverly Sieman and Sylvia Crest could also be former cops, girlfriends, wives, or both? Somebody had to do the clerical work, Hamilton thought in his chauvinistic mindset.

Interestingly, each of them was a managing partner in at least one of the eight LLCs they formed. What did the other LLCs do? What was the connection to Frankel and Watson in Orchard Hill? He was a bit upset he had not recognized Frankel and Watson's names the first time around.

CHAPTER 60

Daniel Pak did not take long to get back to James. "I have a name for you."

James let the silence fill the phone line. "He will contact you. Can I give him this number?"

"No." He gave him a different number for a throwaway burner cell number he had purchased just for the occasion. "Do you have the name?"

Pak was very cryptic in his response. "Kim, Ku-pun un kunin imnida." He gave only the last name and that he had been a soldier in the South Korean Army.

"He will contact you when appropriate. You make the financial arrangements. I take my percentage from him. An-nyong-hi kye-sip-si-o."

"Is that all I get? Kim? It's like Smith in our language. Do I get a first name?"

"No." The phone went dead.

James had his plan in motion. Now he needed the details.

He called Sparrow Hill City Hall, speaking in broken English with his feigned Korean accent. "This is Lee Kim, Kim's Kitchen. We catering event for city staff on Friday. My assistant fail to get location to deliver food. Can you help? And want to verify the number of people."

It was too easy. *Why would Sparrow Hill have a workshop at the Orchard Hill Trusdale Inn? Because there is not one hotel in their little town.* He answered his own question.

His burner phone vibrated. Only two people had that number.

"Can we meet?"

"When and where?"

"Noon tomorrow at the Orchard Hill Trusdale Inn coffee shop at 222 North—"

"I know where it is. You buying lunch?"

"Cho-k'o mal-go." *Certainly.*

CHAPTER 61

Howard spent the next few days s dealing with several issues. Every time he went to the bathroom, someone would ask, "Hey, Hamilton, out of Patrol, huh? Got a desk job now? It's about time. What are you doing in Narc?" The questioning was endless.

He went to the city website to look at the photos of Watson and Frankel once again. It was the same picture that hung outside the City Manager's office. He committed their faces to memory in case he ran into them during the investigation. He tried to recall if he saw them on Sunday but quickly shook that off. *They wouldn't get their hands that dirty,* he decided.

He stiffed in a call to the security company. Posing as a police officer from Pasadena, he inquired if they were hiring off-duty cops.

"We're always looking for good cops," was the response. The voice on the other end directed HH to their website very politely and advised him to apply online. They did not ask for his name or take any other personal information.

The next step was the SSI website. *Pretty impressive* was his first thought—no photos of the principles but a lot of glitzes showing off their client list. Faceless security in their event-appropriate attire at events like the Golden Globes, Country Music Awards, and golf tournaments all around Southern California and even the New York City region were featured.

He eventually found the list of ownership and many event staff. He didn't know anyone or recognize any names other than Tobias Spacek and William Marcus. There was no doubt they were all prior law enforcement or current cops moonlighting. Because of his political contacts, he thought that Marcus was possibly the conduit to Watson and Frankel.

His investigation led to the Motion Picture Association of America, or MPAA, and the Recording Industry Association of America, RIAA. He found they worked closely together on pirating counterfeit movies and music. Nothing about jeans, of course. The MPAA and RIAA may not be interested in the movies or CDs' actual sales, but they would be interested in who was doing the counterfeiting. But it was hard to figure out who to contact.

He sat down with Barber to get advice about where to go next. After going over everything he had, he was getting a little frustrated. "What you have here is good information, HH. No worries. Let me sit down with the Lieutenant and see where we go from here. In the meantime, I have something new for you to work up."

Barber reached into a file drawer and pulled out a thick folder that appeared old and in disarray. "We've never had the opportunity to update this, Howard. But, with your new position, this gives us a chance to get moving on it."

"What's the file?"

Barber turned it around for Hamilton to see. "One of the signs of a good intel officer is being able to read things upside down, but I don't think you've had that class," he said jokingly.

"I got pretty good doing it with Sgt. Bennett in Patrol, but I'll work on it."

"This is the old file on all of the various organized crime figures in the South Bay. As you can see, it's a bit outdated. It shouldn't be much work but do some research on who is in the zoo around here. Who's dead, in prison, or still out there somewhere."

Barber moved the file directly in front of Hamilton.

"There's more here in this drawer," he said, pointing to a cabinet against the wall. "It may take some research into different databases, some snoopin', and surveillance. It may also mean touching base with LASD, LAPD, and the FBI. Just be careful and give us a heads-up before you do."

"What about that?" He pointed to the Sundown project.

"I'll let you know, Hamilton. Just sit tight."

CHAPTER 62

Howard walked into the office on Thursday at his usual time. After his first caffeine fix, he started lining up information on his latest project, Organized Crime in the South Bay. He would just label the file OCSB in case anybody was snooping around. *Who knew there was any organized crime around here?*

By nine o'clock, he had skimmed the file Barber had provided and started to go through items in the cabinet. There were old chronos from a decade ago, newspaper clippings, and a few mug shots.

Rikelman came out of his office with his first cup of coffee.

"HH, nice work on this project." He was holding the folder Howard had given Barber yesterday. "Let's take a walk upstairs."

"Where are we going?" he asked.

"Chief's office." They took the stairwell in silence to the third-floor administrative offices.

Rikelman walked into the Chief's office like it was his own. "Chief, I have Hamilton here if you have any questions regarding his investigation."

They exchanged cordial greetings and, with the Chief motioning them to sit, sat at a six-foot conference table next to a large window overlooking the employee parking lot.

"How're you doing, Howard?" the Chief said. "Geoff and Marcia ..."

"We're good, Chief. We're all adjusting but settling in as good as can be expected."

"Glad to hear it. I hope you don't mind, but I've chosen to invite someone else to this meeting."

The Chief got up from the table and asked Janet, "Is he here yet?"

"He just walked in, Chief."

Howard stood to greet the newest member of the meeting, the City Manager.

"Mr. Rollins, sir, didn't expect to see you, sir." Now Howard was very concerned. Dealing with top-level people like the Chief and City Manager was not something he was comfortable with. *Where is all of this going? Is this about the organized crime project or what?*

CHAPTER 63

The Chief gave an overview to the City Manager about the Sundown project. He explained the several business entities, their ties to one attorney, and lastly, the involvement of two Orchard Hill city councilmen. Howard was amazed at how much detail he knew about what was not even a completed investigation.

Rollins asked the first question. "How long did this take you, Officer Hamilton? I understand you just started the new assignment last week?"

"Yes, sir. It took me a few days, but my training course on intelligence helped a lot."

"One more question. Do you think anyone, I mean our Council people, Frankel or Watson, is aware of this investigation?"

"No, sir, not to my knowledge."

"Let's keep it that way for now, Officer, I mean Detective Hamilton."

Rollins made eye contact with the Chief.

"That'll be all, Officer Hamilton," the Chief advised. "You're free to go. Lieutenant, can you stick around for a few minutes?"

Rikelman snapped to attention. "Yes, sir."

Howard walked out of the room in a bit of a daze. *What's going on? There was not enough in that investigation if you can call it one. It's just information. I didn't see any crime. Maybe the lack of a business license. Was that a big deal? What's going to happen to the guys from the POA? What's going to happen to the councilmen?*

The Chief followed Hamilton to the door, closed it, and returned to his seat. There was silence in the room for about ten seconds.

"Sir," the Chief said, addressing Rollins, "I have a plan of attack on this if you hear me out."

After another thirty minutes, the Chief, Rollins, and Rikelman agreed on the course of action. But it would be Rikelman who would put the pieces together, with a bit of help from one of the Chief's old friends.

CHAPTER 64

James and Kim met for lunch at the Orchard Hill Trusdale Inn coffee shop. The place had seen better days. Perhaps prime for remodeling or demolition, the Trusdale Inn was not a destination point any longer. It served its purpose as a meeting spot for the local business community, chamber of commerce, and other local community groups to gather and socialize. That and perhaps a clandestine rendezvous or two kept the developers at bay before it would become a piece of folklore history.

But who would vacation in downtown Orchard Hill? No one would say, "Oh, let's spend the weekend at the Orchard Hill Trusdale Inn." It was just not a sought-after vacation spot. But business got done there every day. Local businesses put up out-of-town guests for a few nights, but very few families were ever to frequent its slightly old and outdated rooms.

James spent two cups of coffee and a breakfast roll telling Kim what he wanted. "Let's take a walk." James motioned as he paid the bill.

They walked the parking lot perimeter. "You pick out where you want to park, but I think the best access is over here." James pointed to the rear loading area where deliveries were made.

There was a fire exit door that led to the rear stairwell of the twelve-story structure. It only opened from the inside. There was no exterior door handle.

"This is where you can come in."

"It's locked for the outside entrance. How do you expect me to get in?" This was the most Kim had asked since their initial meeting.

"Tomorrow morning, I'll come by and put some conductor tape on the inside lock mechanism. Then, all you will have to do is put a piece of metal, like your car keys, against the door latch area here," he said, pointing to the doorjamb, "and it will unlock from the inside. It releases the circuit and gives you just enough slack in the door to open it from outside. Do you see that?"

"Ne, hal-su it-sumnida." *Yes, I see.*

Next, James took him through the front lobby and walked him to the rear door they had just been to from the outside. Interestingly, no one challenged them. The stairwell was directly opposite the exit door and went to every level of the hotel.

"I walked this area last week." He directed Kim to the stairwell and pointed in the air. "Take these stairs twelve floors to the penthouse. *Ji-guk-hi, kon-gang ham-ni-da.*" We both enjoy good health. Let's walk it together."

They arrived at the top floor a little winded but feeling energized. "Here's the door to the conference room and penthouse, and here's where the meeting is. I will have conductor tape on this doorjamb," he said, pointing to a replica of the door on the first floor.

James examined the door and jiggled it, and it came open. "What luck."

They walked into the room to get the layout. The eight wooden tables had been set in a horseshoe design, but tablecloths and settings were not yet displayed. "This should be easy, Kim. I have a photo of your target in the car. He'll be easy to pick out."

"How many will be in the room?" Kim asked.

"Not sure, but I think only six or seven."

172

They walked back down the stairs the same way they came up. There was no one using either the stairs or alcoves as they descended. "Follow me to my car." James pointed to his Lexus LC 500 sports car.

"You do well." Kim smiled.

"Never mind what I do. I will Venmo you half tonight, and when you let me know the job is done, I will send you the rest. I will be busy all day with my fiancée. Song Ba-lan-t a-in Nal." *It is Valentine's Day.*

James got his briefcase out and handed him a photo of Svenson. He had taken a picture of the press release he found on the internet when he discovered who Paul Svenson was.

"Ko-map-sum-ni-da." They exchanged *thank yous.*

CHAPTER 65

Hamilton walked out of the meeting thoroughly confused. He did not think he had done much with the information compiled. It was nowhere complete by any stretch. He needed much more information on the females and wanted to dig into the LLCs.

He sat back at his desk for a few minutes, staring at his screen, trying to collect thoughts. *Collect, analyze, and evaluate. Collect, analyze, and evaluate.*

The file on organized crime figures in the South Bay stared back at him. His discussion with Guy Coyle was becoming more evident.

"You may never arrest anyone in that assignment," he had said, "but the information you develop turns into intelligence when you can evaluate, analyze, and use the material for a specific purpose or reference."

He knew his strategic information was not going to result in anything more than knowledge. But what good was it?

Rikelman finally returned from the meeting and motioned to meet in his office, with the door closed.

"Right now, all I can tell you is that the Chief and City Manager are very pleased with your work. We have a plan, and I'll fill you in as we go forward. Nothing more to do with it for now."

"But …"

"No buts, Hamilton. I don't have time to discuss this further, so …" He pointed to the door. "Oh, and no matter what, don't go near Sundown this weekend." Norman Bates was alive and well. "And do not say anything to anyone about this."

He was yearning for the blue suit right now. Maybe he would just go downstairs to his locker and make sure he had everything ready for his shift tomorrow.

His phone vibrated. It read "Amanda Johnson."

"Happy Thursday the thirteenth, Amanda," he said.

"It's a lucky day for you too, Howard. You're lucky this isn't Friday the thirteenth. That's bad luck, but Thursday the thirteenth is good luck, and tomorrow is still Valentine's Day. Are you still working tomorrow night?"

He was going to avoid the question. "Did you know there is a Friday the thirteenth about every two hundred twelve days? I bet you didn't."

"I didn't, smarty-pants."

"And did you know that people like you, who have a fear of Friday the thirteenth, have triskaidekaphobia?"

"Of course I did." She laughed. "But you still didn't answer my question."

"Yes, I am still working tomorrow night."

"What time are you off?"

"Why?"

"We could just meet for drinks or something."

"It's always hard to tell, but with the holiday and it being Friday night, I'll probably get stuck with some OT."

"Are you trying to avoid me, Howard?"

"No, ma'am, just trying to be real here. It's always hard to predict. The streets could get weird, that's all. Even though it's not Friday the thirteenth."

"Well, there is a full moon."

"Well, Amanda, I hate to say it, but that just ensures trouble."

She was getting nowhere, and he could tell she was feeling rejected.

They were both right.

CHAPTER 66

If he was going to make this new assignment work, he needed to utilize his organizational skills. Clare had trained him well. His black-and-white was always pristine, he had all the tools in his briefcase, and the go-to bag was full of everything he would need. His office would be no different.

"Sgt. Barber, got a minute?"

"Sure, HH. Whatcha got?"

Howard posed the question he had wanted to ask for a few weeks. "What *stuff*," he said, putting his fingers in the form of quotes, "do we have for good surveillance work?"

"Not sure you have enough time today to get my standard class on all the shit we have. It's all locked up in that room," he said, pointing to a door that Hamilton never saw opened. It was labeled "JB."

"Tell you what. Here's the key. Go through everything, and when you're done, let me know if you have any questions. We can talk next week about it."

Howard gladly took the key with a nod.

"By the way, Howard, do not take anything out of there without signing it out. That's a felony around here if you know what I mean."

"I assume that means you would get the wrath of Norman Bates."

"You got it. But I'm the one who controls it, so you know whose ass it'll be."

After tidying up his workspace with a dust rag and cleaner, he spent the next two hours locked in the James Bond room, as it was called. Everything was lined up on shelves, labeled, signed for, and dated for last use.

On one side were all of the various types of cameras. There was handheld night vision equipment and drones with cameras. On the back shelf were various recorders, including voice-activated pens, bug detectors, audio jammers, and one of the fascinating items, the voice changer. The sign on it said, "Even your mother won't recognize your voice."

There were GPS tracking devices of all kinds. A complete countermeasure kit called the 22 must have cost thousands, he thought. There were data recovery sticks, SIM card recovery equipment, lock picks, and a small item called a road star, designed to disable a car. He would have to ask Barber about other electronic devices because he didn't understand their use.

After spending over two hours in the JB room, his favorite item, and the one he would probably use the most, was a plastic Starbucks coffee cup, Venti size, with a built-in camera and voice recorder. He laughed to himself. *I like coffee, but I guess the spy gadget people force you to drink Starbucks.*

He removed the top of the coffee cup and peeked in to see the electronics. *Maybe I have to come up with a way to use it when I'm not also drinking a Peet's at the same time.*

Next to it was another great piece of equipment. A water bottle with a built-in camera and mic. This one you could drink from and record at the same time. *Cool.*

It was a small room with everything jammed into tight spaces. He was getting a bit claustrophobic, so he decided to lock up and put the key back in Barber's desk. As he started to close the door, he saw a set of keys hanging from the sign-out clipboard. The tag said, "Shop 007." What was that? He had to ask someone but didn't want to appear too naïve—again.

CHAPTER 67

Hamilton returned to his computer and researched counterfeit jeans. He was surprised to see what came up. Counterfeit Jeans was a Canadian rock group out of Edmonton, Alberta, Canada. Who knew?

He finally found the information he was looking for. Counterfeit jeans were a $24 billion industry that started to appear in the mid-1990s and exploded in the early 2000s. Jeans had become so fashionable that the top of the line went for significant three digits. Just for jeans. Some of the most expensive were those that displayed fake mud or grass stains but were just part of the fabric. There were at least seven different makes of jeans he had never heard of, like 7 for All Mankind and Balman. *What happened to Levi's? Who comes up with this?*

He drilled down and could not locate a specific agency that investigated counterfeit jeans. *Must be the Department of Consumer Affairs,* he thought. He'd reach out to them if the investigation on the swap meet continued. And now that was a big if.

The most exciting part of his research taught him that counterfeit jeans should not be worn as a fashion statement. Sometimes one could not tell the real from the fake unless they were part of the garment industry that manufactured them.

It was also interesting to find the most prominent use of fake jeans was in the retail world of returns. People bought the fake jeans at a swap meet like Sundown and returned them to retail stores to exchange for a different size. The retailer would not know they were taking back a fake and giving them a real pair of jeans in exchange, or just giving the cash refund.

The retail world's biggest losers would be stores like Nordstrom that had a very liberal return policy. He knew about Nordstrom because Clare had been jokingly referred to as the "return queen" by her friends.

It seemed like every day was a lesson in something new. It was going to be an exciting assignment after all.

CHAPTER 68

He walked by Barber's desk and saw the Rotator. The Rotator was a hard copy file of current events taken from the watch commander's twenty-four-hour log for the last few days. It also contained internal memos, training information, and death and funeral notices for retirees from OHPD. Where the name Rotator came from, he never knew. Perhaps it was just a moving commodity that never seemed to sit still. Or maybe it was just OHPD folklore and custom that had passed by using technology. Rolodex came to mind.

There were the usual calls for service summaries, the amount of available time the dispatch center carried to show how much time was spent on calls versus the available patrol time. Howard saw the death and funeral notice for Harvey Stevens. It was next week, Thursday, at 10:00 a.m. at some nondescript church in Hermosa. He would calendar it. He had to go.

Stevens had been a reliable supervisor—until AJ Johnson, Amanda's husband, had been killed. Howard remembered what a mess that night was. Then the announcement of his retirement, his divorce from Val, and ultimately his moving out.

He had electrocuted himself while moving boxes from his garage to his pickup. So the rumors went, Val was going to get the house instead of getting a piece of his pension. She had listed it with Lieutenant Hospian's real estate office because she had worked for Hospian toward the end of her career. Word was out; she was moving out of state somewhere.

He had some time to kill, so he decided to look up the death report online. He had found a way to tap into other South Bay PD's report systems at the intelligence school. Rather than call Hermosa, he would just browse their system.

It was easy to find. Hermosa had closed it out as an industrial accident. *That was quick*, he thought.

He printed out a copy of the death report along with the autopsy examination. The coroner had confirmed the cause of death. Photos were taken of Stevens but not included in the report. It did indicate that Stevens was barefoot, wearing jeans and a T-shirt at the time of the incident. A frayed electric cord was sitting in a pool of water from a leaky water hose inside the garage. It seemed simple enough.

Everyone else was already EOW. *Hell, it's Thursday the thirteenth, and after four days of ten-hour shifts, what's a few minutes?* He had been so conditioned to patrol, where you could not go EOW unless relieved by another shift, that he didn't realize no one was going to relieve him. He just had to go home.

He was putting some files in his briefcase when it dawned on him. *Wait a minute.*

Didn't somebody say that the reason there was not going to be a retirement party was because of the circumstances of their divorce? And that Val was having an affair with someone? And that someone was a contractor who had been remodeling their house? At least that was what the dolphins were saying.

Who was the contractor? What type of work was he doing? Had they already filed for divorce? Was it still pending? What about his life insurance policy through the POA? We are all worth more dead, but who would get Steven's pension and life insurance? They had no kids.

Should I call Barber, Rikelman, or the Chief? Fuck, am I the only one who thinks there's something wrong with this picture? Am I the paranoid one, seeing bad in everything?

He completed his tour of duty a little bit after four and made sure his desk was neat as a pin, with pens and paper put away, his blotter cleaned, and his laptop computer shut down and packed away in his briefcase. He locked all files and drawers to keep away from those prying eyes.

He decided to think more about his first patrol shift in more than three weeks. Monday was another day. He was going to be ready for tomorrow.

CHAPTER 69

James and Mary Ann were going to have the entire Valentine's Day for themselves. It would be brunch in Redondo, a walk on the beach, shopping, maybe some lovemaking in the afternoon, and an early dinner in Koreatown.

The combination of tulips and deep red roses filled his condo and threw Mary Ann into a sense of euphoria he had never seen. She was spending more time at his new place than hers. He overwhelmed her with Valentine's cards and flowers that expressed his affections much more than he could. It wasn't Valentine's Day; it was Valentine's Week.

They were dressing smartly for their planned brunch when his cell phone rang.

"I-ri chom o-sip-si-o, I-ri o-si-o!" It was Kim asking James to *come here.*

"Where is here?" James asked quietly, whispering into the phone so as not to disturb Mary Ann while she dressed.

"At the hotel."

"Why?" James asked in a low tone of voice. He decided that this conversation was going to be all Korean due to Mary Ann's proximity.

"Too many people in the room. I come early. Check to make sure."

James asked how many people were in the room.

"Ten or twelve. I can't handle it alone. You come help."

He had to think fast. How was he going to handle treating Mary Ann to her most favorite day and taking care of this matter at the same time?

James was trying not to show any emotion. Mary Ann was within hearing distance, even in the spacious condo. "Not yet."

"I will meet you in the parking lot."

He looked at his watch. It was nine thirty. "One or two o'clock, if that's all right," James whispered in Korean.

Kim let James know he was good with that arrangement.

James strolled into the bedroom/bath area where Mary Ann was primping. "Everything OK, James?"

"Of course. Just have a minor issue I have to take care of around two this afternoon."

"Oh, no. I thought this was our day."

"It is, dear. I have something to do—a little surprise for you. I'll only be gone for an hour. Then we can nap, fool around, and get ready for the best dinner you will ever have."

"Can't wait," she cooed, flipping her long brown hair in his face.

"Me neither. For a lot of reasons."

James had a massive walk-in closet. Because he and Mary Ann were not living together, he gave her the smaller closet for personal use. He walked into his closet, took out a key, removed a few items from an old trunk, placed them neatly in a black plastic bag, and added them to his briefcase.

CHAPTER 70

There was always the opportunity to pass information in Patrol or even an end-of-watch radio call to the next shift. The uniform would hang in your locker until you returned for a new shift, regardless of what happened that day. Driving home, whether it was a ten-minute commute or a two-hour drive, your day was done when the reports were completed and you went end-of-watch or EOW. Then, home to the family until the next shift.

Hamilton was starting to realize that his new assignment was not going to be anything like Patrol. No one took over after he left the station. It was all his work, his cases, and there was no handoff to someone else.

It was all-consuming. *How can you not think about your cases, read up on what is going on in the law enforcement world, and not even think about what you would do when you get back to work?* The phantom was lurking in the backroads of his mind. Was it going to get him? Take the place of Geoff and Marcia? The memory of Clare?

He thought about the phantom more and more. He and Clare had seen *Phantom of the Opera* four times. Each time, it reaffirmed to him there was no real phantom. It was that all-consuming commitment to your craft. Christine had wanted to become a legendary opera singer. To reach the pinnacle, she had to give up many things to concentrate on her performance. That may have included giving up her lover, Viscount Raoul de Chagny. The phantom was the need for Christine to commit to her singing and not to Raoul. She had to choose between the love of her life and her love of the stage. Which would it be? He wondered if anyone else saw the irony.

Howard had seen detectives like Dave Nieman, who regularly worked homicide cases. Nieman had a family but lived at either the station or in the field when his cases needed working. He was fanatical.

Everyone used to joke you would not want Nieman on your case if you were the bad guy. He would never let go. He would fuck with you; make you think he was watching you every minute of every day. His relentless pursuit was legendary. His partners used to say that his passions were his work, sailing, and his family—in that order. The name of his sailboat said it all, *Tenacity.*

Howard was finding himself becoming much too aware of his new job. Was it a job? An assignment? Or a calling?

So now, he had to do a drive-by, just to check out something. It wouldn't take long. Not on a quiet Friday morning. At the same time, the kids were in school. *Grab a Peet's, go for a drive, and do not even think about putting in for overtime for what I am about to do.*

CHAPTER 71

The kids left for school, and Howard was on a mission this bright and early Friday morning. His phone chimed. Who was on the phone for him this early?

"HH, Donny here." Simpkins didn't call him that often, but when he did, he usually had something substantial.

"Whatcha got?"

"Your buddy, the Chief, is in trouble."

"What do you mean my buddy? He's not my buddy, asshole, and what trouble could he be in?"

"We know you're a pipeline, but that's OK because most of us like the guy. He's a street cop's Chief."

"Listen, he is not my buddy. Get over it. What trouble is he in?"

"Well, you know the City Manager and him are on the POA shitlist. And they have two councilmen on their side. They all want to get rid of him and the CM. And now the city just got sued for something Hotel did at three o'clock in the morning. They want to ream their asses. Starting with the Chief and then, because the CM hired him, the Council wants to axe him as well."

Simpkins was talking too fast for Howard to absorb it all.

"Whoa, Donny, whoa."

Howard was looking for a place to sit and think about what Donny was telling him. "What did Marty do?"

Marty Hyatt had picked up the nickname "Hotel" the minute he landed at OHPD. You didn't have to be a rocket scientist to figure that one out.

"Marty and your boot trainee Alcazar were patrolling the northside business alleys a couple of months ago on graveyard. I think it was about three in the morning. They stopped three douchebags in a beat-up piece-of-shit car who were cruising the alley with their lights out. Marty lit them up, got all three out, separated them, and tried to find out what the fuck they were up to."

Simpkins was trying to calm down. He had worked himself into a frenzy, trying to get all the facts out.

"Are you in the station, Donny?"

"No, I'm in court. That's where I heard about it. From the City Attorney's office."

"Well, from what you said, what the fuck is wrong with it?"

"I'm not done."

"Go on."

"Well, they run the guys for warrants, search the car, and come up with zilch. They keep them separated, and finally, one of the suspects admits he works at the auto parts store near where they stopped them. Marty asks him to empty his pockets on the car's hood and finds a key to the business. It sounds like, well, you know, he would come back and burglarize his place of business. What the fuck else would you be doing at three o'clock in the fuckin' morning?"

"Makes sense to me," Howard agreed.

"Well, now it gets dicey. Marty takes the time to call the emergency number on the business, but there's no answer. They said he tried several times." Simpkins paused again to catch his breath.

"Any use of force?"

"Nope."

"Go on."

190

"That's it, HH, that is fuckin' it. They're suing for false imprisonment, illegal detention, and a few other rat-fuck things that make no sense. One of the guy's aunts or uncle is a big-time civil rights attorney, and they're going to make a big fuckin' thing about it. Take it to the press and say the Chief and Marty are out to get them. They had to kick them loose, but get this. Their investigation took forty-five minutes. I think they just threw the City Manager under the bus because he's in charge too."

"What the fuck, Donny. Come on. None of it makes sense. Remember that study that said our average time on a traffic stop or radio call was twenty-three minutes? Well, this was only twenty-three minutes doubled. Hell, under those circumstances ..."

"And they want, get this, five hundred thousand dollars from the city, plus attorney fees and punitive damages. It turns out one of the guys was on his way to a big-time college with an athletic scholarship or something and may not get it because of this."

"Now they're making this stuff up," Howard said out of exasperation.

"Thought you ought to know, HH, seeing as how you and the Chief ..."

"Knock that shit off, Donny. I told you, we are not friends, asshole."

"Well, either way, he's in trouble."

Howard thought about it for a moment. "Hey, Donny, the Chief was at home in bed when Marty and Alcazar were in that alley. And the City Manager, well ..."

"Doesn't matter, HH. He's the Chief, and the CM is in charge of the city. The Council is going to have a field day. And so is the press."

CHAPTER 72

Howard had pulled to the curb to finish the conversation with Donny. He was going to compartmentalize what he heard for now and concentrate on his current mission.

He arrived at his destination: 333 North Maple in Hermosa, Harvey Steven's former residence. It was a typical, quiet, early Friday morning in a tree-lined beach community and residential area. A gardener was cleaning up across the street with a Volkswagen engine on his back, blowing leaves to the next neighbor's yard. A mailman was making his rounds, feeding the curbside mailboxes their daily ration of bills and junk mail.

He had been to Steven's house maybe one or two times. Both were brief visits. Howard got out of his car and decided to be a little curious. He could tell the house was empty. No furniture, no For Sale sign. It just sat there waiting for something else to happen. The yard was pristine, with marathon grass, boxwoods lining the walkways, and impatiens blooming with pink and white blossoms.

What was he looking for? He didn't know. Was he going to find Val here? He doubted it. Harvey Stevens wasn't going to reappear from the dead or come from behind a tree to scare him. The garage was closed. He would not try any doors and didn't want to even think about looking into where Stevens had electrocuted himself. No, that was not why he was there. Why was he there?

He walked to the garage side and saw a new air-conditioner, or what appeared to be a new air-conditioner. New lines were going into the house from the compressor. They were freshly wrapped with new insulation and sealed, so no creepy, crawly creatures could use it as a conduit to get in the house.

You don't need too much air-conditioning at the beach, so they must have had an ancient one that needed replacement, particularly if they were going to sell it. After all, the house is over thirty years old.

Makes sense. Looking closer at the compressor, he saw it was seated on a hard plastic stand to ensure the air circulation would flow freely in all directions.

On the side of the compressor was a sticker: "For service, call Hanson's Electrical" with a phone number. It was new, freshly stuck on the new conditioner for maximum visibility.

"I wonder if that was the contractor that Val ..."

Hamilton's thoughts faded away. *I wonder if Hermosa is looking at any of this.*

CHAPTER 73

James had to give this situation some more thought. While Mary Ann might not like it, he had something that needed to be handled—today.

He excused himself and went to the underground garage's storage area, where he kept more personal items. He stuck them in his trunk with the briefcase and returned to the house.

"Let's go to brunch a little early, Mary Ann. I must take care of some business around two this afternoon if that's OK. It shouldn't take me long. We can still do a walk on the beach and get ready for a great dinner in K-town."

"Well, James. If duty calls. I understand. I just may come back and take a nap."

As predicted, lunch or brunch on holidays like Valentine's Day would be crowded. The Chart House in Redondo had their reservation for a window table, but the wait was still almost thirty minutes.

"You're a bit distracted, dear." It was a casual comment meant to solicit a "What's on your mind?"

"I am. Many things to think about. Work, our wedding, and, most importantly, what to get you."

"You don't have to get me anything. This ring and the wedding band must have cost a fortune."

"You deserve it. And so much more. You've made me the happiest …" James let the word hang out there like a fishing line hoping to catch its prey.

"I'm the happy one."

"We both are, I guess."

The time went quickly. A light mimosa with a steak salad for him, a salmon Caesar salad for her, and a shared Reece's Pieces cheesecake made the afternoon perfect. He could have done without the waitress hovering over them, wanting to get ready for her next big tip of the day. He saw they had stretched the day past one thirty and closer to two o'clock.

"I think someone else wants this table," he said, half joking but more than willing to surrender it.

"If naps weren't invented yet, I would be the one to patent them," Mary Ann said humorously.

"I'm jealous. But I promise I'll be right back as soon as I take care of some business."

"You better."

CHAPTER 74

Howard returned home to get ready for his first night shift in a long time. He left a note reminding the kids he may be late, but the overtime would be to their benefit. Being a mom and dad was getting hard to figure out. Where did one begin and another end? He had never left notes before, before … when Clare was around. He reminded himself to check in with them around five or six that night.

He went to work an hour early. He dropped into his new office and found a couple of the narcs finishing up some paperwork.

"How's the new job, HH?" Eddie L asked. The PD being what it was, nicknames were for everyone below the rank of Sergeant. Eddie was Eddie L because he had such a confusing last name—Laskowich or something like that.

"Still can't find my ass yet, Eddie. Got nobody to follow. This job is brand-new, so not sure what my next step is."

"Believe me. Rikelman and Barber will keep you busy, no doubt."

He opened his computer with just a hint of what he wanted to do. He checked his emails, looked at some websites given to him by Barber about organized crime, and found another new project from Rikelman and Barber. They were teaming up to load him up. Eddie L was right.

The new project looked even more exciting than organized crime work. But HH had another priority right now—Hanson Electrical.

The California State Department of Corporations' files held a wealth of information. Stanley Hanson was a very successful contractor. Just his home address made the statement. Googling him, he found Hanson to be an upstanding community member, but in Sparrow Hill, not Orchard Hill. That just meant he had more money. A Chamber businessman of the year, a frequent contributor to charitable causes, and, most importantly, being a longtime widower made him the catch of the century in the South Bay.

Hamilton checked his DMV record for a photo. Not a bad-looking guy, but he still looked like a fugitive. Didn't they all on DLs? He did a criminal history check and found only one DUI twenty years ago. "Val did well," he mumbled. There would be one last question before he determined a course of action.

"Sergeant Blair Rydell, sir, how are you?"

Rydell was the head of HR or Personnel, whatever they were calling it today. He did the background investigations for new hires, and Hamilton contacted him when he was training Michael Alcazar.

His name generated the common nickname "Golden" for two reasons. He was a golden boy, so named for the anointed because, according to many, he was destined to be a lieutenant or higher if he kept his nose clean. His last name was also the same as the singing legend Bobby Rydell, who now toured with Frankie Avalon and Fabian, both icons from the 1950s rock and roll era. They were dubbed "The Golden Boys," so Blair was a twofer.

"How's the new job, HH?"

"Going well, sir. Like any new gig, can't find my ass yet." They laughed together. "I have a stupid question for you. I don't know if you know, and don't know if I have the right to know, but I have to ask it anyway."

"OK, shoot."

"Did Harvey Steven's life insurance policy beneficiary ever get changed?"

"From what to what?"

"I don't know, but he and Val were getting a divorce, and I just wondered."

"Interesting you say that, Howard. The Chief and I were talking about that yesterday. It turns out their divorce was not final, they didn't have any kids, and he never came up here to make any changes from when they were originally married."

"I see."

"Are you asking about this in an official capacity, or are you just nosey?"

"Well, I am the new intelligence officer, and it's my job to gather information, and I am a confidential employee, sir," he said, trying to make light of it.

"I see where you're going, Hamilton, and I like it. Let me get back to you."

His next call was to Hermosa homicide.

"Hermosa PD, Detective Graham. May I help you?"

Hamilton identified himself and advised he was inquiring into the death of Sgt. Stevens.

Silence.

"I worked for Sgt. Stevens here at OHPD and was wondering ..." He stumbled with his words.

"I heard you classified the case as an industrial accident or something like that."

"Yes." It was a very curt reply.

"Can I send you some information for you to look at?" Hamilton had to be very careful here.

"What kind of information?"

"Just some information I came up with."

They exchanged email addresses.

CHAPTER 75

James said his casual farewell and drove to the Orchard Hill Trusdale Inn to meet Kim. He found him exactly where they had met yesterday. It was a spot that was to the rear of the hotel, where deliveries were made. There were no hotel employees or delivery trucks to be seen. This late in the day, all deliveries had been made for the weekend.

Kim was smoking like a chimney. James could see three or four cigarette butts outside the driver's door of his car.

"That stuff is gonna kill you, Kim."

"Gotta die from something," Kim joked.

Kim was dressed in a green T-shirt, low-cut combat boots, and camouflage pants. His outer Cammy shirt was unbuttoned and worn to hide his weapon of choice.

"Glad to see you dressed the part. I brought mine also."

James went behind a large tree and quickly changed into similar clothes he had brought with him for the occasion. He did add one item. His over-the-ankle combat boots, green T-shirt, Cammy pants, and untucked green buttoned-down shirt almost matched Kim's.

"What was your rank?" James asked.

"Ha-sa." *Staff Sergeant.* "And you?"

"Teajwa," *Senior Colonel.*

"Wow. You see any action?"

"A-ni-yo, Kun-ui hak-kyo." *Not much because of my medical degrees.*

James opened his shirt to display his Beretta 92 FS 96 Series fifteen-round-capacity handgun.

Kim opened his shirt to show a Daewoo K5 thirteen-round-capacity semiautomatic. "They let me keep it. This is what enlisted *bo-byong* swine got."

"Yes, but yours is Korean made. Mine is Italian. I think you have the better *mu-chang*, no?" James was trying to bolster Kim's ego, suggesting he was the real warrior with a better handgun.

"We see," Kim said proudly. "Reason I need you is I go to the room and act like I in wrong place. Ten or twelve in room. Too many people. Your man in a bright blue shirt. Others more casual. Easy to spot."

James went back to his car trunk, obtained an item, and went behind the tree again. He stripped his shirt off, added a bulletproof vest, put his shirt back on, and handed Kim another vest he had brought with him.

He looked Kim in the eye. "Put it on."

He had not told Kim that some in the group were cops.

"Good idea. We can handle it. Ready, *Ku-pun?*" *Soldier?*

CHAPTER 76

Howard closed his office computer and readied for his shift. He was hoping it was not going to rain tonight. He wouldn't be ready for that event. He took the stairs to the locker room in the basement. Donny Simpkins was putting his uniform on. Simpkins was never in good physical shape. He was called the doughboy and for a good reason.

"Donny? Are you looking for some OT too? It looks like you're having some trouble buttoning up." Hamilton added a chuckle.

"Yup. And you know, asshole, you don't have to notice everything. Patrol is a little shorthanded until some of the boots get off probation, so I decided to help out. If I can get these trousers on." He struggled but finally achieved his goal.

"Me too. Maybe we'll see each other tonight."

"I don't know. They got me working the north end, and you're on the south side. Did you see the lineup?"

"Yeah, but who knows what'll happen. See you in roll call."

Hamilton walked into the briefing room and barely knew anyone. Many new faces. He did recognize Tenery and Mel Flowers and gave them a silent nod of recognition.

When Donny sat down next to him in the back row, the chant from the less tenured uniforms became, "Ka-ching, ka-ching."

Donny directed his comments to the front of the room. That was where those still in training were required to sit. "You guys will understand someday."

One voice from the front said, "We already do, sir."

Bennett walked in behind the back row, clipped Hamilton's ear with his forefinger and thumb, and had an "I'm here now" attitude. He read off the assignments. "Lincoln 75 is back with us. Good to see you, Officer Hamilton."

"Good to be seen, sir."

Bennett covered a few new orders that the Chief had put out. One had to do with a new report form, but the other caught his attention.

"Just a reminder from the Chief," Bennett said in a formal tone. "Review your life insurance policies you have with the city and the POA. Make sure your beneficiaries are up to date. And current. Nobody wants it all to go to your ex-wife, now do they?"

Donny and Howard smiled at each other. *We know where that came from* was the underlying message.

When the briefing was over, Howard hurried to the kit room to check out his favorite black-and-white, Shop 885. It was gone.

"Who's got it?" he asked Will, the kit room coordinator.

"Flowers."

He looked up, and Mel was dangling the keys mockingly.

"This is all I got," Will said. "Sorry, HH. Didn't know you were working Patrol anymore."

"This is a piece-of-shit car, Will."

"All we have left."

He saw Mel Flowers as she gloated her way to the back lot to put her gear in Shop 885. "I guess if someone had to get it, it should be you, Flowers."

"You took good care of it, Howard. Now it's my turn."

In more ways than one, Mel. It's your turn in more ways than one.

CHAPTER 77

"Lincoln 75 clear and available for calls," he advised dispatch. It was starting to get cloudy. Could it rain? He repositioned his body cam as it rubbed against the seat belt.

"Lincoln 75 10-4, good to have you back," said the familiar voice on the radio waves. Since Clare's passing, people at OHPD had been walking on pins and needles, unsure how to deal with him. Howard knew it was up to him to make sure everyone at his home away from home was comfortable with his situation. His upbeat attitude had to be shown to all. Yes, he had his grieving time, but now things were getting back to normal—whatever normal was.

He met Donny for a quick Peet's coffee and worked his way to the city's south end. For a Friday night, Valentine's Day Friday night, it was eerily quiet. But it was early.

He knew he had a choice. Think about Clare or not. He was feeling like his old self—curb-to-curb vision, head on a swivel, and examining people, cars, and license plates the way he used to. He was again in his comfort zone. Was it that easy? It had to be. His life depended on it.

CHAPTER 78

It was becoming twilight on this Valentine's night, with a hint of rain. Lights in the parking lot to the rear of the Trusdale Inn came on automatically as dusk approached. Traffic noise from the main street could be heard in the distance.

James went over his game plan one more time with Kim.

"I'm here only to back you up. You're getting paid to take this guy out. Understand?" Kim nodded. James continued in his native language. "Nobody else gets hurt, just this guy," he said, pointing again to Svenson's picture.

"And Kim …" James looked him in the eyes again. "Ko-map sum-ni-da." *Thanks.*

They quickly slid a tool into the doorjamb and made the connection to the conductor tape James had installed the day before. It easily opened.

They huddled inside the alcove of the stairwell. "Let's take the first six levels, take a breather, and then work our way up to *yol tul,*" James advised, referring to the twelfth floor. Unfortunately, he was not in as good shape as the more athletic Kim.

Reaching the sixth floor, they heard voices in the stairwell. James could see the ready in Kim's eyes. Using sign language, James put his finger to his lips to be quiet. He looked down the stairwell and saw two bodies huddled on what was the second landing.

He laughed. They were having sex. He held up both hands to Kim, made a small fist with one hand, and moved the other hand's finger in and out, simulating sex. They both grinned—probably employees.

They took advantage of the noise and moved quickly up the stairs toward the top floor. Their combat boots on the linoleum floor were as good as slippers on tile, making no noise at all. The loudest echoes came from the grunts and groans several flights below.

They arrived at the top floor and paused. Both were motivated— one by passion and one by money, the perfect combination. There was no need for conversation. Both knew what needed to be done. Each pulled black ski masks over their heads. It was time.

James used his trusty tool to activate the conductor tape. The door easily relaxed in the jamb. There was no handle to open from his side, so he leveraged the heavy metal door slightly open with his hand.

"Ka-so." *Go.*

CHAPTER 79

Kim was the first in. He quickly announced, "Hands up! I want to see all hands. Hands up. This is a holdup. We want your money, and I mean hands up."

He slid along the back wall to make sure he could see everyone. He then moved to the center of the horseshoe-shaped tables. Taking a combat stance, Kim waved his Daewoo handgun back and forth and, for effect, fired two shots into the ceiling. He made eye contact with the man in the blue dress shirt. He concentrated on the left side of the horseshoe, where the target was standing. Song took the right side, holding half of the room at bay.

The entire group was startled—en masse. One of the participants started laughing. Then a few others. "Good job, Chief. Made this an entire training day. Quite a …" the following words would have been "a situation simulation," but the Chief's face said it all. It was not a simulation. Reality was rapidly setting in.

Kim kept shouting commands. "Hands up. Hands up." He had their undivided attention now. Eye contact was necessary on both sides. Kim's military training kicked in as he focused on his target and sight alignment.

"Put your wallets on the table. Ladies, get your purses out. All money and jewelry on the table." Kim's English was perfect. They knew how to follow directions.

James pulled out a plastic bag from his side pocket and scooped up the wallets that lay on the table. He said nothing to anyone. It was Kim's show.

Kim knew what to do. He would alienate the blue shirt, try to get him angry, and then take care of business as if he was merely reacting to the confrontation. It worked.

Svenson dropped his hands and shouted at Kim, "What the fuck do you think you are doing? We're not going to take this bullshit. Do you know who we are?"

Kim looked him in the eye for that brief, indescribable moment that told him he was a dead man. "I don't care who you are." The sights on his Daewoo lined up perfectly with Svenson's chest. One shot from his handgun served its purpose. Easy, in the ten ring. Less than five feet away. Center mass. Kim smiled.

As he stepped forward to admire his work, he let down his guard. The man next to Svenson, tall, a bit heavyset, handlebar mustache, and massive arms, used his strength and grip to grab Kim's weapon. They struggled. Kim's gun went off again.

James saw what was going on and dropped the bag. Was Kim shot, or did Mister Mustache get hit? He didn't know, but he could not have Kim overpowered now. With one swift movement, James struck Mustache on the side of his head with his gun and watched him fall to the floor. The concussion pushed Mustache backward, knocking over a portable whiteboard easel that was on wheels.

Mustache stumbled, tried to catch himself, and pushed the easel against the wall as he fell. He slid down until he sat on the floor with his head leaning against the whiteboard tray. James had no idea that a bullet from Kim's gun had entered Mustache's side, almost near the armpit, during the struggle.

Two people to his left dropped their hands and moved toward the fallen man. "Van! Van!"

J. C. De Ladurantey

The toxic but familiar smell of cordite gun powder permeated the air.

Only fifteen seconds had passed since the entry by Kim and James, but it became an eternity to all in the room.

"Don't anyone move," Kim ordered.

There was that moment when the group realized this was not a simulated situation. They had only collectively entertained it for perhaps seconds, but it was enough of an advantage for Kim and James to get the upper hand.

That was about to change.

Song reached down to pick up the bag of wallets. Kim was reacting to being grabbed by Mustache.

Within those few moments, those in the room who knew how to act did so. It would not be a reaction but an assertiveness that came with the job. Training embeds one with the innate ability to respond without thinking, and this was the time to kick it into gear.

CHAPTER 80

In deference to their City Manager, the Sparrow Hill PD members were asked not to come to the team-building workshop armed with their off-duty weapons. Getting a new Chief, particularly one from outside and with no municipal law enforcement experience, meant there needed to be some adjustment time. The CM knew it, and the new Chief did as well. The members of the PD, however, did not leave their training in the locker room.

Without saying a word, as Mustache and Blue Shirt went down, White Golf Shirt and Parks Director went for Kim, tackling him immediately after he shot Blue Dress Shirt. White Golf Shirt kicked Kim's gun hand, using both hands to push his arm up and shake loose the handgun, and for good measure, he kicked him in the face. The weapon dropped to the floor. Untucked went low with a football-style tackle waist-high, causing Kim to fall onto a table, breaking the legs and going face first into the tabletop.

More shouting as black Untucked and Tan Golf Shirt detective went for James as he turned toward them. He was no match for the detective, who aggressively went for James's weapon by pushing it out of the way in a sweeping motion everyone had been taught at the police academy. It was gun takeaway 101.

The City Manager realized the seriousness of the situation immediately. Let his police officers do their job while he did his. Someone had to call the police. Trying to keep his composure, he ducked out the door, stood in the stairwell, and punched in 911. He was immediately connected to OHPD dispatch.

"This is Jim Hines, City Manager, Sparrow Hill."

He said it like he was reading a grocery list. His quiet demeanor kept him from losing his mind. He had to stay calm. He had to concentrate. He could hear the scuffling going on, but this call was needed more than his intervention in the room. There was no time for the shock to intellectualize or put things into a rational context.

"We are at your Trusdale Inn, on the penthouse floor. There's been a shooting. Two people have been shot. They are both police officers. I need an ambulance. No one is armed. Repeat. No one is armed but the gunmen. Two suspects are still in the room. I don't know if they are a part of a larger assault team or not." His voice echoed in the stairwell, so he had to cup his hands over his ears to listen to the 911 operator.

"Stay on the line if you can, Mr. Hines. We'll have help there as soon as we can."

Hines could hear the dispatcher broadcast. "All units and Lincoln 75 and Lincoln 77. Shots fired, Trusdale Inn."

She gave the address, reading it from her call locater screen. There was no doubt where it was, with only one Trusdale Inn in the city, but she did it the way she had been trained. She looked to her supervisor, who knew what her question would be, and got a nod. "Lincoln 75, proceed code three, red lights and siren. Lincoln 77, code two only as I have R 25 from Fire also en route, code three."

The OHPD dispatch center was taking charge of the airwaves to make sure all knew what to do. "All units responding to the shots fired at Trusdale Inn, I'm bringing up the floor plan for the hotel on CAD. Watch for it."

After 9/11, the city identified vulnerable locations that might require entry in an emergency. The Orchard Hill Planning

Department, in cooperation with the Fire and Police Department, had digitized floor plans of all critical businesses in the city.

Hines wanted to go back into the room but knew what his job was now. It was to be the linkage to OHPD. He needed to feed information to the dispatcher so everyone could do their jobs.

CHAPTER 81

There was no chaos inside the penthouse conference room. Everyone knew what needed to be done. Even with no one having weapons or handcuffs. After just two minutes, control was finally taking over.

White Golf Shirt shouted to anyone in the room as he straddled Kim, who was now face down on top of a broken table. He was spewing spittle as he wrestled his suspect to the ground. "Anybody with shoelaces, give 'em to me now!"

Untucked straddled Kim, holding his legs firmly with each hand, while Parks Director controlled his head and Brown Golf Shirt tied his hands behind his back with shoelaces. He was shouting over the panic. Everyone knew why he wanted them.

Miss Finance Director, who had been invited to talk about the city budget, composed herself and casually walked over to a corner where Kim's Daewoo K5 had been swept from his hand by White Golf Shirt. *Someone better take care of this. It might as well be me.*

Someone shouted to her, "Pick it up by the grip. We need prints."

"Got it!" she said.

On the other side of the room, after using their tactics to dislodge the gun from his grip, Tan Golf Shirt and White Dress Shirt wrestled James to the floor. James was shouting now. He kept screaming, "Svenson, Svenson!"

"Svenson, you son-of-a-bitch." He was spitting saliva as another set of shoelaces was being used to tie his hands.

Parks Director, a former NFL football player, used his defensive tackle experience to sit on Kim's back while someone else held his

214

head and shoulders and Brown Golf Shirt finished tying his hands and held his legs. Now the swarm technique was being used on both Kim and James. They had enough laces to tie the feet of each of the shooters.

There had been no time to sense danger. Everybody just had to act, invoke their training, and do what had to be done.

CHAPTER 82

"Lincoln 75, roger," Hamilton calmly responded to dispatch. "Can I get 77 and Sgt. McGinty on the side channel?"

Both McGinty and Simpkins acknowledged the request.

"Sarge, I'll take the front entrance and see if we have someone like the manager to meet us. If it's righteous, you may need to set up a command post in the parking lot. I'll let you know. Donny, can you get the backside?"

He heard two 10-4's.

"L 75, be advised the reporting person is on the twelfth floor. We have contacted the manager, and he will meet you in front. Fire Department paramedics are en route." Dispatch had done their part to ensure communication was open.

"Roger that. Can you connect me with the RP via telephone line?"

"Here it comes," the dispatcher responded in as calm a manner as possible.

Hamilton activated his body cam, pulled in at a strategic angle to the hotel entrance, opened his door, and stood behind it until he could see someone coming to meet him.

He had a Trusdale Inn badge, but just for safety's sake, he said, "Sorry, gotta do this. Put your hands on top of your head. Turn around. Take off your suit jacket and walk toward me, backward."

The manager did as instructed. Hamilton gave him a cursory search and told him to put his hands down.

"Tell me what you have."

The manager outlined the situation.

One of his staff was on the penthouse floor when she heard two shots, a lot of shouting, and furniture slamming. "All I know is I think we had shooting up there."

"Who's up there? Do you know?"

"The city staff for Sparrow Hill. They had a workshop planned. I think the PD was involved."

"Oh, shit." Howard's statement was a complete description of the circumstances. It was the simplest expletive he could muster. Just then, his cell phone buzzed.

"Hamilton," he shouted into the speaker.

"Here's the RP, L 75." The phone reconnected with a few clicks.

Sgt. McGinty drove up, parked, and walked toward him. Hamilton held his hand up to show he was on the phone. The threat of rain was becoming very real. Would the mist turn into sprinkles? Would the sprinkles turn into droplets?

McGinty opened his SUV command post vehicle with a big screen facing the tailgate. He brought up the floor plan as provided by Dispatch.

"This is Officer Hamilton, Orchard Hill PD. Who am I talking to?"

"My name is Jim Hines, and I'm the Sparrow Hill City Manager."

Hamilton put the phone on speaker so that McGinty could hear. "Go on. Tell us what you have up there, sir."

Hines gave him a summary of the shooting, the suspects, and two PD members who had been shot. He did not know the condition of either the officers or suspects.

"How many suspects, sir? Can you describe them? What are they wearing? What type of weapons do they have?"

Hines responded, "I think there are two, but I don't know. All I saw were handguns. They have camouflage clothes, like they're soldiers or something. Oh, and you should know. None of our PD in the room are armed. Long story."

Donny quickly scanned the hotel's floor plan on his terminal and chimed in on the side channel. "I've got the back area covered. I asked for another unit. They're on the way. Nobody else back here right now."

Hamilton responded, "Roger, stay put. We have shots fired upstairs on the twelfth floor. Two down, and I don't know about the suspects. Two males with camouflage clothing. They should be easy to spot."

CHAPTER 83

McGinty had heard enough to make a tactical plan. He announced to his team, "we do not have time for SWAT, so listen up!" He called over the paramedics, asked who was in charge, and was introduced to a Fire Captain.

He gave them a brief version of what they had, pointing to the first floor, stairwell, and twelfth-floor penthouse on his screen.

"I need your paramedics to go with my team to the twelfth floor. We have shots fired, and we don't know how many casualties. Let me know when you're ready."

"We're not going in there," the Captain said.

"What?" McGinty was incredulous. "What the fuck? What do you mean you're not going in there? We have people down. I don't know whether they're civilians or suspects, but they need to be taken care of."

"We have a policy that you guys have to clear the scene of any shooters before we enter. Our job is to treat the wounded. I'm not sending my people in unless it's safe."

"What the fuck? Are you kidding me?" McGinty looked at Hamilton and the hotel manager for support. They both shook their heads in despair.

There was a moment of silence that could have lasted longer, but there was not that much time to spare. Everyone looked at each other as Hamilton's cell rang.

"This is Hines. Update. I have two PD down, and the rest of us are controlling the suspects. We have no guns up here other than what they brought. Can I get some help?"

"On the way," Hamilton said.

"Sarge, you give me Donny, and we'll go in. Just need to relieve him from the rear perimeter."

McGinty directed two other patrol units and an LA Sheriff's unit that had heard the call. He advised dispatch he would need additional units. He walked over to his equipped SUV and handed Hamilton a Heckler & Koch Gambi semiautomatic rifle with a scope and fifteen-round-capacity magazine that all supervisors carried for just this type of occasion.

"Used it in the last training day, sir. Got it," Hamilton responded.

He met Donny in the lobby. He advised the manager to lock down the elevators and monitor any fire doors from their office's video board.

"Sarge, I need someone here with the manager to monitor the video cameras at the desk. Can you give me someone?" Hamilton spoke into his shoulder mic, and within twenty seconds, Flowers was walking into the lobby. He filled her in on what he needed and turned to Donny.

"Activate your camera?"

"Way ahead of you, HH. You mean we gotta use the stairs up to twelve?"

Donny looked at Hamilton with a *what the fuck?*

"Let's go to seven and take a breather, then go in."

He reached for his cell phone. "Mr. Hines, we're comin' up."

"Donny, remember from the floor plan. I'll go in first and go to the right. You go to the left and cover everybody."

CHAPTER 84

White Golf Shirt, Brown Golf Shirt, and Parks Director had controlled Kim, who continued to yell they were hurting him. Miss Finance Director took possession of both handguns, placing them in table napkins, while Parks Director and Tan Golf Shirt were still trying to control their suspect, who was squirming and trying to get loose.

Then, for some reason, Kim stopped struggling, but no one was aware.

Hines stuck his head in. "The police are on their way along with paramedics. Won't be long now," he announced.

"Chief!" one of the participants shouted. "Sergeant Vanowen. He's not breathing. Fuck, I think … I think he's dead. Oh, Jesus," he cried out.

There was another shout. "Chief, Svenson is bleeding like crazy. I grabbed some napkins and a tablecloth to hold down on the wound, but he's going fast. Where the fuck are those paramedics?"

Just then, there was a loud bang as two uniformed OHPD officers burst in through the side door—the same side door the shooters had come through.

"Police! Police!" The shout was meant to get everyone's attention.

"Hands up, everybody! Hands up! Hands up! Where we can see them. We don't know who's who yet."

Simpkins was breathing heavily after taking the last set of stairs. Hamilton had maintained his composure, but Simpkins was sucking air.

Hamilton's order was immediately obeyed. Neither Donny nor Hamilton knew who was who in the room. They would have to figure that out, and quickly.

"Spread out. Move away from the bodies."

Hamilton directed Donny to move to the first suspect and cuff him while keeping his rifle scanning the room. He threw Donny his cuffs. Then Donny moved to the second suspect and cuffed him. He could see Donny was exhausted. The combination of running up twelve flights of stairs and the adrenaline rush was taking its toll.

"Anybody else? Where is Mr. Hines?"

The oldest member of the group stepped forward. "I'm Jim Hines, Officer. It's OK. We just need paramedics. Fast."

"Don't anyone move just yet. Where are the weapons?" Miss Finance Director pointed to the two handguns she had picked up and placed on a side table, wrapped in a cloth napkin, away from everyone. There was silence in the room.

"I need to know if there are any other suspects. Anyone in this room that is not already cuffed."

"No, sir" was the collective reply. Hamilton saw that Donny was still struggling from exhaustion.

"Donny, take some deep breaths and relax. We got this."

Hamilton finally felt comfortable enough to lower his H&K. He spoke into his shoulder mic. "Need paramedics here ASAP. Suspects in custody, code four, but we need medical. Have the manager reactivate the elevators. They can come up faster, but damn it, get them here."

His frustration, the adrenaline rush, and mental exhaustion were all coming together at once. He hoped he made sense.

Two individuals broke ranks and returned to tending Svenson. Donny moved to collect the guns while everyone else tried to do whatever they could to make themselves useful until the paramedics arrived.

CHAPTER 85

Was it an hour? A minute? Two minutes? No one knew, but it was way too long. The first paramedic team arrived and was immediately directed to Svenson and Vanowen.

"Is there another team coming in?" someone shouted. "We have other people here that need to be treated."

"Right. They're a little behind us," one of the paramedics shouted back. There was enough frustration to go around the room, and it would not dissipate any time soon.

"Who gives a shit about the suspects." It was an emphatic statement and not a question. "Vanowen is gone, and this team is on Svenson." No one would remember who said that.

The second paramedic unit finally arrived and was directed to both Kim and James. James was shouting epithets in both English and Korean. Nothing was coming from Kim.

The paramedics stabilized Svenson and covered the body of Vanowen. They ordered two gurneys over their radio but then reconsidered. "Better bring four."

Hamilton got on the radio. "We do have a code four but at least one fatality, maybe more. I think we'll need to have our CSI unit and all notifications made."

Dispatch quickly responded, "Already in progress, L 75."

McGinty came up on the side channel. "I'll be up, Hamilton, but let's stay off the main frequency. Too much media attention already."

McGinty quickly switched channels.

"The media are vultures when it comes to this stuff. They monitor our main frequency but not this one. If they knew what happened here, they'd be here in swarms. Let's keep it off the air for now."

"Good call, sir. That's why you get the big bucks," Hamilton responded. There was no humor intended. It was true. So very true. Hamilton tried to relax his command presence, but it was not easy. He didn't know who was in the room. He hooked his new best friend, the H&K, over his shoulder and wiped the sweat from his burning eyes.

He looked to see Donny take possession of the handguns and search the room for other possible evidence. Donny was not going to talk to anyone. He was exhausted but focused on both suspects.

So it fell to Howard. Hamilton introduced himself and Donny.

Finally, Hines introduced himself more formally and introduced the Chief of Police for Sparrow Hill.

Hines gave everyone a rundown in the room, including all PD staff members, the workshop facilitator, and the finance and parks director. Hamilton pulled the Chief aside. "Chief, I know you know this, but this is going to be quite an investigation. We need to isolate everybody for the detectives and make sure no one talks about this until you've all been interviewed."

"Thanks, Officer, er Hamilton." The Chief glanced at his nameplate. "You're right. I just got lost here for a few minutes. We'll regroup and make sure we do this right. Thanks."

The Chief turned to all in the room. "OK, everyone, listen up." Hamilton could tell this was a moment of truth. Men were crying, and he could see the anguish and despair on every face. He looked at the bodies on the floor and back to the participants. All eyes focused on the Chief.

He gave directions in a very matter-of-fact way, in a low but firm tone of voice. The Chief separated everyone and told them to wait until the detectives showed up. "Let the paramedics do their job. Back off and take some deep breaths." Hamilton was unaware of the circumstances leading up to the workshop, but it looked like everyone was falling in line with the Chief.

Hamilton took a step back, trying to move toward the door quietly. It was then he saw the one person who could make sense of this–Detective Supervisor Dave Nieman!

All will be well, he thought.

CHAPTER 86

There were four bodies down in the room. Two needed medical attention, but it looked like the other two were more than likely deceased.

Hamilton looked over the shoulder of those providing the needed assistance. He didn't know either of the two Sparrow Hill PD officers. He saw the struggling suspect, still yelling and shouting in two languages, controlled by Donny and a few of the Sparrow Hill people, and decided to move closer to the other suspect in case he was needed for control purposes.

The paramedics were getting ready to roll him over from his stomach to his back in hopes of possibly resuscitating him. While the suspect looked gone, he knew they could perform a miracle with the medical unit's state-of-the-art equipment. Hamilton glanced back at the struggling suspect as the noise level increased. He compared the clothing each had worn and saw they almost matched. He then walked back over to the larger suspect, still trying to resist, and saw an embroidered name on his shirt's right pocket.

It read *Song*. He looked at the face again and said, "I may know this guy."

Having heard the comment, Detective Nieman walked over and asked, "How do you know him, Hamilton?"

"I'm not sure yet. Where did I see that name? That face? Let me think about it."

He continued to stare at Song, trying to recall the name and face that had momentarily triggered him.

"Not sure we can save this one," the paramedic treating Kim shouted to the room.

"Who cares?" said the Chief as he held Kim's legs in futile anticipation of him being revived.

Hamilton walked away and took his gaze out the expansive window to the parking lot twelve stories down. He saw the rain coming as he looked to the mountains in the distance and city lights that were coming on, signaling dusk.

This was the guy he gave a break to on New Year's Day. The double-parking doctor. He remembered the name Song.

He passed that information on to Nieman, not knowing its significance at this point, other than for identification purposes.

After working on him for fifteen minutes, the paramedic attending to Kim announced, "This one is gone, DOA." They opened his shirt to reveal the bulletproof vest he had used.

"We'll have to wait for the autopsy, but if I was to take an educated guess, his larynx looks crushed from somebody sitting on his back, and the vest cut into his neck and shut off his breathing," the paramedic announced, without any intent to seek agreement.

Everyone looked at the two-hundred-eighty-pound Parks Director who had been sitting on Kim's back for at least ten minutes. Some wanted to congratulate him or thank him, while others just continued to feel shocked and relieved.

A few members of the PD walked over and touched him lightly on the shoulder with *It's going to be OK*. Others appeared unsure what emotion was appropriate, one way or the other. The emotions in the room ranged from frustration to anger, relief, and shock. Who was in what state was hard to tell.

Hamilton watched Nieman take control of the room. He could only stare at the guy's body in the blue shirt, who he found out was Sergeant Vanowen. Paramedics were still working on Song and the other Sparrow Hill PD person who appeared to be still alive, but barely.

CHAPTER 87

The rest of his shift was becoming a blur. There would be a quick debriefing in the parking lot with McGinty and the other uniforms on duty. He knew from experience there would be paperwork to write up on everything he and Donny did. He would then be interviewed by somebody and immortalize it for the follow-up investigation.

He and Donny took the elevator down to the lobby. Smartly, the manager only had one elevator working, and it was limited to the police and fire personnel involved. No press, hotel guests, or lookie-loos allowed.

He walked outside to meet with McGinty at the command post and return the rifle to its rightful owner. He was met with flashing lights, TV cameras, and cell phones taking pictures as he unharnessed the rifle that had been his mainstay during the incident. "I'm sure glad I had this, Sarge. It felt very comfortable knowing I had some firepower going up there." McGinty gladly took the weapon and replaced it in its locked holder in the rear of his SUV.

It was now raining. Droplets took the place of sweat on this humid night. It was a night that would never be forgotten.

Both Donny and Hamilton were wiping rain and sweat from their brows and trying to get the adrenaline off as well. But endorphins were something they could not just wipe off.

Donny broke the silence. "I may not be good enough for Baker to Vegas," he said, referring to the longstanding annual run across the desert by law enforcement teams throughout the country that occurred every spring, "but I know I better start running again. Those stairs kicked my ass."

"Mine too, buddy, and I still run." They both laughed away their fatigue. Hamilton took a poke at Donny's belly. "Want another doughnut?" They laughed a little too loud.

McGinty quickly rushed over to silence them. "Hey, with all the media around here, you do not want to be seen laughing. Particularly when they start wheeling out the bodies. The cameras will be rolling, and they'll take photos of everything, but the only thing on the front page will be you two guys fucking laughing."

"Yes, sir" was the joint response. They wanted to laugh at that statement as well but deferred it to a much, much later time.

"Here's how it's going to go down." Sgt. McGinty called all OHPD units that responded to the scene to meet at the command post. He looked around to make sure he had everyone's attention and there was no media listening.

"The detectives at the station will interview 75 and 77. Tenery and Flowers, stay here to monitor the media and help me keep this CP going for a while. Everyone else, give me a memo about what you did and turn it in before your EOW—time, assignment, and where you were during this operation, all that shit. Got it?"

"Got it, sir" was the group reply.

"Now, the decision's been made that the Sheriffs will be investigating with our detectives. You may or may not be contacted by someone from LASD. I don't know. Don't panic or think you need a POA rep with you. It's just routine. Got it?"

Another collective "Got it, sir."

"Anybody hurt or hungry?"

"Hungry!"

"Too fuckin bad," he whispered. "Get back to work and make sure you stagger when you do your reports. We still have calls from dispatch to assign. With this rain, there are probably a few accidents out there. They've been holding a bunch of calls for you. All except L 75 and 77 get the hell back to work."

The last response was "*Oh*, 75 and 77." Lips were smacking.

"Fuck you, guys," Donny and Howard said in a low voice, remembering not to smile. "And girls," Donny added after seeing Flowers in the background. "Equal treatment." It was all about the gallows humor now.

Everyone was quiet as they wheeled out the first body. With resuscitation still in place on the first one out, Howard whispered to Donny, "I think that's their media guy, Svenson. I've seen him on TV before. He may still be alive." The gurney was quickly placed in the ambulance, and red lights and sirens faded into a wet and windy night.

Flashbulbs were shooting off like firecrackers, even though most pictures were being taken by cell phones. Media cameras continued to collect their footage for the eleven o'clock news.

Next came Song, still shouting in a hoarse, raspy voice to anyone who would listen. The sheet covering Song did not go all the way up to his neck, so there was ample display of his Cammy uniform. He was accompanied by Red Walker and a Sheriff's detective. The cameras and iPhones continued flashing, zeroing in on the uniform, but everyone except Song kept their mouth shut and their faces grim.

Right behind Song's gurney was the body of Vanowen. The face was covered, sending a message of its own. A left arm slipped from under the sheet and hung there listless, alongside the rail of the gurney.

The last four-wheeled gurney out had a sheet covering Kim's face and most of his body. Combat boots sticking out the end of the gurney were the only telltale signs of who this guy was.

There was a lot of cleanup to do by everyone involved.

CHAPTER 88

By the time they had been dismissed from the scene, it was 2130 or 0930. Both L 75 and 77 still had to be interviewed by detectives. While they were not directly involved in the deaths of anyone in the room, they were the entry team that witnessed everything that transpired immediately after the shooting.

They both took off their Sam Browne gun belts, placed them in their lockers, and went to the report-writing station, sitting separately but within talking distance. They didn't need to compare notes. Each of them wrote separate but comparable statements that would become part of one of OHPD's most historically significant investigations. Body cam footage was downloaded into the system, and end of watch could not come soon enough.

"Happy Valentine's Day, Howard," Donny said without taking his eyes off the computer screen.

"Oh, shit, that's right. I almost forgot. Same to you, buddy. You and the Wolf doing anything?"

Howard was referring to Officer Pat "Don't call me Patricia" Wolford, who had picked up the nickname Wolf. Donny had been dating the Wolf ever since he split up with his wife. Howard caught them both in the weight room one early morning. Donny was getting a blowjob from Pat, and thankfully, only Howard was there. The rest, as they say, was history. They had been a couple since the incident and his separation. Hamilton was never sure which came first, the separation or the head job.

"All this weekend. I figured I'd get some OT, and we'd spend some time tomorrow. Going to need it now."

Howard could not resist. "Need what?"

"Screw you, HH," he responded. "At least we can smile here."

"Yeah. How are you coming on your report?"

"Engineering it right to EOW. As usual."

"Me too." Hamilton was drilling a hole in his computer screen, staring, and thinking about the day, the events they had been involved in at the Trusdale Inn, and one other thing as well.

"I think I'll go up to my new office to finish this. Do you mind?"

Donny looked up from his screen. "No, but let's both meet McGinty at about 2345 and let him know we did our stuff separately but finished about the same time."

Howard said, "McGinty's not stupid. He knows we're engineering. He used to when he was one of us." Howard was describing the all too well-known division between sergeants and above and the street cops.

"Hey, Howard." Donny stood up to stretch. "Everybody knows you'll be a supervisor soon. One of *them*. You're now one of the golden boys."

"Ah, bullshit, Donny. It's just me and always will be."

"Yeah, right." Donny laughed. "But that's OK. I already know enough about you. I know where the bodies are buried."

"What bodies?"

He had a phone call he wanted, no, needed to make.

CHAPTER 89

He walked into his new office, knowing he would be alone for the rest of his shift. He had downloaded his report to a thumb drive in the report-writing room and decided to use his office's quiet to give it more thought. He would give it one more edit. But something else was gnawing at him as well.

Should I do it? … You are a fool, Hamilton. You are an idiot not to do it. You'll be sorry … You need to …

He had her on his *favorites,* so he didn't even have to look her up in his contacts.

Too easy.

"Hi, Howard. Saw you on the news tonight." Caller ID had done its work.

"Yeah. Pretty scary thing. Glad it's almost over."

"What do you mean? It looks over to me."

"Not till the paperwork is done. It's never over until then." He looked at the clock on the wall. It matched what his computer told him: 2315.

He was just going to say it and hope for the best.

"It's still Valentine's Day, Amanda. Want to meet for a drink?" There was a long silence that neither knew who was going to break.

"Well, I'm not dressed to go out. I've been curled up on my couch with a glass of red wine, watching you on the news."

"Oh, I should have known. Sorry. I just …" There was another pause that needed to be filled.

"Do you want to come by, just for some red?"

"Maybe I better not. I'm all sweaty. I'm still coming down from all of this."

"All the more reason, Howard."

"I don't even know where you live. Did you move back in with your parents?"

"No. I have a condo. In Lomita. Just ten minutes away."

She let that last piece of information linger out there like he was on a ledge. He took the last step off. "What's the address?"

CHAPTER 90

He emailed his report to McGinty and waited for it to be electronically approved. In the meantime, he went to his locker, took off the uniform, dressed in his civies, and went back to the office. He did not want to meet face-to-face with McGinty or anyone else. He wanted to make sure his report was approved and then go EOW with dispatch.

He returned to his desk, saw his report was signed off. There was a note from McGinty that he did not need to stick around to be interviewed tonight. The dicks would catch up with him on Monday. He shut his computer down, whispering to it, "See you on Monday." He needed to do that for closure.

Lomita was a mixed bag. He would classify it as a quiet city, a lot of industry, and some throwback neighborhoods from the 1950s and early '60s. It was a community off the radar, policed quietly by the Sheriffs, and never known for anything useful, threatening, or indifferent. Now, Amanda Johnson was its newest resident.

It was not a gated condominium project. It was tucked neatly away into the side of a hill, which gave it a sense of being hidden and secluded. It was away from the madness that almost every other community out there wanted to be. It had its piece of solitude. The rain had been reduced to a drizzle, but the night also brought mist from the nearby ocean. It made for a bewitching setting.

He at least had washed his face and took what was jokingly known as a "whore's bath," using paper towels and soap from the station men's room to at least make himself presentable. His hair was still damp. He hoped he did not give off his body odor. He should have showered at the station, and he knew it.

"Got red?" Howard said as he took her offer to enter. She opened the door with a smile and a glass of wine. She wore sweatpants and a T-shirt emblazoned with the USC Trojan logo, her dead husband's alma mater, AJ Johnson.

Looking for something else to say, he blurted, "Go, Trojans. I hope they have another good year." He lifted the glass to hers as a toast. He realized that James Song was also a graduate of the prestigious school located in South Central Los Angeles.

"They will, Howard." She paused, looking from head to toe at her visitor. "You look tired, but wow, you've been working out, haven't you? I can tell. How are you doing after all this?"

She walked to the couch. He decided not to follow and sat in a comfortable lounging chair that faced a muted TV. She curled her legs under and took a sip of wine.

"I'm good, I guess, but those guys from Sparrow Hill aren't. And, yeah, I've been running and doing some light lifting. You inspired me. It seemed like every time I saw you, you were coming from the gym. I need to get back in shape." He filled her in on what he knew of the events that had transpired.

"The media had some of it, but you filled in some holes, Howard." The way she said his name was different from other times. *She said she had been drinking when I called. Was it the wine?*

"They rarely get it right, Amanda. You know that." He wanted to take that last statement back, sure she would associate it with AJ.

He looked around the small but efficient living room. Very well decorated. He could see there was a lot of thought and creativity that went into her new home. The lighted candles should have been a warning.

She walked over to him and refilled his glass. She returned to the couch, looked at him, then the muted television, and then back to him. He looked at the clock on a side table.

"Three minutes to midnight. It's still Valentine's Day. Happy Valentine's Day, Amanda." He raised his glass in another toast.

"Thank you, Howard. Happy Valentine's Day to you." She walked over to the chair, pulled him to a standing position, put her arms around his neck, and kissed him gently.

At first, he didn't know what to do. His last kiss had been almost two years ago. It was Clare's kiss. She was not Clare, and this was not Clare's kiss, nor her lips. It was someone else.

CHAPTER 91

His cell phone rang. "Dad, Dad, are you OK?" It was Geoff. Howard didn't know where he was. He had to collect his thoughts. Looking around, he was on the floor in a living room. *Where am I? Am I naked?* He realized he was in his Tommy John underwear. He thought for a moment until it all came back to him.

He held the phone for just a minute, collecting his thoughts. "I'm, I'm just leaving. I'll be home in a few minutes. You kids OK?"

"Yeah, we are, Dad, but we've been watching TV and saw what was going on and saw you. Marcia spotted you right away, coming out of the hotel, holding a rifle. Geez, Dad, why didn't you call? Are you OK?"

He glanced at the clock again: 3:00 a.m.

"Sorry, Geoff, I just … got busy." The wine, the adrenaline, and the passion had taken their toll. "I'll be right home and fill you guys in."

He was talking to a wall and felt arms around him from his back. Amanda squeezed him, putting her head in the middle of his back and her arms around him.

Their Valentine's Day kiss at three minutes to midnight had worked its way to three o'clock in the morning. He remembered her lips were moist, soft, yet energized. Her kisses were unlike anything he had experienced in a very long time. Not bad or good, just new. Her lips had been softer than he expected. Her tongue had met his with a hunger that came from him as well. And that proved to be dangerous. When hunger meets hunger, there is a collision that becomes uncontrollable.

He reflected for a moment on what happened before the phone call from Geoff. He turned around to hold her, hold her in silence. He remembered they had worked their way down to the carpeted floor. The soft, fluffy, out-of-date beige carpeting was way too comfortable. They were gentle with each other—almost timid, not wanting to shock or scare the other away. But it was more than either of them could handle. Clothing came off slowly, and he marveled at her bronze body that complemented her green eyes. Everything seemed to make her body more radiant, even the carpeting.

He recalled they lay together, kissing, fondling, and caressing each other like it was the first touch and first time for each. It was. Amanda had wanted him to relax. "You've had enough work tonight, Howard. Allow me." She straddled him, gently moving to place his manhood inside and just let it be.

They stared at each other, knowing that they were each asking permission from their respective spouses to engage. No words. Only thoughts that collided. It was like two trains traveling on separate tracks, a far distance from each other, finally coming together, meeting, combining, and gradually joining in one direction.

The coupling had been exhausting. Each had been released from what had been holding them back. Finally, they were free to have an experience outside of themselves. They had fallen asleep on the floor, holding each other, with a muted television still on and a red wine bottle, gladly empty.

Then Geoff had called.

CHAPTER 92

He slept until almost noon. Breakfast was delivered at 1130, with Bentley prominently resting at the foot of the bed. The kids were very good to him. They made a Peet's run and treated him to Valentine's candy and a card, where they both had written heartfelt thoughts. It would be a Valentine's Day weekend he would never forget—for many reasons.

They were becoming young adults, right before his very eyes. They each seemed so self-assured, exuding confidence and maturity that he had not paid much attention to until recently. Geoff would graduate this year, and Marcia would be a junior in the fall. Where did their high school years go?

This weekend would be theirs, together, and he would share some of his harrowing escapades at the Trusdale Inn. He would leave out the blood and trauma and make it sound like a simple newspaper story, which it was now.

It would be Sunday night when he was drawn back into the abyss that was OHPD. Rikelman called to advise him he would be loaned to the homicide table for a few days next week. They were shorthanded due to vacations and needed to wrap up the Trusdale Inn shooting within the week. Most of the investigation, primarily the shooting itself, would be handled by the Sheriffs, but OHPD had agreed to support them in the areas they needed assistance. One of those was in Howard's area of expertise and job knowledge.

"They found out you knew one of the suspects," Rikelman said in a bit of an accusatory way. He cleared his throat rather loudly. "Care to tell me about it?"

Howard explained his run-in with Song on New Year's Day. "It wasn't much, but I gave him a break when he was double-parked, unloading his car for a Rose Bowl party. I may have met his wife, too, but I am not sure. He abandoned the car in the middle of the road and had forgotten he left it in the street with the driver's door wide open. I had to go into the backyard to find him."

Rikelman laughed. "Oh, thought he might have been a friend. Sorry. Sounds like a good ticket."

"It was only a warning because it was New Year's." *Only Rikelman would have written a ticket like that,* he thought.

"Anyway, they'd like you to report to the EOC at 0730 tomorrow. Just for a few days. Check in with Nieman. The Chief has approved it, but he asked me to call."

"Got it, sir. Will be there."

"Sounds like a hell of a caper for Valentine's Day, Howard. Glad it all turned out well and none of us got hurt. Did you know any of the Sparrow Hill PD guys that were killed?"

"No. Hey …" He paused. "Did the other one die? Svenson?"

"Yeah. Thought you knew."

"No, I was EOW at 2400, sir." He flashed back to the gurney being wheeled out and loaded into the ambulance. It was all so surreal.

Rikelman brought him back. "All that and no OT?"

They both laughed at the only funny thing about the evening—at least at the cop shop. The kids thought he had worked three hours

244

of overtime, but they wouldn't see his paycheck. Not with direct deposit.

Getting home at three in the morning was not part of the job—not that night anyway.

CHAPTER 93

Monday, Monday, can't trust that day. Howard was convinced the song had been written with him in mind. He chose a powder-blue dress shirt, no tie, brown slacks, and a dark blue sports jacket, just in case he had to go in the field.

The homicide detail working on the Trusdale shooting was nicknamed and moved to the emergency operations center or EOC. Howard remembered the last time it had been used. He got involved with Johnny Bresani, a disgraced ex-cop from OHPD, who became Howard's informant for a big cartel narcotics case.

Bresani was shot to death by LASD SWAT in a warehouse in Irwindale. The EOC had been set up to monitor five to seven cars from Mexico smuggling in several types of drugs, from coke to meth and fentanyl. The seizure went well, except for Bresani and his business partner being killed in the shootout. No loss.

The EOC was in full swing. *Did they get there at oh dark thirty to set this up?* The Chief had made the unused room on the second floor an emergency operations center. Simulation exercises that went into the planning for significant events had paid off for the Department, much to the anti-LAPD sentiment's chagrin.

While they had not planned for multiple shootings, the Department had planned for an earthquake, fire, flood, and civil unrest. So, for planning purposes, they were not that different.

Hamilton walked into the foreboding atmosphere of a twenty-four-seven operational setup, in a room with no windows but organized as only OHPD could. The energy was unmistakable.

Nieman welcomed him to the team. "Hey, Mr. Intelligence. Grab some coffee and come over here." Howard put a Peet's dark roast pod in the Keurig machine and grabbed a buttermilk doughnut.

I could get used to this.

Hamilton had the utmost respect for and a little bit of fear of Nieman. He knew his shit. And he knew he knew. He had the requisite short brown hair, a little too much stomach, and a small mustache that Hitler would have admired. His everyday uniform was short-sleeved shirt, red tie, and brown slacks, with an assortment of accouterments on his belt, including a handgun, ammo, and handcuffs.

Homicide detectives rarely had to wrestle with their suspects. That was only on television or in the movies. Hamilton thought Nieman would probably lose that fight anyway because he was not in the best of shape. But he didn't have to be. He had Johnny "Red" Walker and Hans Rollenhagen working for him, and they were all the gunslingers he needed.

"Whatcha got, sir?"

"Tell me again how you know one of the suspects, Howard. Should be interesting." Nieman looked at Walker and Rollenhagen, who feigned interest.

"Well, I'll tell you, sir, but not these assholes." He paused. "What are you lookin' at?" He pointed to Walker and Rollenhagen. They were just laughing that Howard had become a part of the A-team in one fell swoop.

He told the story for the umpteenth time, it seemed.

"And you didn't write him up?" Walker jabbed.

"Fuck you, Red. It was New Year's Day."

"But if you had written him a cite, we would have him in the system."

"Wrong!" Howard had him.

"You wouldn't know a cite if it hit you in the eyes. It would have been a parking citation with no driver listed. It would have gone to the registered owner, but it wouldn't put him in our system, *asshole.*"

"OK, kids, let's get to work," Nieman said, recognizing it had already deteriorated. "And, Howard, can you get me the address of where you met Song?"

"Sure. I'll look it up in the CAD system history file."

Howard picked up his coffee and returned to the horseshoe tables. Nieman stood up. "Here's what we need."

He gave Walker and Rollenhagen the assignment to go to the impound lot and go through Kim's and Song's cars.

"Find out everything you can about what level of preparation these guys made. We labeled the cars as evidence, so no one has touched them since Friday night. Well, if the truth is known, it was Saturday morning."

"And me, sir?" Howard asked.

Walker and Rollenhagen were waiting to make sure they got the better assignment.

"Howard, you just finished intel school, right?"

Howard nodded.

"Here's what I need from you. We seized the suspects' cell phones. They had them in their pockets, and we got the coroner to turn them over to us. They're booked as evidence in our property room. I want you to go down and check them out. Go through them with a fine-tooth comb. See who's on their contact list. Check both phones and see how many times they called each other and anything else that comes up. Got it?"

"Got it."

"And, Howard, you do know how to do that, don't you?"

"Well, sir, I took the class and knew the software, but I may need to contact my instructor to get some prompters. But it'll get done."

"I want to beat the Sheriffs to this, HH. We may be a team, but I want OHPD to shine. Get my drift?" He whispered so as not to be heard by the LASO detectives at the other end of the room.

"Yes, sir."

"By the way, Hamilton, you're mine for a few days. Regardless of what patrol says, I need you here. Redondo and we are taking over policing for the Sparrow Hill PD while they get debriefed and go through a shitload of counseling. They're doing twelve-hour shifts between the departments, but I don't care how much OT they promise you. Turn it down. Got it?"

CHAPTER 94

He was getting excited about being a part of investigations from a variety of sources—from the most extensive shooting and triple homicide in OHPD history to a swap meet that marketed questionable merchandise to his latest project on organized crime. *What was that all about?* He better look before they asked him about it. Later, he agreed. *Bigger fish to fry here.* He was now officially swimming in it.

He went back to his office with the two cell phones, after checking them out of the evidence room. Both were iPhones, and the latest model XS something or other. First, he would have to contact the DEA instructor who taught the class on cell phone analysis, Dennis Packer. He would walk him through his first effort. He put in a call to Packer and was advised he was on another line and would call back.

He remembered Packer told the class that Apple would disapprove of using their iPhones in television and movies if the bad guys were using them. Product placement was a big business in the media industry. Apple wanted to ensure its products and their logos or distinct devices were seen in only a positive light. They definitely would not have approved the use Kim and Song developed to pull off this caper.

Packer called back. They exchanged catch-up information since his attendance at the class and then got down to business. Hamilton explained what he had. He wanted to download all recent phone calls to see if there were any standard numbers to identify other parties involved in the crime. Packer was familiar with the incident at the Trusdale Inn because of the news coverage.

"So, who's doing the investigation—you or the SO?"

"Well, it's a joint investigation, but because we have two PDs involved, the SO is taking the lead." Knowing that Nieman wanted to beat the deputies to some information, he still did not want to share the competition's dirty laundry.

"Well, HH, I'm afraid I have some bad news, buddy."

"What's that?"

Packer paused and tried to be as brief as he could. "It doesn't matter whether they're dead or alive. You'll need a search warrant to get the information off the phones."

"I can do that."

"Sounds like a pain, but you just want to protect yourself and the department. There could be a bunch of civil suits and all that bullshit, even if the two suspects are dead."

He corrected Packer. "Only one of the suspects is dead. Anything else?"

"Yes. Two things. The warrant is easy. It's a short form. Get a DA to sign off on it and fax it to the on-call judge. Second, your agency may not like it, but the SO has a great piece of equipment. It's a digital forensic tool called an RTL Aceso. Get the warrant and take it to their electronics unit in East LA. They'll do the work for you. Otherwise, you can do it by what they call brute force acquisition. You've got ten tries to get the right password. Then it will lock you out." Packer was still lecturing in his strong baritone voice.

"Thanks, Dennis. Big help. I'm going to put you in my favorites so I can call you."

"Hey, HH, this shit took me ten years to develop, and you're on day one. Remember that. Anytime, bud, anytime." Packer gave him the name and phone number to contact at the electronics unit.

He knew Nieman was not going to be happy with this. But he would provide him with Packer's rationale for going by the rules—at least this time.

CHAPTER 95

He got the predicted reaction and the go-ahead from Nieman.

As if on cue, Carrie Wade, the PD's favorite DA, walked into the room. Hamilton had used her for legal advice on several cases, including the death of Ginny Karsdon and all the legal work needed with the Bresani case.

Wade was a godsend. She was built like an NFL fullback—broad shoulders, thick body, powerful legs, and muscular arms. Not fat or obese, just powerful. And her work with the PD was just like a fullback. She blocked and paved the way for runners to get to the goal line.

Not so coincidently, she had the forms with her. She provided the on-call judge's name and number and almost dictated the probable cause needed for the warrant.

"You are a brainiac, Carrie. Don't know what we would do without you." Hamilton spoke for many at the table.

"My job is to keep you guys out of trouble. It's easier doing it right rather than just winging it. Just might take you a little longer."

Nieman and Hamilton connected via the eyes, and he got the message to get his ass moving.

He decided to get out of the EOC and stop by his office. He made the call to the Sheriff's electronics unit.

"Bring your department ID, search warrant, and phones. Anything else you think we may need. Do you have the passwords?"

"No, ma'am."

"We'll figure it out. Bring as much as you have on the owners of the devices."

Howard put together his file and was waiting on the search warrant approval from the judge. DA Wade had written most of it, but he was still listed as the Affiant. The format looked straightforward, something he could do next time on his own. He would keep a copy for his files.

"Detective Hamilton, line two." Joanie made the statement so only he could hear.

"Who is it?"

"We have a policy here that we don't ask that question, Howard. If someone calls asking for someone in this office, we just let you know there's a call. No screening of your calls." Joanie had made it a point to educate him on all the office's procedures, but he had not heard that one.

"Hamilton. I mean Detective Hamilton. How can I help you?" He figured he better go by the policy of giving a greeting, then his name and the offer to assist.

"Detective Hamilton. My name is Mary Ann Kowalski." There was silence as she paused after providing her name.

Hamilton did not know who this was. Or did he? "I'm sorry, ma'am, Mrs. Kowalski. Is there something I can help you with?"

"It's Miss Kowalski, but I am … or was … I'm James Song's fiancée. We were getting married before …"

"I understand. Sorry I did not connect your name to his. Is there something that I can help with?"

Hamilton was trying to figure out why she would reach out to him. First, it didn't make sense. And then it did.

"You may not remember, but you were the officer that gave James a break on New Year's. He left his car in the middle of the street."

Howard said, "Right, right, I remember."

"Well, you came into the backyard, and I saw you. You were very kind and didn't give us a ticket. You were in uniform." She paused.

"Yes, there were a lot of people in the backyard. Sorry. I don't remember meeting you there."

"Oh, I didn't introduce myself then. I just saw how you dealt with the situation and how you dealt with James."

"OK ..."

"The reason for my call is ... well, I've been interviewed by the Sheriff's detectives several times this weekend. I'm not sure what they wanted, but I tried to help out as much as possible. They wouldn't tell me anything about James and what he did. I only know what I saw on television Friday night. It wasn't good. I saw you on TV and remembered you. Is there a time we could talk? Can you talk to me, or do I have to deal with those other guys?"

Hamilton mulled over his options. "Where do you live, Miss Kowalski?"

"Right now, I'm at James's place. I'm here in Monterey Park."

"Coincidently, I'm headed out to East LA. Can I swing by this afternoon?"

"Sure." She gave him the address.

"That's right near where I'm going. See you at about 1330. I mean one thirty."

He stared at the phone.

CHAPTER 96

The signed search warrant came through on the fax while he was on the phone. He went back to the EOC to pick up some papers. He looked around to see who he could tell about the conversation with Kowalski. Nieman was nowhere to be seen, and he sure as hell wasn't going to tell Walker or Rollenhagen. Or the Sheriff's detectives. *Fuck it. I'll call Nieman on my way to the SO.*

He packed up as much of the case as he had, put the cell phones back into their evidence bags, and piled everything he could think of into his briefcase. Then he signed out to the SO lab and grabbed the keys to the UC.

He plugged in the address to the SO lab in the car's GPS, took surface streets to the on-ramp to the 91 Freeway from the South Bay, and headed east. So far, the traffic was not too bad.

He always marveled every time he left the boundaries of Orchard Hill. The streets went from clean to filthy, from no debris to nothing but debris, from no graffiti to graffiti. He saw couches and old washing machines left on the side of the road, shopping carts, and who knows what else. The county and LA city could not keep up with the municipal decay caused by the accumulation of neglect. Not his fight, and he knew it. It made him appreciate working in a city that cared about its image.

He was going through his mental checklist, and it dawned on him. *Geez, I never called Amanda back after ... after Friday night. Not good manners. How bad is that? And it's now Monday.* He mumbled and brought up his cell phone.

"Siri, call Amanda Johnson."

He was very excited to talk with her. They had finally consummated their relationship, and he wanted to see her again. Soon. If truth be told, she went after him until he caved in. Now, she had him. And it wasn't bad at all.

"This is Amanda."

"Amanda, HH here. Thought you had caller ID?"

"I didn't look. Sorry," she lied.

"Hey, I am so sorry for not calling you over the weekend. I didn't get up till late Saturday, and the kids …"

"Howard, that's OK. I was going to call you too, but …"

He turned north on the 710 Long Beach Freeway from the eastbound 91. He was driving hands-free, but he was waving them across the steering wheel as if he was talking to her in person. Traffic had slowed a bit because everyone's destination was downtown LA.

"Well, thanks for that. And now I've been loaned to homicide to work on this case from last Friday night."

He wanted to tell her a bit of it, but she interjected. "Howard, the reason I was going to call is …" After that, he was trying to figure out or interpret a little bit of silence.

"On Sunday, my parents and AJ's got together. We, we used to do that quite a bit."

He let the freeway traffic drown out the quiet of the cell line. Or did he lose the cell phone connection? He wasn't sure. She came back on.

"I, I happened to mention …" Howard could tell she was struggling. *Just let her talk. It's just like interviewing a suspect. Just let them talk.* Maybe add in an umm for effect. He did.

"I told them … I told them we went out for a drink. Some wine. I didn't tell …"

"Well, we didn't go out. We stayed in. But that's fine." He smiled into the phone.

"They both got upset." Then there was another unhealthy silence.

"How so?"

"They always wanted AJ to play football. That's what he loved. Being a policeman was something he wanted to do, you know, for the benefits and all. If he had gotten picked up at the combine by a team, he would have left the department."

Howard was slowing and moving to the far lane to get off at Cesar Chavez Way.

Howard nodded to no one. "I understand, but …"

She said, "Let me finish. They don't want me to get back into the department, police work, you know, in any way. I tried to tell them that we're just friends, but they didn't buy it."

She had blurted it all out in one breath that then descended into a more deafening silence.

The sound of traffic, tires screeching, and horns were all that he heard. There was no accident, just people in a hurry to go nowhere.

"So, I take it this means …" He didn't have to finish his sentence.

"Yes, yes, it does, Howard. I'm sorry, but I guess blood is thicker than, well, you know what I mean."

He had to ask. "Is this something you want, Amanda?"

He pulled into the Sheriff's lab parking lot, letting silence fill the void of the mental anguish he was feeling.

"I don't think so. I don't know." Both were holding their breath to control their emotions.

"Are you still there, Howard?" There was no traffic noise to drown out the silence.

"I promise you, Amanda, I will still keep you in my *favorites*."

"Me too." More silence.

They exchanged "Take cares."

CHAPTER 97

The Sheriff's electronics office was in a nondescript building that could very well have passed for being abandoned. The parking lot had not been swept in months or longer, some windows were boarded up with plywood, and there were too many empty parking spaces.

The problem he saw was that half of the county facilities looked like they were abandoned buildings. It was just that no one wanted to flaunt their image, for fear of being painted over with graffiti, or worse. It was a community that had given up and sunk to its lowest common denominator.

He checked in at the front counter after finding the suite that quietly said "Sheriff's Lab" on its door. He waited on a wooden bench in the lobby that must have been a castoff from a park that didn't need it anymore.

He thought about what had just happened to him.

Did I just get dumped?

He laughed to himself. He was just a bit numb over the call with Amanda. Was it the blue or anything to do with police work, or was it his ethnicity? He thought everyone was past the ethnic issue. It had to be the blue. Not everyone was cut out for the job. It wasn't like they were going to get serious. Or was it? He could hear the conversation in his head.

Amanda, you don't want to be a police widow twice, do you?

"Detective Hamilton?" He quickly snapped back to the present. He'd have to digest that thought a little later.

The Sheriff's technician introduced herself. "I'm Trinka Prado, lead here in the electronics unit. Did you bring the search warrant?"

He handed the two forms faxed by the judge. Trinka was a carbon copy of Carrie Wade. She was built like a fullback, with robust features that sent the message she would not take any shit from anyone.

"I see you got Carrie Wade to help with this. She sure knows her stuff. I love working with that lady."

"So do we. Don't try and steal her from this side of the county. She's ours in the South Bay," he joked.

"We'll see. Whatcha got?"

He opened his briefcase and took out the evidence bags containing the two phones. "This is from that homicide in Orchard Hill last Friday night, huh?"

He nodded. It was a triple, but he did not want to get caught up in semantics.

"Saw it on TV. Pretty messy."

She walked over to a box that looked like one of those old computers from the 70s and 80s. It had a small screen and a series of ports in the front. Prado hooked phone lines up to the cell phones from the box and started punching in numbers and codes.

"Got any passwords?"

"No," he quickly answered. "Do I need them?"

"It would make it easier."

"I'll tell you what. I'll give you the file here. This is Kim. That's his phone," he said, pointing to the black iPhone.

"You may be able to figure it out from all of our background data on him. Here's his booking slip and arrest report. In the meantime,

I can call somebody who may be able to help with the other one. Can I use your phone?"

She nodded and took the file. Howard moved to the farthest desk and dialed the number Mary Ann Kowalski had just given him. She answered on the first ring.

"Miss Kowalski, this is Detective Hamilton. I'm just a few minutes away. But I have a quick question. Do you know Mr. Song's phone password?"

She gave him 2843. "Thank you. I'll see you in about twenty minutes."

He walked back over to Prado. "Here's the password for that one," he said, pointing to Song's phone."

"I got the other one, and ... we are in," Prado said, hitting the keys with a smile of satisfaction.

"What was it, if I could ask?"

Prado was now showing her excitement. "People are victims of habit. You know, with cells, you get up to ten tries on a password. I got it in three. Pretty good, huh? My best was two."

"So, what was it?"

"Too simple. I tried Kim's DOB. Then I got a hit with his street address number. Bingo!"

She beamed with the sense of pride that only working in the electronics unit could provide.

CHAPTER 98

He walked out of the Sheriff's electronics unit with a one-year history of each cell phone. Prado was kind enough to print everything out on a high-speed printer. Unfortunately, their furniture and technology were stuck in the 80s and 90s, but their copy machine was not. At least the county sprang for that.

Not being familiar with the east side, he plugged Kowalski's address into his GPS. Seven minutes and five miles to Monterey Park.

It was a cul-de-sac with medium-rise condos spread out in a contemporary architectural setting. He counted four five-story glass, steel, and concrete structures that looked alike but faced different directions, obviously for the views. *Very nice*, he thought.

He found her building, parked the car, and walked into the lobby. He pushed the button for Song-Kowalski, and Mary Ann buzzed him into the elevator. Everyone he passed was Asian. Was Mary Ann?

She answered the door and, at the same time, answered his own question. No. She extended her hand. "Officer, I mean Detective Hamilton, welcome. Come in." He entered an expansive hall that led to a great room with metal-encased windows from ceiling to floor and a view of downtown Los Angeles that was breathtaking.

She motioned him to sit in the white overstuffed chair that provided the best view. "I remember you now," he said a bit uncomfortably. "You were in the backyard with some friends, watching the Rose Bowl game on New Year's."

She smiled awkwardly. "Yes, and you gave James a break and were very kind."

"It was easy. He was nice as well. And who wants to give out a citation on New Year's?" They both laughed to continue the icebreaking.

"Well, Miss Kowalski, Mary Ann, may I ask what the purpose of your call was?"

"I've been giving a lot of thought to what happened. The Sheriff's detectives just wanted information on James. So I tried to give them as much as possible. But they didn't give me anything. I mean information on how he was injured, what he was doing there, you know. I'm a bit lost here."

"I think we all are, ma'am." He was still unsure of why he was there. He was not going to offer her any information right then. "It's still early in the investigation. Do you have the names of the detectives you talked to?"

She gave him their business cards, and he copied the contact information. He knew who they were but did not want to give her any indication.

"I saw that you were there. On television, I mean. I recognized you."

"Yes, ma'am."

"Did you shoot him?"

"Oh, no, ma'am. He wasn't shot. They didn't tell you?"

"No." She shook her head, and he could see she was in pain and a bit confused.

"First, can I ask you some questions? Then I'll try to answer yours."

She nodded.

"Tell me a little bit about ... your fiancée." He paused, not sure how to pose the question.

She told him about how James was first generation, his time in medical school, and his service in the South Korean Army. She finished with how they met and a bit about his parents.

"His father's a federal judge?" Hamilton asked, reacting with surprise.

"Yes, and they're devastated by the news. Well, I don't know how much you know about Korean culture, but James's parents are more ashamed of what he did than the fact that he's injured so severely. Parents take great pride in their children's successes and are devasted by their failures. Their pride has been pierced. They keep apologizing to me like it was their fault, not his."

"That is strange—I mean different," Howard commented.

"Not if you know Asian culture, Detective. I've learned a lot about it since we started dating."

CHAPTER 99

The conversation continued regarding her relationship with James and their plans for getting married.

"Are you going to stay here, Miss Kowalski?" he said, waving his hand around the room.

"Please call me Mary Ann. And no, I don't think so. This was James's home, but I stayed here a lot. I have another place closer to my work. But, quite frankly, I'm not sure what I'm going to do." There was a silence that churned about the room for a statement that had no response.

She then went on to explain her work.

"It's hard to make any decisions right now, but … I'm sure you see. I'm about the only non-Asian in the building. I don't speak the language very well, and while James was very Americanized, he liked living here. But now …" She drifted off.

"Mary Ann," he said a little uncomfortably, "what can you tell me about the guy that was with him? Kim? We don't know too much about him."

"The other detectives asked me the same question. I don't know him. I don't know how James knew him."

"They dressed alike. Both had camouflage clothing. Each had a handgun."

"I never saw any clothes like that, and I didn't even know he owned a gun. He did have a box in the closet that he kept some of his military stuff in."

"Can you give me a tour?"

She walked him down an expansive hallway with antiseptically clean walls and flooring. It was like a hospital setting. The bedroom area opened to another expansive view and then pointed to his closet.

"You have matching walk-in closets?"

"Yes," she said. "I never go in there. It's his little domain with suits, shoes, and other items."

"May I?" he asked.

"Be my guest."

Hamilton walked into the closet and saw an older brown trunk covered with some form of leather and metal protectors on each corner. It was sitting underneath the various suits hanging neatly, lined up by color, from light to dark. There was a lock on the trunk, but it was a key lock, not a combination type.

"Do you have the key?"

"Oh no. I didn't even know that was there. I don't go in there." Hamilton told her the sheriff's detectives might come back with a search warrant to investigate the trunk contents.

"The key may be on his car key ring," she offered.

"We'll look at that." He took a picture of it with his cell phone, just for the record.

"Did you tell the detectives about this?"

No, they never asked. We, I mean James also has a storage locker downstairs in the garage."

"I think they'll be back, so just let it sit for now." He surmised they might be getting the search warrants for the home and office and were planning to return. At least he hoped so. He made a note to remind them about the trunk and the downstairs storage area.

"Anything else, Mary Ann? I've taken up a lot of your available time."

"Detective Hamilton, I have nothing but available time now," she said, drifting off again to wherever one goes under the circumstances.

"But ... you were going to tell me how he ... he was injured."

CHAPTER 100

They returned to the great room and took their original seats. The view had not changed, but Howard still marveled at the majestic towers that were Los Angeles. There was no graffiti, debris, or roadways in need of repair from this distance. But he knew it was all there. It was an unkempt city that was beautiful only from a distance. Yet it was as majestic as he had ever seen it on this clear, brisk day. The tall buildings held secrets, camouflaging what was only seen from within its city limits, perhaps somewhat like those in Monterey Park and Orchard Hill.

"I'm surprised the detectives didn't go over that, but I'll tell you as much as I know."

"If truth be told, Detective, I never asked them."

He made another note to tell the detectives that he had told her how her fiancée was injured. However, he still had no idea why he was there in the first place.

He explained that when he entered the room, James was being controlled by several of the people. "The meeting was a team-building workshop with Sparrow Hill Police Department and some other city officials, including the City Manager."

"Sparrow Hill police?" She sat up straight, her back separating from the cushion on the sectional couch. "Oh, I ... didn't know." She looked away.

"The press didn't have all of that information at the time, and I'm sure you didn't want to read the newspapers later. But, yes, the PD was there, but they had been asked not to bring any firearms into the meeting. I think the Chief and City Manager may have had some concerns there. Why, I don't know."

"Did James shoot anyone?"

"I don't know, ma'am. I'm not sure. That's why we're still investigating. We, Orchard Hill PD and the Sheriff's Department, are working on this together. The detectives can give you more information, and I've made a note to tell them you wish for some closure here."

"You're right, Detective Hamilton. I have not read the papers or watched the news. It's all so devastating. I'm sure you realize. Do you know the names of the other people, the officers that were killed?"

"Yes, ma'am. It was Paul Svenson and Tom Vanowen. They were both sergeants, and I think Svenson was their press relations person."

It was her silence on the mention of Svenson's name filling the room.

She wanted to change the subject rather abruptly. "You still haven't told me how James was hurt."

"I'm sorry, Mary Ann." His uncertainty of how much to disclose held him back. He would not tell her about Song's facial injuries from the feet of one of Sparrow Hill's finest. More than likely, the jail hospital staff would clean him up. "To the best of my knowledge, and the Sheriffs can verify it with you, he was almost asphyxiated. See, he was wearing a bulletproof vest. So was Kim. But when they went to subdue him, they had no cuffs or any kind of restraints. All they could do is hold him down. They called 911, but by the time we got there, well, it was too late."

He felt like he might as well tell her as much as he knew. She probably needed it for some closure.

"Someone sat on his back to control him, and someone else held his legs. They didn't realize he was wearing a vest. I think it pushed up against his larynx and cut off his breathing, damaging his throat. The detectives can fill you in, or you can get a copy of their report."

He paused, realizing he was now giving out way too much information. "I'm sorry, Mary Ann, Miss Kowalski. I may have told you too much. I think I should go."

She was once again stunned into silence but was not going to tell him what she was thinking. He was concerned he had somehow crossed the line on what information he provided. Finally, she stood and turned toward the door.

They walked down the short hallway.

"This is a beautiful home, Mary Ann. I'm sorry this all happened."

"Yes, it *was* a beautiful home, wasn't it?"

CHAPTER 101

He walked slowly back to his car, gazing at the four buildings that looked alike but had so many separate secrets inside. Living in these structures was so different. Where did they barbeque or play catch with their kids? There was no lawn to mow or driveway to hose off. Or garden to plant. Elevators?

He admitted to himself there were many ways to live your life. *Choices that one makes dictate many things to each of us. Back to the case, Howard*, he thought. *Back to the case.*

Did he provide too much information? What did he learn? Who was the detective here?

He hesitated to start the engine. It appeared Mary Ann cared for Song. She didn't show as much emotion as he had after losing Clare. He saw no tears. Why was that? He had been on an emotional roller coaster, while Mary Ann appeared to deal with her situation very matter-of-factly. She had James for less than a year, and he had Clare …

Would they continue to be engaged? Would Song stand trial for murder? Would he ever be able to talk again? Would she still marry Song after all of this? Where did Song get a bulletproof vest? How could she get through this? Why was he there, for crying out loud? There were so many unanswered questions. And this was not his case. Would he ever know all the details?

He was interrupted by the chirping of his cell phone. He knew who it was by caller ID. "Hello, Guy," he said, trying to surprise him.

"Hello, Howard," Coyle said, laughing into the phone. "What are you doing to my quiet little city of Orchard Hill? Turning it into a war zone?"

Guy was laughing. "I move here, and there's an officer killed in the line of duty, a satanic cult homicide, a major drug deal, and now two other officers are killed? What the fuck?"

"Hey, don't blame me. I just work here. How've you been otherwise?" Howard said, smiling into the phone. He started the car to put him on speaker. "And, believe me, you don't even know what other shit I'm into."

"What do you mean?"

He went on to tell him about the intelligence position, a few details about the Sundown case, and the latest update on the Trusdale Inn shooting. He now knew how to get back on the freeway and to the haven that was Orchard Hill.

"I was working a quiet patrol overtime shift on Valentine's Day and look at what happened. I'm feeling like a shit magnet."

"I'm beginning to think that too, HH."

"I just got through interviewing a girlfriend or wife of one of the suspects. Well, she was a fiancée and not a real wife yet. But I feel like she interviewed me more than I got anything from her." He pointed the Dodge Charger to the 710 Freeway south, working to the 91. Traffic was much better going that way, at least at that time of day.

"Word to the wise, Howard, you better watch out what you tell the family on this case. I saw one of the suspects' father is a federal court judge. So, they'll be thinking of civil action against your city and Sparrow Hill."

"Oh. I hadn't thought of that, Guy. Good advice. But, as usual, it might be too late. I think I may have told her too much. Got to get back to the barn and do some damage control."

"These things tend to blow up in your face years later. In civil court. When the emotion of the case is long gone. That's not exactly why I called."

"What's going on?" Howard queried.

"Tom Vanowen." He let the name stand out there as if suspended in space.

"Yes?"

"He and I worked together back in the late 80s when he was on LAPD. We worked a traffic car together on PMs. Back then, we handled all the traffic accidents on the south side. He went through the ninety-two riots, and his wife told him he had to quit because of all the violence. She thought he might get hurt. He fought it and fought it, and in the mid-nineties, I guess, he opted to lateral to Sparrow Hill."

"Wow," said Hamilton. He flashed back to the gurney carrying Vanowen and realized what his family was going through. That was one death notification he would not have looked forward to, and he was glad it was not his to do.

He had a heck of a time getting in the lane he needed to be in to get off the 710. He talked into the windshield as he swerved to avoid a plastic chair that must have fallen off a truck. *People.*

"Yeah, with his LAPD training, he did well and made sergeant quickly. So, his wife talks him into changing jobs from South Central to a nice quiet suburban community like Sparrow Hill, and, well, go figure."

"That is … amazing, Guy. I never knew him, but I never got up to the Hill very much." He finally found his lane.

"Well, your Chief will probably remember him, but I don't know if he knows that story. Have you talked with him lately?"

"The Chief?"

"Yeah. Your Chief."

"A few weeks back when I went into this job. He gave me a doozy of a case right away. I'll have to tell you about it sometime over coffee."

"Remember, Howard. I don't mean to lecture you, but …"

"Coming from you, I never view it as a lecture, Guy." He turned on to the 91 Freeway and saw brake lights. *Damn.*

"Hey, you know experience is doing it right after doing it wrong. Back in the day, we got in trouble and were sued by a group of dissidents for having an intel file on them."

"Really?" Hamilton was trying to concentrate on what Guy was saying and at the same time maneuver around a fender bender that had slowed traffic.

"Really. But guess what?"

"What?"

"They subpoenaed our files into federal court. And they were shocked at what they found."

"Geez, Guy, you are wringing me out here. Tell me."

"We turned over an intel file, and it was nothing more than newspaper articles from the *Times*, a few underground papers, some magazines, and the internet. Anybody could have done it. Instead, they took us to task over information that was public knowledge and dragged us through the courts, costing the city a lot of money."

"Over newspaper clippings?"

"Yep. The media has better intel than any PD or three letters of government operation. We got taken to task by the ACLU, the Cochran's, Yagman's, and others. They are all bottom-feeding attorneys that eat from the public trough. And we're the low-hanging fruit."

"Well, you know, Guy, LAPD is just the punching bag for the courts, TV, and newspapers, and those guys are the punchers. So, we little guys sit and watch you get beat up time and again. They usually don't pick on us."

"Your turn will come up. Trust me." There was a pause, "Anyway, my turn to buy next time."

He got off the 91 Freeway, heading back to the South Bay, surface streets, and Orchard Hill—from streets where everyone littered, and no one picked up to clean streets that were swept regularly. From ghetto art to clean and orderly, he saw the transition. But he still thought it might not be as safe as he thought it was.

CHAPTER 102

He was in a hurry to get back to the station to meet with Nieman. First, he had to let him know he may have screwed up big-time. He also had to tell him to get a search warrant for Song's condominium if they had not done so. That trunk and storage area might have held some other jewels of evidence as well.

He walked into the temporary command post in the EOC. Nieman, Walker, Rollenhagen, and the two Sheriff detectives were all still there.

He was trying to figure out how to deal with the situation. Should he just announce his screwup with everybody there? Talk to the SO detectives separately? But, no, he had a better idea.

He pulled Nieman aside. As he was walking away with Nieman for their private conversation, Walker shouted out to him.

"HH. Heard what happened at the Sundown this weekend?"

"What do you mean?"

"Looks like you're busy. When you are done with the boss, we'll talk."

He nodded and followed Nieman to a closed-off area of the EOC. He was not going to admit to making a mistake. Instead, he would give Nieman the facts and decide if he overdid the information to Kowalski.

"Earlier today, I got a phone call." He then explained how Mary Ann saw him on television, their previous meet on New Year's, and his visit with her.

"I may have told her a little too much about how Song was injured. The Sheriffs never said anything about it to her, but she told me she never asked them either."

"OK, let me think about it." Nieman maintained the stern look he always had, regardless of the situation.

"Oh, and she showed me where he might have gotten the camouflage outfit he wore."

"What do you mean?"

"They have separate closets. Ms. Kowalski gave me a tour of the house and showed me his walk-in closet. There's a trunk with a lock on it. The key may be on his key ring that's booked with his property. She has no idea what's in there. I think we need to get a search warrant and check it out. He also has a storage area in the underground garage."

"Those idiots didn't get a warrant for his office or house yet. I better get them on it right now," Nieman said as he started to walk away.

"One other thing." Hamilton paused. "This may or may not be pertinent. The fiancée doesn't live there. She stayed there a lot but lived here in the South Bay. I guess she could permit us to search without a warrant."

Nieman paused. "I'm not going to take the chance. While this is a criminal case, the civil aspect bothers me enough just to get the warrant. Anything else?"

"I got some good intel from the Sheriff's electronics lab. Just must go through it, analyze it, and write it up. I should have told you where I was going, but I couldn't find you. Sorry."

"Hey, Howard. You gave me some good info. I don't think you screwed up. I think they did," he said, referring to the Sheriff's detectives. "But we'll fix that."

The emphasis on "you" and "they" made him feel a bit better.

CHAPTER 103

Hamilton went back to the working tables. "Hey, Red, you asked if I heard about Sundown. What about it?"

"I just know what I heard from the POA. But the dolphins are running with it."

Dolphins was a code for rumors that were more than likely genuine but had not been verified. That was because dolphins loved to gossip, according to the trainers at Sea World. And so did police departments. So that was how it all started.

Red decided to jump right in.

"A couple of the board members worked security there this weekend, and they got raided by some investigative unit. I don't know much more than that. I always thought something weird was going on at those outdoor farmer's markets or swap meets, whatever they are. I'm glad I don't shop there." Walker tried to laugh, but no one saw any humor.

"You dress like you do." Howard could not resist. There was laughter and then a momentary silence.

Rikelman walked into the room. "Hamilton, front and center." At least he had a smile on his face. "Let's go to my office."

Was he going to get chewed out about what he just told Nieman? For not checking in with him and leaving the station? He signed out. Wasn't that enough?

"Chief wants to see us in ten minutes. You and me. Know what it's about?"

"Gee, Lieutenant, how would I know? Maybe it's about this case?"

"I don't think so. The Chief's up to speed on it as far as we know. He knows that one of our victims is an old friend of his from LAPD. The guy lateraled to Sparrow Hill because his family wanted him to work in a safer community. Go figure."

"Yeah, I heard," he said, not wanting to mention who he heard it from.

"Get your files on everything you are working on. Not sure which issue the Chief wants to discuss."

They walked up the stairs to the third floor, where the air got a little bit thinner. The joke was because the brass, dispatch, and the Strategic Planning Unit, along with HR, were all up there. But, of course, only visitors used the elevator.

They walked into the Chief's reception area, where his administrative assistant, Janet, held court. She was the most influential person in the Department. She had worked for three different chiefs before this one and had every commanding officer by the balls. They knew it, and she did as well.

The only mistake in her entire career was she wanted a husband with a badge and made every effort to find one. Late one night after a city council meeting, she had been caught by the City Manager giving a motor cop a head job under a burned-out light in the parking lot. Unbeknownst to her, the cop she had her eye and lips on, Wally Harris, was one of the department's biggest cock hounds. She should have known better. She apologized to the City Manager, and all was forgiven.

Cities like Orchard Hill had secrets. Some went unnoticed, and others only those in the know knew. Wally Harris had since retired.

He had a son, Dean, who was now an OHPD motor cop. That was from wife number one.

His second wife birthed James, who was ten or twelve years younger than Dean, eventually found his way to OHPD, was a recent graduate of the Police Academy, and had just made his probation. Wally hit it big on the third try, marrying a widow who was a victim of a burglary and worth a lot of money. Hence the retirement. They moved to Sparrow Hill.

Janet settled for the OHPD Juvenile Division psychologist, Ted Rankin. Then, all was well with the world. And Orchard Hill.

Hamilton followed Rikelman into the Chief's crowded conference room. There were two seats left at the far end of the table. He saw the Chief, Mr. Rollins, and four others he did not know.

He gently placed his files on the table and took a seat.

The Chief opened the meeting. "I would like to have everyone introduce themselves. It's the first time we've all been together. But first, let me introduce Lt. Ib Rikelman and Detective Howard Hamilton." They each acknowledged.

"Good to see you again, Detective Hamilton, and congratulations on your new promotion." Rollins wanted everyone to know that he was in the know about the PD.

The Chief asked Rollins to introduce his guests, but Hamilton thought he knew who they were. "This is Mayor Martha Gottlieb, councilwoman Lee Straus, and councilman Don Diego." The requisite nods were exchanged. Unfortunately, the business attire gave it away. Everyone looked like their photographs on the city hall walls.

He was right.

The Chief jumped in and introduced the only remaining

unannounced person in the room. "This is Bob Dolson. Bob, tell them what you do and why you're here."

Dolson was dressed in a sports jacket, white dress shirt, and slacks but no tie.

"Hi, everyone. As the Chief said, I'm Bob Dolson. I'm the Chief of Investigations for the Music and Film Industry Association of America. Back in '06, we merged with the Motion Picture Association of America. You may have heard of the MPAA and the Recording Industry Association of America, or RIAA. We are now known as the MAFIAA."

He laughed at the connotation of Mafia. Everyone immediately got the joke and humored him.

"Well, the Chief and I go back to our LAPD days, and a couple of weeks back, he gave me a call. Many of our investigations involve counterfeit reproductions of movies and recordings. It's a massive underground economy, internationally and here as well. These cases are hard to prosecute. We do like to seize as much of the fake products out there as we can."

Hamilton and Rikelman looked at each other knowingly.

"Well, the Chief asked if we could look at a couple of things occurring in Orchard Hill. Primarily at Sundown."

The two council members were starting to squirm in their seats. Rollins sat up a bit straighter in his chair, glancing at the Mayor with an "I told you so" look.

Dolson continued. "The location is a bit strange because half the lot is in your city, and the other half is in the county. It doesn't matter to us because we enforce federal and state laws."

Hamilton was figuring out what had happened even before Rikelman, but they kicked each other under the table, trying to control a smile.

"With the help of some investigation by your department, we found that there were several locations throughout the county that had similar, if not identical, setups. The level of counterfeit movies and recordings was astronomical. The bottom line is that we seized over five thousand movies and ten thousand fake CDs in each of the four locations. It was massive."

Dolson reached down and opened his briefcase, pulling out photos to support his statements.

"The vendors were all controlled at the top by a drug cartel from Mexico and San Salvador. We found the manufacturing location in the City of Industry at a huge warehouse. We don't know yet if the operation owners knew everything was being laundered from a drug cartel. That's still under investigation."

The Chief stepped in to add more information to the table.

"What we found was that none of the vendors had a state tax license, but they were adding state tax to their sales and not reporting it. Then we found they didn't have a business license to conduct these sales in Orchard Hill or the county."

Rollins raised his hand to be heard. "And you have to remember that we have a one-cent city tax that not many of our communities do in LA County. That's why we have such a great city and can keep our streets, parks, beaches, and city facilities looking good."

"And this was all right in front of all of us." The Chief swept his arm around the table with a somewhat accusatory implication, like everyone should have known.

Hamilton and Rikelman looked at each other again. They both knew what was coming next.

CHAPTER 104

The room fell silent, and the Chief realized his error.

"That's not to say that anyone here should have known. I guess our business license office should have known, but that's water under the bridge."

Everyone nodded in agreement. Hamilton could tell that the council members were already figuring what was coming next.

Dolson continued. "Our investigation also found a few other things."

The Chief and Rikelman, along with Hamilton, exchanged eye contact.

"There were several organizations that governed this operation throughout the county. LLCs were formed, and a network of people oversaw each location. The makeup of these people was interesting. One is the Mayor of a large city in north county, and two are council people right here in Orchard Hill."

Rollins said, "I don't want to interrupt your presentation here, Chief Dolson, but I want to set the record straight for our council members here."

He turned and looked at Gottlieb, Straus, and Diego. "This involves council members Doug Frankel and Ron Watson. But I'm sure you've already figured that out."

They nodded.

Dolson took back the floor.

"Let me be clear here for everyone. We don't know if any of the owners knew they were selling counterfeit products. Yet. We're looking at that now. But right now, the biggest issue we see is administrative and not criminal. All we see is a failure of the vendors to pay their taxes on the products, possession of counterfeit movies and CDs, and selling them without a license to do so."

"Are we going to know about our council members' level of involvement?" Rollins threw the question out to Dolson on behalf of the other two members, who were not inclined to ask any questions.

"Of course, but again," Dolson said, sitting up straighter, "this is a bit hard for the Chief and me to deal with. But believe me, we understand. I would love to put everybody involved in jail. But until we find out who knew what and where the money flows to, the MAFIAA wants this handled administratively."

"Why is that Chief Dolson?" Rollins asked on behalf of Gottlieb, Straus, and Diego.

"I've been in this position for five years. We rarely prosecute anything criminally. It's all done from an administrative or civil perspective. The industry does not want to become bogged down in the criminal arena and takes great pains to deal with these matters civilly and outside the media and, quite frankly, out of the criminal justice system. What we do is turn over the information, in this case, the intelligence gathered by OHPD and my people, to DEA or perhaps even to our county-wide drug task force, LA DUECE."

"I see. So, it will still get taken to another level, right?" Rollins was starting to understand the process.

Dolson jumped right on it. "Yup. We, my team, may not do it, but with the intel we've put together, it'll get taken to a logical conclusion by somebody with higher initials than MAFIAA. It just may take some time."

A few people in the room got the intended poke.

The Chief tried to wrap up the meeting. "We'll keep everybody apprised of the results of all of this. I think the only other person we should have invited to this was our city attorney."

Mayor Gottlieb finally spoke. "Why is that?"

"Because we need to ensure that none of this information leaves this room, ma'am. I think he would reinforce to everyone the need for confidentiality at this point."

The Chief realized he may have insulted them but still held firm.

"I think we realize that Chief. Council members Diego, Straus, and I have heard enough." Gottlieb stood and reached over to provide the politically correct handshake to Dolson and the Chief. She nodded to Rikelman and Hamilton, and the elected officials made a quick exit.

CHAPTER 105

Dolson started to put his photos and other work papers in his briefcase. "Chief, good to see you again. Sorry it was not under better circumstances. We still have a lot of work to do on this. I'll be in touch."

The Chief stood to shake his hand and walk him to the door. "If everyone else could hang on, I just want to say goodbye to Bob." The walk continued to the waiting area, where Janet was talking to a records clerk.

"Bob, I cannot thank you enough for your help with this. Let me tell you. These were great circumstances, not bad ones. I'll fill you in later. Keep in touch, and we'll have a drink together soon."

"Chief, you know I love this shit. Anytime we can stick it to some cartel guys and some politicians, well, that's what we live for." He smiled as he winked at Janet.

He walked back into his office, where Rollins, Rikelman, and Hamilton were engaged in small talk.

"How do you think that went?" The question was posed directly to Rollins and not the other end of the table.

"Couldn't have been better, Chief." Rollins and the Chief exchanged mental high fives.

Rikelman and Hamilton looked at each other, a bit perplexed by their reaction. But neither of them was going to say a word.

The Chief spoke first. "I want to thank both of you for some great work on this. Howard, I first want to say I heard what you did on Friday night, and while we lost some people that are dear to us, you performed very well."

Rollins added, "I got a call this morning from Jim Hines, the City Manager of Sparrow Hill. He echoed the Chief's statement. Sad situation. I don't know how you do it, but I know it could have been much worse. Thanks."

"Training, sir. Just good training." Hamilton realized he had to say something.

Everyone was now standing. Rikelman asked, "What's going to go on with this case?" He was referring to the folders with Sundown typed on the tab.

Rollins said, "Well, Lieutenant, this file will go in my bottom— no, make it my top—drawer. It's February. We have a local election coming up in June. The Chief and I have been advised by these two council members they wanted to see us gone. And the POA is backing their play."

The Chief said, "Detective Hamilton. Your intelligence report indicated that there were two members of the POA working security at Sundown."

"Yes, sir."

"Well, it seems they did not have work permits to do that job. I didn't want to discuss this with the other two council members in the room, but we will be dealing with this matter"—he paused for effect—"administratively. There is a reason we need to know what off-duty jobs our officers chose to engage in. And this is one of them."

There was that word again.

More smiles were exchanged between the City Manager and the Chief.

"Any other questions?"

CHAPTER 106

There comes a time when discretion is the better form of courage, or valor, and this was one of those times. Rikelman and Hamilton escaped from the third floor and returned to the more comfortable Narco/Vice office. Rikelman directed Hamilton into his office and closed the door.

"Here's the deal, HH. Nobody here knows jack shit about what you did on this except Barber and me. The only people who know anything about what's going on were the people in that room. Got it?"

"I understand, but—"

"The POA has no idea we snooped on them. They don't know who blew the whistle, but the Chief can handle that part of it. Not having work permits for a place like that was stupid on their part. Hell, they may not have approved it, or when it got reviewed, they would find out the place didn't have a business license. Who knows?"

"You know, I didn't do that much, Lieutenant. I mean, a simple inspection, checking a few databases. Unfortunately, this thing got way out of control."

"That's why they call it intelligence, HH. You took some basic information and weaved it into one of the most significant political cases this city has seen. At least lately."

"Fuck me. I had no idea this thing would mushroom like this. Should I be watching my back?"

"The Chief and I have your back, and it stays right here in this room. Got it?"

"Got it. But remember, I must live with those guys down there. And I've been feeling like a shit magnet recently." He paused just to look around the room.

"I have a few things to catch up on, and then I'm EOW. Anything else, sir?"

"Isn't that enough?"

Hamilton was swimming in the intrigue that surrounded him. But he did have a little work to do, so it was back to the Trusdale Inn caper.

He returned to his cubbyhole and opened the computer file provided by the Sheriff's electronics lab. He obtained the records on the cell phone history for Song. He then reviewed Kim's phone information and plugged in his magic software.

There it was. It was that easy. Howard had correlated numbers from Song to those from Kim and found a common denominator. The dates were significant in that they were all close together. They had called the same number several times, and that number had called each of them. Another simple click showed the owner.

Pak's Clothier in Monterey Park, specializing in high-end dress suits for the Asian businessperson, was a business. He found the owner, Daniel Pak. There was an extensive rap sheet for Pak, so he printed everything out and took it to Nieman.

"This is great, HH. I think we now have the connections we need with all of this. I'll let the SO do the grunt work on this and tie it up in a bow. Just need to figure out Pak's involvement."

CHAPTER 107

Today was one of those days he wished he had a long drive home to go over everything. He reflected on his accomplishments on the drive to East LA and the Sheriff's office, and it gave him time to sort through the bullshit.

He had been assigned, or at least loaned, to the homicide investigation from the Friday-night massacre, got moved into the EOC temporarily, and received a call from the significant other of one of the suspects. He drove to East LA for the first time in a long time. On the way, he got dumped by Amanda Johnson, who told him they could not see each other anymore.

He went to the Sheriff's electronics lab and picked up some data from the two suspects' cell phones. And then he met with Mary Ann Kowalski and was given information he was not sure what to do with. He received a call from Guy Coyle telling him to watch his ass with the information he gave to Mary Ann, then found out one of the dead Sparrow PD guys, Tom Vanowen, was friends with Coyle and the Chief. *What the fuck?*

He then returned to the station, got called to the Chief's office for a powwow with the Chief of the MAFIAA, the city manager, mayor, and two council members, only to find the whole Sundown caper going in somebody's files. *What the fuck?*

The software he recently discovered located a third person in the triangle with Song and Kim, and who knew where that would lead? He was officially swimming in it now.

On the way home, his car radio was playing an oldies song from the 90s. "Two out of Three Ain't Bad" by Marvin Lee Aday, better known as Meat Loaf, was pounding through the speakers. His parents would have cringed at 90s music being referred to as "oldies." *Symbolic or what?*

The line that struck him was "I want you, I need you, but there ain't no way I'm ever gonna love you." Amanda probably heard the same song and thought of him. Or he hoped so—at least for a moment.

The Mamas and Papas also were right. *"Monday, Monday, can't trust that day. It just turns out that way."*

CHAPTER 108

The dolphins were running the show now. Hamilton was hearing from several sources that the Redondo and Orchard Hill Police Departments would patrol Sparrow Hill's city for eight days and nights. Counselors were reluctant to return the department to policing their city, but mutual aid from the two largest cities in the South Bay made the residents feel comfortable.

But not the press.

Jim Hines and his Mayor became the spokespersons for the incident, even though it took place in Orchard Hill. Everyone was OK with that, primarily because Sparrow Hill did need to go through the grieving process and mourn. The city had to express how they released the pent-up anger and grief enveloping this small community.

There was a tremendous outpouring of sympathy, empathy, and sorrow, but it only lasted two days. It was then that the media turned the tables on the Sparrow Hill Police Department, the city, and the community. The focus became the two assailants. Was there too much force used by the members of the team-building workshop? Was the dreaded chokehold used to control them? The media raised doubts about what occurred, and people in the community did not know who to believe.

The city leaders were in disbelief, and then anger raged at the possibility their police department could do anything wrong. The community and its leaders became enraged. There existed a strong desire to connect with the citizenry to inform and show support.

Overnight, a memorial fund was established for the families of Svenson and Vanowen. In one week, $130,000 in donations from residents, businesses, and other organizations was raised. A memorial service was held in the city park, which turned into a rally supporting the department and its members.

Jim Hines and his Mayor went on the offense. They shielded all department members and city employees from the relentless pressure of the media. The city's leaders took the hits and were resilient in their defense of the department's actions. Churches and schools rallied on behalf of the city. But more than anything, it became a healing process for an entire region of the County and its municipalities.

The District Attorney's office would take months to conduct their investigation, but the city and community had closed the case without any formal resolution. The officers and city employees were justified in using the necessary force until the imminent threat had passed. Everyone who needed to know knew. The media be damned. Everyone involved needed to put their lives back together.

CHAPTER 109

Working patrol was always easy. Go EOW, take off the uniform, carefully place the city's troubles in your locker, and go home.

The new job? Not so easy. Too many things to think about. Too many *different* things to think about.

"Well, Dad, at least you're home on time tonight," Marcia said with a soft jab to the midplex.

"Hey, lighten up. Friday night was one of a kind. Where's Geoff?"

"He'll be here. He's bringing dinner. KFC, if that's all right. I'll set the table, and we'll be ready by six. Do you realize he'll be graduating from high school this year? Actually, in a few months?"

"Can't believe it myself. He's not been very talkative about it. Maybe Geoff will tell us what he wants to do next. Think he knows?"

"I don't know. He's been quiet with me as well." Marcia set the table and then worked on a salad. She was developing her routine now, he noticed.

"Maybe tonight's the night we pin him down. I'm going to check my emails. I'll be ready by six."

Howard went to his small office, which was no larger than a closet, and opened his emails. Nothing significant. Nothing from Amanda. But he knew that was it for them. No more. Too much blue for the family, and he understood it. Even though Amanda had been something, he could … never mind.

Up popped a new email from, of all people, Lieutenant Rikelman. He recognized his email address. *How did he get my personal email? Well, he is a detective.*

It read:

    HH. Heads up. City Council has called
    an emergency meeting for tomorrow
    afternoon.
    3 p.m. May want to tune in. It'll be
    on the local cable channel. FYI, NB.

It was all in bold. *What is this about? And what's with signing it NB? Does he know his nickname?* Of course, he did.

"Hey, Dad, Geoff's home. Six o'clock. Off the computer. Dinnertime." Marcia was picking up right where Clare had left off.

"Did you get the extra crunchy?"

"Just for you, Dad. We got the regular crunchy or whatever it is for us." Geoff looked happy to see everybody. He had one of those shit-eating grins that told everyone he was holding on to something special.

They all sat down, did a quick "Bless us oh, Lord," and opened the boxes of chicken. Marcia had placed a community salad bowl on the table and passed it around, along with the mashed potatoes and gravy.

Geoff started giggling.

"Anything you want to tell us, Geoff?" Howard asked.

Now he was laughing with a piece of chicken in his mouth. "I got into Arizona State. I just got notified today at school. A formal letter should be in the mail soon. Can you believe it?"

"Wow, Geoff, that's great," Marcia cheered. "I was, we all, were wondering what you were going to do after graduation."

"Congrats, Geoff," Howard said in a somewhat subdued celebration. "But did you apply to any local schools? And, by the way, when were you going to tell us? How come I didn't even know about you looking?"

"Just ASU."

"Oh, when were you going to tell us all?" The emphasis was on *all*. He didn't mean for it to be accusatory, but it came out that way. "Pass the salad, Marcia."

"I think I'm going to get a partial scholarship, too, Dad."

Marcia picked up on the issue on the table. "Well, I think that's great, Geoff. I'm glad it wasn't an East Coast school or even Texas. Arizona is pretty close. You'll be coming home on all the holidays, right?"

Howard looked to Marcia with a "Thanks for saving me" head shake. She decided to change the subject.

"So, Dad, are you ever going to become a eucharistic minister at St. Elizabeth's? You did the training, and then ..." Her voice trailed off because it had been a long time since they had talked about their mom.

"I've thought about it. I talked to Deacon Rex but not Father Art. It may be time, but I guess I'm not sure of anything anymore. Except that I have two wonderful kids."

The silent consensus gave each of them some solace. But each would deal with it differently.

CHAPTER 110

"Can we talk about Mom for a minute?" Howard threw the question on the table, hoping for a unanimous vote.

"Sure," they said in unison.

"I'm not sure how to phrase what I have to say, so …"

"Spit it out, Dad. We can handle it."

"I know, but I'm not sure about me. But here goes. I got a call from the DA's office about, about the guy who … was in the accident with Mom."

Both Geoff and Marcia set their forks down and starred at the half-filled salad bowl. "What's going on with the case?" Geoff asked.

"The guy has been in the hospital a long time and finally pled guilty to illegal street racing, reckless driving, and a few other things, including … vehicular *manslaughter*," Howard said. He then realized he emphasized the word manslaughter a bit too much.

Marcia spoke first. "That's a lot to take in, Dad."

"I know." There was an uncomfortable silence.

"What's next?" Geoff added.

"What's next is the sentencing. The DA wanted to know if we wanted to attend the sentencing hearing."

"Would we have to testify?" Marcia queried.

"About what?" Geoff asked Marcia in a rather condescending way.

"Hey, no, Geoff. No testimony. We would sit there in court and listen to the arguments from the DA and his attorney about how much time he should get in prison. Then we would hear the judge's decision. Maybe."

"What do you mean maybe?" Marcia was now getting flustered.

"Well ..." Howard tried to get the kids to make eye contact instead of just starring at the table. "Sometimes the judge needs more time to think about it. Look at his criminal and driving record, if he has one, and just hear his side."

"Does he have a side?" Geoff asked with a bit more forcefulness.

"I don't know, Geoff, and I don't care. I mean, I care about what he gets, but ..."

Marcia jumped in. "We could all go to court and sit there for hours, waiting for the trial, and then the judge would say, 'I'll think about it'?"

"It could happen like that, yes."

"You know, we've gone through a lot these last few years or so. We've been hurt and are just getting our lives back together." Geoff was taking the high road. "He gets what he gets. What difference does it make if we go there? Do I even want to see what he looks like? No. Do I care what his sentence is? Yes. But I can do that from a distance. They'll notify us, won't they? What do you guys think?"

"All in favor?"

"Those Sun Devils have a great football team, Geoff. But boy, it sure gets hot in Tempe."

They all agreed on the heat.

It was time for a glass of red. But just for the adult in the room.

CHAPTER 111

All he could think on the way to the station was, *I hope Ruby Tuesday is better than Monday, Monday.* It was still bothering him that Geoff had announced his choice of colleges without any family input. Not that it would have mattered. At the same time, he pondered that Geoff could make his own decisions. But he knew Clare would be a bit upset if she were…

He spent the first few hours cleaning up everything from yesterday. He did an interview summary of Kowalski, closed out the file on Sundown, and had his second cup of Keurig coffee and a buttermilk doughnut, compliments of the detective squad room. He put the money in the jar using change so people could hear coins. It was schmoozing time at the coffee table.

Walker saddled up and opened the conversation. "So, Howard, tell us a bit about your new job. Intel Officer. Sounds cool."

"Not much to tell, Red. Just getting my feet wet and trying to find the men's room, you know."

"What the fuck does that mean?"

"It means that I'm developing the job with the guidance of Barber and Bates—I mean Rikelman. I'm trying to take each day and build on it. Someday, I hope we can work together to solve homicides, but right now I have a major learning curve."

"That doesn't tell me shit, HH."

"I know." They both laughed it off.

"Detective Hamilton, please report to your office." It was a page over the intercom from Joanie.

"Yes, ma'am. Reporting as ordered."

"You have a certified registered letter that needs a signature. It's marked *Personal and Confidential*. Want me to open it?"

"No. I think if it was personal and confidential to me, I should open it. Anyway, don't registered and certified mean the same thing?"

"Be that way, and I don't know, smarty," she said but smiled, knowing it was all in jest.

He took the letter in a playful tug-of-war after signing for it. He tossed it on his desk, looked at it for any telltale markings, and could find absolutely nothing. The return address was Rosecrans Presbyterian Hospital, the addressee was a very formal Detective Howard Hamilton.

Is it a letter bomb? Anthrax? A practical joke? He didn't know. He looked around, but there was no one waiting for him to open it. He bent it, then held it up to the light and shook it back and forth, up, and down. *Should I call the bomb squad?*

Fuck it. It's just a letter. Hamilton opened it neatly with a letter opener, working around the glued flap and the stickers indicating it was certified and required a signature.

He reached in carefully to pull out a three-page letter addressed to him. He looked at the third page for a signature and saw the name of the author.

Dear Detective Hamilton:

Forgive me for using the mail to communicate with you. What I have to say, I do not think I could say in person. At least not yet. First, let me say once again how thankful I am for your kindness. To James and me. As you can imagine, this has been a very trying time for me personally, as well as our families. I do not know where your investigation will lead you, but I must let you know some of the things that have contributed to it. We had planned to get married very soon. It was all based on our work schedule. On Valentine's night, we were going to go to dinner in Koreatown. It was there I was going to tell him I'm pregnant. Obviously, we never made it to dinner, so he still does not know he is a father. During our courtship, I had difficulty being intimate. We overcame that, but only after I confided in him something I had been carrying around for over twenty years. You see, years ago, I was molested. No, I was raped when I was eleven years old. It went on for over two years. Until I was about thirteen. He was a family member—kind of an uncle. I never told anyone. I was too ashamed. I finally confronted him at the ripe old age of thirteen after realizing I was the real victim. I told him that if he didn't stop, I was going to go to my aunt and tell her what he had been doing to me. The things he made me do were so disgusting and disgraceful. I dwelled on it for years. It affected every relationship I had growing up. I still have trouble even talking about it. As I told you, I discussed this with James. But I made a terrible mistake. I never told him who it was, but I found out he discovered his name. I didn't realize it right away. I didn't realize it until Valentine's night. His name is, was Paul Svenson. He worked for the Sparrow Hill Police Department. I had forgotten about that point because we never saw each other at any more family gatherings. He was never at any family function where I was, and I think it was on purpose. I know I should have told you yesterday, but I still cannot verbalize it yet. I hope you understand. I know this is a long letter, but believe me, this is the best therapy I have right now. I do not know how James found him. I didn't tell him. A couple of other comments, and I will be finished with this aspect of my letter and my life. I will move on, bury myself in my work and try to forget. I am still unsure about James and me, but it is too soon to make any decisions. James's parents are humble and honorable people. They are ashamed and embarrassed by his actions. Judge Song will be making a public apology on behalf of all of us soon. They do not know, nor will they ever know, the truth behind their son's honorable deed. Only you and I will carry that. I apologize for involving you in my tragedy. I have not told James's family about my pregnancy. Soon but not now. Lastly, please extend my condolences to the family of the other officer killed. I believe his name was Tom Vanowen I am so sorry. I believe it is in my best interest, personally and professionally, not to communicate any longer with anyone over this unfortunate and tragic matter. I would ask that you honor my request. The best to you and your family. I thank you again, for your kindness.

Sincerely,
Mary Ann Kowalski

CHAPTER 112

Hamilton stared at the letter for what seemed an eternity. He was exhausted just from reading it. But he had to reread it. While he had much empathy for Mary Ann, his biggest issue right now, this moment, was *What the hell do I do with this? Her life was a mess, but I have, we have, an investigation to complete.*

Should he talk with Rikelman about it? Barber? Nieman? Carrie Wade? What would Guy Coyle do? He dwelled on that last thought and figured it out on his own. Mary Ann was confiding in him. The only criminal case left would be against James, and this issue would have a bearing on his prosecution. It looked like Kim was more than likely just a hired gun for Song.

Was there an expectation of privacy here? Did Mary Ann deserve the confidentiality accorded a fiancée under these circumstances? Who got to make those kinds of decisions?

He put the letter back into the envelope and looked at the front. *Personal and Confidential* were handwritten and then stamped again to reinforce the message. He looked around to make sure no one noticed and made a quick copy. He put the letter, envelope, and a copy in his binder for safekeeping. There was only one person to confide in.

He went to the stairwell that led to the third floor.

"Janet, is the Chief busy? Can I see him?"

"Of course, Howard. Have a seat. As soon as he gets off the phone, I'll let him know you're here."

She was so accommodating. Who knew? He had been on the job for almost ten years and only once or twice had been to the Chief's office. Now it was becoming a habit he was not sure he wanted. It was like a revolving door, with him up there for one thing or another.

"The Chief will see you now," she announced.

The Chief came around from behind his desk and motioned to sit with him at the small conference table.

"So how's the big detective doing, Howard? Do I get to call you HH yet?"

"Of course, sir, you can call me anything. You're the Chief."

"Well, nicknames around here are very possessive, I find. But thanks for the OK. What can I do for you?"

Hamilton placed his notebook on the table and paused to take a breath. "Chief, yesterday I received a call from Mary Ann Kowalski."

"Who is that? Wait a minute. The name is familiar, but ..."

"She is the, *was* the fiancée of James Song. From the Friday-night shooting. The guy who was injured, not the shooter, Kim."

"OK."

"She asked to see me, so I went out to Monterey Park to see her because I was in the area to go to the Sheriff's lab. Well, you don't need to know all that."

The Chief could tell he was nervous. Hamilton explained the incident with Song on New Year's Day, unsure if the Chief knew any of that information. He did not.

"OK." The Chief was letting Hamilton relax a moment.

"Today, I received a letter. This letter." Howard opened the binder showing the envelope containing the three pages.

"I think it's relevant to the criminal case, but because it was marked Personal and Confidential to me, I didn't know what to do with it. I didn't know who to turn to, sir. This is when information turns into intel, but I also think this is more than confidential and privileged somehow. Should I give it to the Sheriffs, Detective Nieman, Lieutenant Hospian, or Rikelman?"

"May I?" The Chief reached for it, and Hamilton slowly, almost reluctantly, slid it over to him.

"Do you mind?" the Chief asked.

"No, sir. That's why I'm here."

"Should we hold it for prints?" the Chief joked, not sure Hamilton got it.

He picked the letter up by an edge to emphasize that he considered it evidence. Then he took out the three pages and set the envelope down, noting it was marked twice for Personal and Confidential.

It took almost five minutes for the Chief to read it. He then went back and reread it.

"I had to read it a couple of times, too, sir."

He got up from his chair and walked over to close the door so even Janet would not know what was going on.

CHAPTER 113

The silence in the room made the paneled walls feel like they were pulsing. The movement of the chairs, as slight as they were, amplified the squeaks. It was a cacophony of noise that overtook the quiet. Each took turns staring at the letter and then at each other. Hamilton broke the quiet.

"I know, Chief. I know."

"I've got to think about this, but let's just bounce a few things off the wall here. And I want to remind you," the Chief said with a smile, "you are a confidential employee, HH."

"Yes, sir."

He walked to the window overlooking the employee parking lot. He seemed to watch people come and go, socialize, and get in their cars and drive away. Or was he?

"You know, this was a murder for hire. The reason for the hire doesn't matter, does it? I mean, let's just say that Svenson was Mary Ann's ex-husband or lover. The motive here is revenge for something. What that something is doesn't matter. Or does it?"

Hamilton could see where the Chief was going with this. He knew he would agree with whatever he decided.

"It's like many things here, Howard," he said, using a more formal designation now. "There are things that deserve to just be in a folder—some things in the top drawer, some in the bottom drawer. Quite frankly, we must look at prosecution in this case. But this could make it ugly. Very ugly. I would hate to see this on the six o'clock news." He looked away, staring at a dark television monitor.

"With your permission, because it was written to you in the manner she chose, I need to meet with the DA and City Attorney. This," he said, pointing to the envelope and its contents, "cannot go in my bottom drawer or top drawer. Do you understand? And, quite frankly, I'm not sure how to handle it. If I had a preference, and I do not, I would like to see if the investigators on this case, our people and the Sheriff's, would come up with this on their own. Without Mary Ann. I don't know."

"Of course, sir. But if it came to light, it would only hurt people. Too many people. Too many families. How do we find justice in this situation? There is just too much hurt to go around, don't you think?"

Both the Chief and Howard had to let the quiet sink into their collective decision-making.

"I do. Thanks, Detective, for bringing this to my attention." Perhaps the official designation of his rank was to mean something.

"It will get handled. Just remember, every city has its secrets. I guess Orchard Hill and Sparrow Hill have a few more than we expected."

"Yes, sir." There was a long pause. "Will that be all?"

"Isn't it enough?"

"Yes, sir."

Hamilton was not going to bring up that he had a bottom drawer, and another copy was living there.

The Chief walked him out to the reception area, where Janet was at the ready. "Thanks again, Detective Hamilton." He turned to Janet. "Can you get in touch with Deputy District Attorney Carrie Wade and John, our City Attorney, and have them come to my office ASAP?"

CHAPTER 114

For some reason, taking the back stairs had always cleansed the mind. It was like leaving everything in his locker when he hung up his uniform after a tough shift, whether he was going up or down.

He checked in with the homicide team at the EOC. It looked like they had everything covered. Much to Nieman's satisfaction, The Sheriffs were getting the search warrant for Song's office and home. He made sure they specified all home areas, including closets and storage areas, in the affidavit. There would be no need to indicate the trunk in Song's closet because it would portend that someone had already discovered it. They would find it. Police work could be so touchy at times.

He was highly concerned about his meeting with the Chief. Had he betrayed Mary Ann's confidence? Would Svenson's name be all over the papers as a child molester? His loyalty was clearly with the Department and the criminal justice system. He felt an obligation here. But he also felt compelled to honor Mary Ann's confidential information. But he wasn't a priest, a doctor, or lawyer, so did she expect he would keep her confidence? What was the Chief going to do?

He stood in the stairwell for just a moment. His thoughts bounced from Mary Ann and James to Clare. As tragic as Clare's death was, there was some finality to it. His grief continued, but all his remembrances were positive. James and Mary Ann had the criminal justice system staring them in the face. Song needed medical treatment that would go on forever, and he was sure to serve an extensive time in jail. It could be decades before any form of closure.

He went back to his office.

The Everlys, Don, and Phil offered to make a run for sandwiches. Howard added his name to the list. *So, we eat at our desks, no time off for a genuine code seven, but it all seems to work out.*

Sometimes they would grab another team to go to a restaurant. Other times, it would be a sandwich on a stakeout, but for some reason, as that old saying went, a good cop never got wet, went hungry, or got off on time.

Joanie reminded everyone there was an emergency city council meeting to watch. What did she know about it? How did she know there was going to be an important announcement?

Someone turned on the office television precisely at three o'clock in the afternoon. The general meeting was usually scheduled for four o'clock, so starting the meeting early was a rarity.

Mayor Gottlieb opened the session with a call to order, flag salute, and invocation. All five members of the council were present on the dais.

The camera focused on the Mayor as she went through her usual routine of reviewing the upcoming council agenda. Then, looking directly into the camera, she spoke. "We have an announcement from one of our colleagues. At this time, I would like to turn over the microphone to Councilman Frankel."

The camera panned to the far side of the dais where Frankel was sitting. He pressed his mic, and the green light was activated and displayed to the public and television audience.

Frankel cleared his throat and looked down at what appeared to be a prepared statement.

"Madam Mayor, esteemed council members, city staff, and the community of Orchard Hill." He cleared his throat. "I have served on the City Council for almost six years. In that capacity, I have been instrumental in bringing to our community a new and vibrant shopping center with a Home Depot anchor, overseen the development of a new school, and was part of the city team to bring in a progressive and professional Chief of Police."

Rikelman, Barber, Joanie, and the remaining unit members who had been doing paperwork were looking on. Silence permeated the room.

Frankel leaned back to catch his breath as he continued.

"I have asked the Mayor if I could have a few minutes today to say how proud I am to have served in this capacity."

He now labored over each word.

"It is with a very heavy heart that at this time, I offer my resignation from the Orchard Hill City Council. I will not be seeking reelection this June and will relinquish my seat to another member of our fine community. I want to say again what an honor it has been to serve in this capacity."

Frankel again held his breath as if he needed CPR. He placed his head in his hands and continued.

"I am struggling with some health issues, personal problems, and I need to devote more time to my business and my family."

It was at this point that he started to sob into the microphone, crying uncontrollably. No one went to his rescue. Mayor Gottlieb let him sit there in his stupor of agony. Councilman Watson started squirming in his seat.

The Mayor and several of the other council members knew the truth.

CHAPTER 115

The silence in the council chambers, on television, and in the office remained past what was a relaxing moment. But then it became even more uncomfortable as Frankel continued to weep.

"Madam Mayor, may I be excused?" There finally was some separation from the moments of solitude to ensure order was restored.

Rikelman looked directly at the screen and remarked, "Beware of bullies who cry."

It was a very profound statement coming from a Norman Bates type of person, Hamilton thought.

"No great loss," the Everlys said in unison.

Rikelman nodded to Howard to come to his office. No words, just a nod.

He closed the door. "I sure have been in a lot of closed-door meetings lately, sir, and I've only been here a few weeks."

"Get used to it, Howard. It's all scary stuff. Are you comfortable with all of this? Do you know your investigation made all of this happen? You better get used to cases like this." Rikelman had to sit back in his chair to read Hamilton's sense of composure.

Howard took a deep breath. "Well, sir, it wasn't much of an investigation. I just did some preliminary research, and ..."

Rikelman held up his right hand and leaned forward. "Hold it, Howard. You're going to find some cases that require you to bust your ass, like the homicides we're investigating out there." He waved his arms to refer to the rest of the station. "Others just need to be uncovered like this one. You lifted some rocks that needed to be lifted, and it was relatively easy. I'll admit that. Had you not done this, someone else would have. It could have been another detective out there snooping around, or it could have been a fuckin' reporter. Or DEA."

"Yeah, I know. I just ... Frankel is an asshole, but to see this go down the way it did ..."

Rikelman sat back and pulled out his bottom desk drawer. "I've got my bottom drawer, and the Chief has his. Your investigation is staying up in his office," he said, referring to the Chief.

"You know he verbally briefed the other two council members and the Mayor privately, but no one has seen the actual report." He shut the drawer with a sound of finality.

"Every city has its secrets. Hamilton. The Chief and the City Manager are only a three-to-two vote away from losing their jobs. You and I are protected by civil service and the Peace Officers Bill of Rights. They're what is called *at will*. They serve at the pleasure of ... got it?"

"I do." Hamilton smiled. It was the second time he heard "every city has its secrets." *Wonder who said it first.*

"You get on the wrong side of a three-to-two, and you're gone. Ideally, you'd like a five-oh or four-one, but that's not always going to happen. Particularly not in Orchard Hill."

"That's quite a lesson in municipal government, Lieutenant. I can't imagine what happens at the state and federal level."

"Me neither, and I don't want to know. But, hey, let's end this. Keep your head down and your powder dry, Hamilton. We're going to have a lot of fun here. I can tell." He was grinning, only like Norman Bates would.

Howard stood. "I can see that, sir."

"Yes, sir, Detective Hamilton. Yes, sir."

What was I going to do before I was interrupted? Oh, yes, look at my next project. I think I've done enough damage with the first two.

He decided to bury himself in his next quest.

Hamilton was now in a rhythm. He sat down, opened his email, and there was Donny with some big news.

> HH: Just an FYI, they settled the Marty Hyatt lawsuit for $250,000. Can you fuckin' believe that? A fuckin quarter of a million dollars? I guess we can't do good police work anymore. Go figure. Rumor was they wanted to contest it but figured it would cost the city more to defend it. Assholes, all of them. Hey, want to come over to dinner at our new place sometime? DS

He opened the folder handed to him by Rikelman a few days ago. It seemed like months had passed with all that had been going on.

> Identify all organized crime figures living in the South Bay and specifically Orchard Hill. Establish a file on each known subject with information on their specific location, business interests, acquaintances, family, and criminal record.
>
> Second, research the known political agitators living in or around the South Bay with a history of

creating social unrest. In anticipation of potential unrest in the future, we will need to identify subjects, residences, acquaintances, business interests, family, and criminal records.

Maintain files to include information obtained from Lexus Nexis, newspaper files, etc. Coordinate with LASO, LAPD, other South Bay agencies, and perhaps even the FBI and ATF.

Hmmm. What could develop from this?

ACKNOWLEDGMENTS

Acknowledgments are long overdue. Writing a book is a team effort, even in its solitude. Some provide encouragement, guidance, and expertise, and others just good old-fashioned common sense.

Sandra D is my confidant and biggest cheerleader. Bill Schilt is a journalist who keeps my writing within the confines of the English language. George Gurney demands more editing to tighten things up. Dennis Packer provided much-needed information on the processes of intelligence.

For more than sixteen years, Tam Nguyen has been my yoga instructor and expert in all that is yogi. She deserves credit for the expertise that went into *Cowards, Crooks, and Warriors* as well as *Twenty-Three Minutes* and this, the third in a series of Howard Hamilton Ride-Alongs.

A special thanks to Dr. Daniel Pak, Los Angeles Unified School District, for his Korean language and culture lectures.

Any errors or technical issues lie with the author.

The insights of a street cop are unique. They may be based upon experience, tragedies, triumphs and perhaps some jaded views of the world. For additional perspectives on how a street cop thinks, looks at life and projects his feelings on others, go to *www.jcdeladurantey. com* and read *HH on Police Work*. Howard Hamilton's views on a variety of topics may give you more insight into the real world of the street cop.

Printed in the United States
by Baker & Taylor Publisher Services